STEVE AOKI
HiROQUEST

GENESIS &
DOUBLE HELIX

CREATOR
STEVE AOKI

STORY BY
STEVE AOKI ◆ JIM KRUEGER

WRITTEN BY
JIM KRUEGER

EDITED BY
CHRISTOPHER SEQUEIRA

CREATIVE DIRECTOR
MATTHEW MEDNEY

ARTIST SCOUT
JONATHAN HANDLER

EDITORIAL & TITLE DESIGN
VOODOO BOWNZ ◆ MOHAMED SAMAH

PRODUCED BY
MATT COLON ◆ JON CAMCHE

PHYSICAL PRODUCTION
HERØ PROJECTS ◆ GUNGNIR

EXECUTIVE PRODUCER
STEVE AOKI

ARTISTS
RING 1 & 2 - FEDERICA DE COTIS
RING 3 & 4 - DARIO SANTARELLI
RING 5 & 6 - PABLO REY ◆ NOELIA YANTE
RING 7 - JONO
RING 8 - EMANUELE PARASCANDOLO
RING 9 - MARCO LUCCHINA
RING 10 - FABRIZIO COSENTINO

COVER ART
FRONT COVER ART - LIP WEI CHANG
BACK COVER ART - LEONARDO VINCENT

CHARACTER ARTIST
ALEXANDRA PAREL
HIEU MAY
TODD BLACKWOOD
JEREMY UZOKA
JONO
KEL

LETTERS
MOHAMED SAMAH

@steveaoki 🔲 🐦 f

SECOND PRINTING
PRINTED IN CANADA

HIROQUEST

CREATED BY
STEVE AOKI

WRITTEN BY
STEVE AOKI AND JIM KRUEGER

GRAPHIC NOVEL CREATIVE DIRECTION BY
MATTHEW MEDNEY

HIROQUEST PART ONE
GENESIS

PRELUDE: THE ANTHEM

Mom? Dad?

Just so you know, I didn't run away from our home, and I didn't drop out of school. And I'm not playing a trick on you. This isn't my "dark sense of humor", as you always say, either. And I know it's been a while since I've been gone and I want you to know I'm alright. I left and I've been gone for so long because I want to make certain that you are alright, as well.

In fact, I hope I can save you. Not just you, of course. Everyone. I hope you'll be proud of me and be glad that you named me Hiro. I know I don't always live up to the name.

I always have to explain to people that it sounds exactly like "hero" but it's spelled with an "I" instead. In fact, sometimes even the scientists I'm now working for pronounce it "Hyro." Why do people always do that?

Anyhow, there wasn't even an opportunity to say goodbye. And I'm sorry about that. I really wish I could have told you about this instead of this letter. I wasn't supposed to even tell you but the scientists said that if I do this right, I'll be back even before you get this, and then I guess I can catch it in the mail before you read it and I'll just come home and say "Hi" instead of "Bye". Does that make sense? Doesn't matter. It's some sort of time travel thing.

Anyhow, there's something bad coming. It's a meteor. It's really coming. I know the news said that it wasn't, but it's really coming. They think it's twice as big as the one that killed all life on Earth like a zillion years ago. Like the dinosaurs, I mean. Bigger than dinosaurs. I'm talking about the meteor that killed the dinosaurs.

As if pollution, disease, war, poverty, acne and how many TikTok followers I have wasn't enough for us to deal with, now there's this too. I know it'll be hard for you to accept, but I let them put me into an experimental test thing after school a couple months ago. It transformed me. Gave me super-powers. I'm super strong now. I have extra sensory abilities and I can even fly now. But none of that is enough to punch the meteor out of the sky, I guess. They gave me these powers for a different reason. It has something to do with assimilating into other worlds and people groups. They're going to make me smarter, too. That's what they say. So I'll be able to understand other cultures and peoples.

By the time you read this, well, it'll be four hundred years ago. Sorry, to me it'll be four hundred years ago. I'm being sent four hundred years into the future to get these rings, ten of them. The rings have powers and operate at different frequencies and the scientists that are sending me to get them say Earth can be saved with them. They say that every ring I get will make me stronger and more powerful. Powerful enough to save the earth. My People. That includes you and Dad, even if I sometimes said you're not my People. You are. Everyone is. I'm going to be a hero.

Each ring also has a code-word of sorts to access the ring's power. So, I guess I have to figure out that "source code" for every planet as well.

I don't know why they picked me for this. Something about a test we all took in one of my classes and how highly I scored. I know what you're thinking. "Me; score high on a test? Is it

April Fools?" Nope. Anyhow, I didn't have to study for it or anything. It was a different kind of a test. The kind that tests things you can't prepare for. You're just kind of born with it, or not. And well, I guess I aced it.

Anyhow, back to the future. They're sending me four hundred years into the future to get these rings and then, when I return with them, they'll be able to use the rings to change the path of the meteor ... or destroy it ... or move Earth in space. I can't remember. They told me. But I wasn't really listening. Ha ha. You know me. Listening has never been a normal power of mine, let alone a super-powered one.

So, I'm supposed to go to ten different worlds and get the ring from each world and then I'll come back.

And don't worry, it's not like I'm going alone. Well, I am going alone, but the three scientists who gave me these powers and are sending me also have prepared for what to expect. So I have really smart people telling me what to do. And you know how well I do with people telling me what to do.

Let me tell you about the Doctors.

First there's Doctor Edina Snow. She's the one who figured out how to send me into the future without disrupting some sort of time-flow. I think it has more to do with bringing me back, though. That's the real issue. They had to do things to change my body so that I could handle the rigors of traveling through time. But they said that when I get back, they'll be able to transform me back to what I was and looked like before. You guys might think that's a good thing, but maybe not. Again, ha ha.

Then there's Doctor Scottski. He determined what worlds I should visit first as I go along the way, and kind of determined the mission I'm on and what to do and when. That sort of thing would normally drive me nuts. But I think that I can trust him. Part of his plan is to use some of the rings I find to help me do what I have to do on the worlds that I visit later.

And finally, there's Doctor Horse. He's kind of in charge of everything. He seems to be the one most worried about how much this is all going to cost. So, I guess he's a little more like Mom. Sorry, Dad. Anyhow, he's the one I want to talk to the least.

Now, they have ways of tracking me on all the worlds I'm going to visit, and all the different types of people and things that I will be interacting with. I know you always said I needed to visit and become aware of different cultures, so I'm about to do that.

Oh, and one more thing. They say that if I succeed, they're going to give me a parade. Probably even have a band make an anthem for me or something. Hope the song doesn't suck.

Anyhow, I love you. And if I don't get all the rings in time, don't worry about me, I'll be safe in the future. No one else will be, but I'll be safe.

There's that dark sense of humor of mine again.

If I don't see you tomorrow, I hope I see you yesterday.

HIRO.

HIRO

AS I WAS

I will never understand, Doctor Snow, why you and the other Doctors thought I'd be a good candidate for this mission to save Earth. I was no one special. I wasn't even smart. If anything, I'm late for everything. Does that make me slow?

HIRO

AS I AM NOW

Well, I'm fast now. And super strong. I CAN FLY. And I have a version of extra sensory perception in the form of a third eye that reveals a lot to me. I'm going to need it. My mission is to get the rings of ten worlds. Ten rings to save my own. I'm the Hero named Hiro.

HiroQuest

RING ONE
ALIEN RING

PART ONE

THE FACTION OF THE ASTRALS

CHAPTER ONE
KULT

"I've got the weight of the world on my back."
Steve Aoki (featuring Josiah)

Doctor Snow? It's Hiro.

I knew you wanted me to keep a log of what I experienced here on this quest.

First of all, and because I said I'd be in communication, I got the first ring. I don't feel like much of a hero, but I keep thinking about the billions of people on Earth and how you told me that getting the rings was more important than anything else and sometimes I would have to do things that were questionable, so I guess this is fine. Also, thanks for amplifying my ability to communicate and speak. I already feel smarter. That said, thinking so much about all the people that are depending on me and stuff like that isn't as fun as it was just thinking about myself, so this is one of those things I hope you reverse as quickly as possible once I get back. So, let me begin.

The transport into the future did not feel good. It was like I was being pulled apart. Twisted. Like a piece of licorice. Cheap licorice. The kind that tears. Maybe as I grow stronger with each ring it won't be as difficult to move between worlds. But even on this world, arriving here, I felt like I was damaged somehow. But I know that you put tachyons in me to rebuild me.

So let me tell you about this place.

The sky is always glittering like there is lightning that never went away. But it also isn't like lightning. It's more like being at a concert. Everyone I meet is constantly looking up. Like the stage is in the sky. Even during the day the sky is glittering like a thousand cameras going off at once. That should have been a clue for me to understand this place. But it took me awhile, just like it always does.

Because everyone is hooded, I never get a great look at anyone. Well, except for one guy, but more on him later.

I know you joked about writing an anthem for me, but that's not what I'm finding here. It's more like chanting. I can't tell if there's a hum to this world or if it's actually the people who live here who seem to be humming all the time. That's what I meant by chanting. And everyone wears exactly the same thing. They all wear robes and hoods and look up into the sky. Like, without ceasing.

I'm trying to get to know who is here, but it's difficult because no one seems to want to have any identity at all. They seem especially identified with whatever it is that they worship. And for my first number of days here, I had no idea of what that was.

I said that there was someone I met here. And he ultimately helped me get the ring. But it was more like stealing the ring. And I don't think it worked out so well for him. But it's not my fault. His name is Pancha.

How we met was accidental. I realized that if I looked like everyone else, I could move around a lot more freely. My antennae and third eye kind of stick out. Especially the antennae. Ha ha. Anyhow, there were giant fields of hooded Kultists (let's call them) all standing there waiting, heads tilted slightly into the air as if they were waiting for something, anything. But I could see that they were still moving, breathing. Still humming. But then I found one that didn't seem to do any of those things. I thought it was a hood on a mannequin or like a dummy or something.

I tried to take the hood and cloak from it, only to realize there was still someone underneath. This was no mannequin. And that is how I met Pancha.

"You don't have a hood?" Those were his first words to me. He didn't say it like he was upset or angry. More like he was worried, and not even for me.

"The Astrals don't like it when we are not cloaked."

"Why?"

At this, Pancha started to laugh, and that seemed to make the weirdness of our meeting all the better. We left the sea of hoods (I call it that because it was like an ocean and also because wherever I looked, that was all I could see) and Pancha took me down some steps into an underground set of hallways that all felt like a maze of rooms that I would find backstage at a theater. Pancha said that at least down here the Astrals won't see me and get upset.

"Who are the Astrals?" I asked.

"The Astrals are all that matter," he said. "You and I don't matter. We only matter because they matter. We don't even really get to show our faces anymore, because they don't compare to the Astrals' faces."

"But everybody matters."

Pancha laughed again.

So, I told him he shouldn't laugh. My third eye opened, the one you gave me to read minds and that gives me a special awareness, and I could see that Pancha could be trusted. And so I began to tell him about Earth and my mission to save it. And all the people on it and about how everyone matters. I told him about how we all dress differently (to a degree, there is a fashion sensibility, of course. And not everyone knows how to dress). I told him about life on Earth. About the life I had that I was trying to save. About how everyone, in other ways besides the way we dress, is different and we all do different things. I told him about TV and movies. And he responded as if he totally understood our love for stars.

I thought he was talking about the stars in the sky and that's why everyone looks up into the air. But it was more than that, Doctor Snow. I kept telling him about Earth. And then I started talking about things like Instagram and TikTok and YouTube and having followers. He froze as if he was thinking a thought that he had never thought before.

"You are your own stars?"

"I guess you could put it that way," I told him. I explained that everyone wants to be famous on my world. To some degree. I explained how some people have followers because they ate bugs. Others sing. Even others animate their faces with big noses or swirly eyes. A lot of people get famous for almost anything. Even the dumbest things. And it's not even like they deserve it all the time. I told him, too, that even those people "off the grid" kind of want to be known for being unknown. I, of course, had to explain what being "off the grid" meant, but it was like Pancha was a sponge. He wanted to know more and more and more.

Then he asked a question.

"How are you going to save your Earth?"

I told him about the ring. About the ten rings. About how I had come from the past.

"The world you talk about where everyone is famous. That's a world worth saving." He said. "Maybe I've been getting brainwashed."

I asked him where the ring was and he was not certain, but he said that the Astrals would know and I would have to get to them, which would be easier said then done, because everyone wanted to get close to the Astrals. He told me to seek out the Tribinal. They would know where the ring was.

When I asked who the Tribunal was, he just said they were more Astrals, but they were the ones who bring the Astrals here and seemed to know more than even the average Astral.

I asked if he would help me.

He paused for a long moment. And then spoke from under his hood.

"If I do help you get the ring, and I was a friend of Hiro, would that make me famous, at least on your planet, four hundred years ago?"

I could tell he did not know what four hundred years meant. But I told him yes. He'd be helping me save billions. If there'll be an anthem for me, I would imagine Pancha would at least get a limerick or something.

I realized something in that moment when Pancha said yes, he indeed would help me. Pancha wanted what we have on Earth. A chance to be known. A chance to matter. What I didn't know was that Pancha and I would have to steal the ring. Or the terrible secret of the Astrals.

Doctor Snow, I think I should also mention that I don't always have a lot of time to send you these logs. Sometimes I speak them into a recorder to be transcribed, and sometimes I go back and write over what I said. And I can get a little lost in the process.

So the translation from what I say to what I write, isn't always clear. Please remember, I'm hardly even in high school. And English was never my thing. Hope you can understand what I'm sending you. Anyhow, back to the Astrals.

THE KULTISTS

They worship the Astrals. And keep their heads covered. It's like their own faces, their own reflections, don't matter. What matters is the object of their affection. I think of this world as populated by Fanboys Anonymous. That said, I don't know if they're all boys because I'm not about to look under their cloaks.

PANCHA

I want to think of Pancha as my first friend in my journey to collect the ten rings. I feel bad about how things went between us. He really did help me get the first ring. But social media is our greatest form of the spotlight, so can I really blame him for wanting to be noticed?

CHAPTER TWO
MOVIE STAR

"We're shootin' for the stars, getting' lost in outer space."
Steve Aoki (featuring Mod Sun & Global Dan)

"The first thing you need, Hiro, is a cloak. You have to cover yourself up."

I told Pancha that I was trying to take his when we first met. He smiled but I don't think he was completely happy to hear this. He said that no one gets near the Astrals without a hood and cloak. In fact, no one gets near them at all if they don't look like everybody else.

"You may be a star on your world, Hiro. But here, you have to look like your nothing. You must look like the rest of us."

He took me into another room where there were hooded cloaks as far as the eye could see (my two normal eyes at least, though my third one wasn't offering me any answers, either). I asked Pancha why there were so many extra cloaks if everyone already had one.

"That's a very good question."

It was a question I would soon find my answers for once I put on the cloak.

We moved out into the throng of Kultists who awaited the Astrals. There was a hum in the sea of Kultists. They knew what was coming … who was coming … even though I did not. And then they began to jump. It didn't seem like gravity was even an issue. They could all jump really high. But they all reached a certain point that they could not get beyond. It was like there was an invisible wall and there was no way to get above it, beyond it.

And then they arrived, the Astrals.

Well, they arrived as an it, first. A giant ship hovered above the sea of Kultists for a long time before it opened up and revealed itself like more of a platform. From this platform, with even more flashes, the Astrals emerged.

It was like the sky was a stage and the Astrals were the stars themselves. Not stars in the sky, but stars like movie stars, music stars. They arrived and hovered on what seemed like floating red carpets at a premiere. They were as alien as you would expect, like in all the ways aliens would be shown in black and white movies. But unlike those aliens, they were so into themselves and wanted everyone one else to be into them as well.

They didn't just want their followers to take pictures of them, they were taking pictures of each other. At least I assume they were pictures. I tried not to watch the flashes too much. I could almost feel a seizure coming on because of how intense it was. Like being flickered at from all sides with the brightest light possible. The Astrals were like the Paparazzi if the Paparazzi saw each other as the real movie stars.

"The Astrals will be very hard to reach," Pancha reminded me. So whatever held the cultists back was some sort of forcefield. As if the fans had to be held back in some sort of way.

So, Doctor Snow, I know that if I was going to get the ring, I would have to get to the other side of that field. To create a force or a wave that could get to the other side of it. You and your team of scientists gave me enough of a sense about it anyhow.

A forcefield, if I remember correctly, is a mix of light, electricity and microwaves. My plan was to ride one wave, sound vibrations, and then catch the electromagnetic wave within the forefield itself. But that would and could only happen if the soundwave was loud enough and strong enough to refract the light waves enough for me to pass from one wave to the other. I don't know if it made any sense. But one wave to another felt like surfing or boarding and that did make sense to me, though I guess that's also kind of the explanation for a drain or a whirlpool so the risk of getting in real trouble was certainly still there.

I really was an idiot for not realizing it sooner. I spent a lot of time trying to figure out how to amplify a sound to make it loud enough to carry me up and through the forcefield once I caught that wave. I know you made me smart, but maybe you didn't make me quick enough. But we'll see what happens with the later worlds.

Anyhow, it was the hum, the chant of the sea of Kultists. I just needed Pancha to move through them and encourage them to chant louder. He told them to tell each other and to pass that message along. I did the same.

And as the chant grew greater and greater and greater, even the Astrals began to notice. But of course, they just looked at each other and took pictures of each other all the more, hardly noticing the chanting below, but believing it somehow just served their own sense of self-importance.

If they had bothered to even look, they would have seen a lone hooded and cloaked figure rising up towards their ship and their photo-shoot.

Instead of flying, it was more like gliding, using as little of my power as possible, I allowed the sound waves and then the transfer to the electromagnetic waves to make the difference. Getting beyond the forcefield and switching waves to glide up felt like being in a plane that was descending through clouds. There was intense turbulence while I soared. But at the same time, I was rising through it as opposed to going down, so I knew that whatever I was doing was right on.

And then I was through. I was on the other side of the forcefield.

That said, I was also exposed. Surely, they would see me now? At least that's what I thought. But their eyes, giant as they were, were so dazed or blinded by the flashes and the lights, they weren't noticing me at all. In fact, I'm sure that wherever place these "photos" get posted or developed must have hundreds of shots of me there, not necessarily photo-bombing the images, but certainly running behind the objects in the shot.

Walking … even running down their version of a red carpet … it was like I was an extra in a movie who got invited to the premiere and no one noticed. No one cared. I hoped that would last long enough for me to get to the ring, wherever that was. I realized then that I really did not have any idea where the ring was or where it would be.

My hope was that maybe whoever "drove" the ship that brought the Astrals here, well, maybe he or she or it or them, I guess, would have the ring I was looking for. My third eye helped me come up with this idea. So, with all the pictures going off behind me, I moved onto the ship.

It was amazing how boring the ship itself was. I expected Star Wars or Star Trek. I would have even put up with Battle Beyond the Stars. Instead, all I found were halls and halls of pictures of the Astrals mounted on the walls. There weren't even windows looking out of the ship, just the pictures. They were so into looking at themselves that they didn't even see or care that they were going through space. It made me remember when my family went to the Grand Canyon, and I didn't even care that much. My mom told me that it was something to be appreciated. Anyhow, this was like that but so much worse.

They also look completely alike. Every picture could have been of the very same Astral. But they weren't. It made me think about how people viewed other people on my planet. I couldn't help thinking that I wanted to be different to what I was. I don't know in what way. Maybe more aware?

Finally, I came to the pilot's seat. Seats. There were three seats. I assumed, though I did not see them, that this is where the Tribunal sat. There was a window there, of course. But also, a lot of mirrors. I assumed that this would be so the Tribunal could be watching himself or herself or itself … well, themselves as well. The only thing was that there was no pilot. I assumed then that the pilot was on the runway as well, having pictures taken and taking pictures,

I looked around at things that looked like they would be used to fly a ship. Part of it looked like the cockpit of an airplane. And part of it looked like a kids' play set. Like a Play-Doh playset. There were these giant shaped areas filled with goop.

My third eye told me to stick my fingers in the goop, and when I did, I felt it.

The ring.

Why they kept the ring in the goop I had no idea at the time. I was just glad that I had found it.

I asked the eye what the source code for the ring was. I instantly knew the word as "Thxii300" which is pronounced "thick-see-ew." I spoke the word, trying to access the ring. But nothing happened. At least not straight away.

Getting out and riding the waves back to the planet of the Kult was not a problem.

The Astrals didn't see me go. They were too involved with themselves. Over my shoulder, I saw three Astrals that seemed to command the most respect. They got more pictures.

More notice. The cameras were flashing, like this was high fashion. This was a superstar status that was so lavish, they had to be the Tribunal that Pancha told me about.

The problem was when I arrived back amongst the Kult. They had watched me get to the other side of the forcefield. They had watched me go down the Astral red carpet. They had watched me go into the ship and emerge and come back.

And they all wanted my secret.

They didn't know who I was. All they saw was the cloak and the hood. All they knew was that they too could walk the red. They too could be special. And they all wanted a piece of me.

THE ASTRALS SPACESHIP

I found the ring on the ship. What's amazing about this ship is that it's meant to be seen. On my Earth it seems like Aliens never want to be seen. Here it's like the opposite. It's all bright lights. Look, up in the sky. It's not a bird. It's not a plane. And it sure isn't a super-anything.

THE ASTRALS

These beings from another world are their own paparazzi and publicists. They may come from the stars, but they also are the stars. If they cough, they want it to be known. They may be their own number one fans, but that doesn't mean they don't want other fans to be treated like number two. That is where the Kultists come in.

THE TRIBUNAL

Even amongst the Astrals themselves, there were three who were signaled out as the most famous, the most important. The Tribunal piloted the ship from whatever world they came from to this one. They would certainly have been the first to discover that the ring was missing.

CHAPTER THREE
MOVE ON

"There's no way to run, no way to hide."
Steve Aoki, Kane Brown and Ricky Retro

The Kultists grabbed and clawed at me, trying to hold on, not wanting me to escape into the ambiguity of the crowds. After all, they all kind of looked alike as well. And I looked like one of them if I kept the hood and cloak on.

Now one of their own, being me, was a star, which meant that any one of them could become a star, or all of them could become stars. They no longer had to look up. They just had to look towards each other. Towards themselves.

Ambiguity? When did I start using words like that? Never mind.

I was on the run. I had no friends and there was no way that Pancha would find me. All I knew was that as long as they tried to hold onto me, I wasn't going to get away from them. I think I wished to be let go harder than anything I had ever wished for before.

And then I was free.

How?

I looked around, and there were still Kultists all around me. But they weren't trying to hold onto me anymore. And more, I had moved from one part of the crowd to another. There was a slight glow that was disappearing from where my hand was. When I looked closer, it was the ring, which glowed a little, and then it stopped glowing completely.

I wished again. Wished to be away, in a different part of the crowd. I wished harder this time, believing that my wish could come true.

And I disappeared and reappeared in another area of the Kultists. Those around me became aware of a new presence in their midst while still others became aware of my disappearance from where I had been. But there wasn't enough time for them to organize or gather or realize a way to stop me.

It was at this point that I realized that the power this ring had was the ability to teleport. I could go anywhere with it. Just by thinking about it. Just by hoping or wishing or ... I don't know, manifesting?

I knew I had to leave, but I thought of Pancha once more without even meaning to. And was instantly teleported back to those underground halls where all the cloaks were. Pancha had returned there. And was waiting for me. Hoping I would return.

"I saw what you did," he said. "You're a star. A true star. And not the kind that eat insects. And I have also realized that if I were to catch you, to trap you, I would be a star to my own people." Pancha almost gloated in his thinking. There was an aspect to his grin that I did not like. He was so kind and helpful when I first met him.

It felt like I had come so far only to be betrayed. And yet I only had one ring. Was I to lose this so soon and therefore lose the lives of all my people?

Pancha grabbed onto me. And harder than the others in the crowd. I think he recognized what I could do. I tried to teleport away but every time I did, he teleported with me; by not letting go he was moved with me.

He began shouting to the others, telling them to grab hold of him and therefore me. More and more of the Kult were teleported with us. We became an amalgamation of beings. How many of these Kultists could this ring move? How many beings could the ring teleport?

The answer to this question was almost immediate.

I didn't have to look up very far to see the Astrals ship come down to the surface of the planet. It was almost like a crash landing; almost. They had discovered my theft. There was no forcefield any longer. The Kultists who were not preoccupied with me departed the area the ship was heading for to be out of the way of the landing.

I realized then just how powerful the ring I had taken was. And just how many beings it could carry. And why it was in the goop in the place where the pilot captained the ship.

The Astrals used the ring for space travel. To teleport from world to world. Across distances guessed at, wished for, in the recesses of our thoughts. That's how they did it. Maybe the goop amplified it to a degree, I don't know. Maybe not. But now, without the ring, they were trapped here.

I had trapped them here. With the Kultists. And with me if I didn't get out of here. But trapped here was better than the death of all of our people. And so I continued.

Pancha grabbed at my hand, the one with the ring, and pulled the cloak and hood from me calling me a pretender. A faker. And he told me that he will be known forever more as the one who stopped me. I pulled away from the others but could not escape Pancha.

He yanked the ring from my finger as I imagined us into a body of water some two miles away. Both of us appeared offshore there as he pulled the ring from my finger. But he dropped it. And it sank below the surface of the water into the murk below.

So consumed were the people of this world with the Astrals that there were abilities they never learned. Like swimming.

I could have left Pancha to drown that day. I didn't, of course. But he swallowed enough water that he was no match for me. I left him on the shore and went back into the water, and dived. It wasn't long before I found the ring. I wished with the third eye and found it glowing even though I wasn't touching it.

I put the ring on and looked at Pancha. He was unconscious. Beyond him, the Astrals were looking everywhere for the ring. And the hooded figure who took it. They weren't looking for me at all. So, like before, they didn't find me.

As I left this world, I couldn't help wondering about all those other cloaks I found. Maybe I would never know why there were so many extras.

Was it because, with any belief, there's the expectation that others will follow to embrace it? Or was it something else? Perhaps the Kultists were there for the Astrals one day because they knew, of course, that fame is not something anyone one can hold onto. Not for long.

Regardless, the hoods might be of good use now. The Kultists' objects of worship were stuck in this place now. Along with them. Maybe they would learn from each other. Maybe my theft would bring an equality to both. I hoped so. Or maybe I was just trying to make myself feel better for what I had done.

I wished that in taking the ring I also gave them something they needed. I'd brought down a false god. I hoped. Of course, it's not that kind of wishing ring …

But as I left them behind, I also feared that perhaps I had doomed the Astrals. It's easy to worship something when it's far enough away. It's hard when you see it up close. That must be true for Pancha and his experience of me as well. I wanted to be a hero and I feared, in this case at least, I was just Hiro.

When I think about Pancha now, it's like a twist of a knife, right in my chest.

This is not as easy, Doctor Snow, as I hoped it would be. The people of Earth are certainly worth it. But I hope the cost to other worlds will not be so high.

THE ASTRALS RING

The Astral Ring has an amazing ability. It has the ability to teleport me from one place to another. The Astrals used it as a way to cross the galaxy so I assume that it can teleport a lot. Maybe we can just teleport the meteor that will kill everyone away from Earth and all it takes is one ring. Not ten?

SOURCE CODE TO
ACCESS POWER: THXII300

THE ASTRALS WERE NOW AS IF THEY WERE KULTISTS

I didn't destroy this world. But I destroyed the way it worked. By taking the Astrals' Ring, I brought gravity to their stardom. I destroyed a world where some are worshipped, and some are not. I don't know, maybe I brought equality. But it's hard to be worshipped and then not. And it's hard to have something you love taken from you. I'm going to have to be more careful with the other nine worlds I visit.

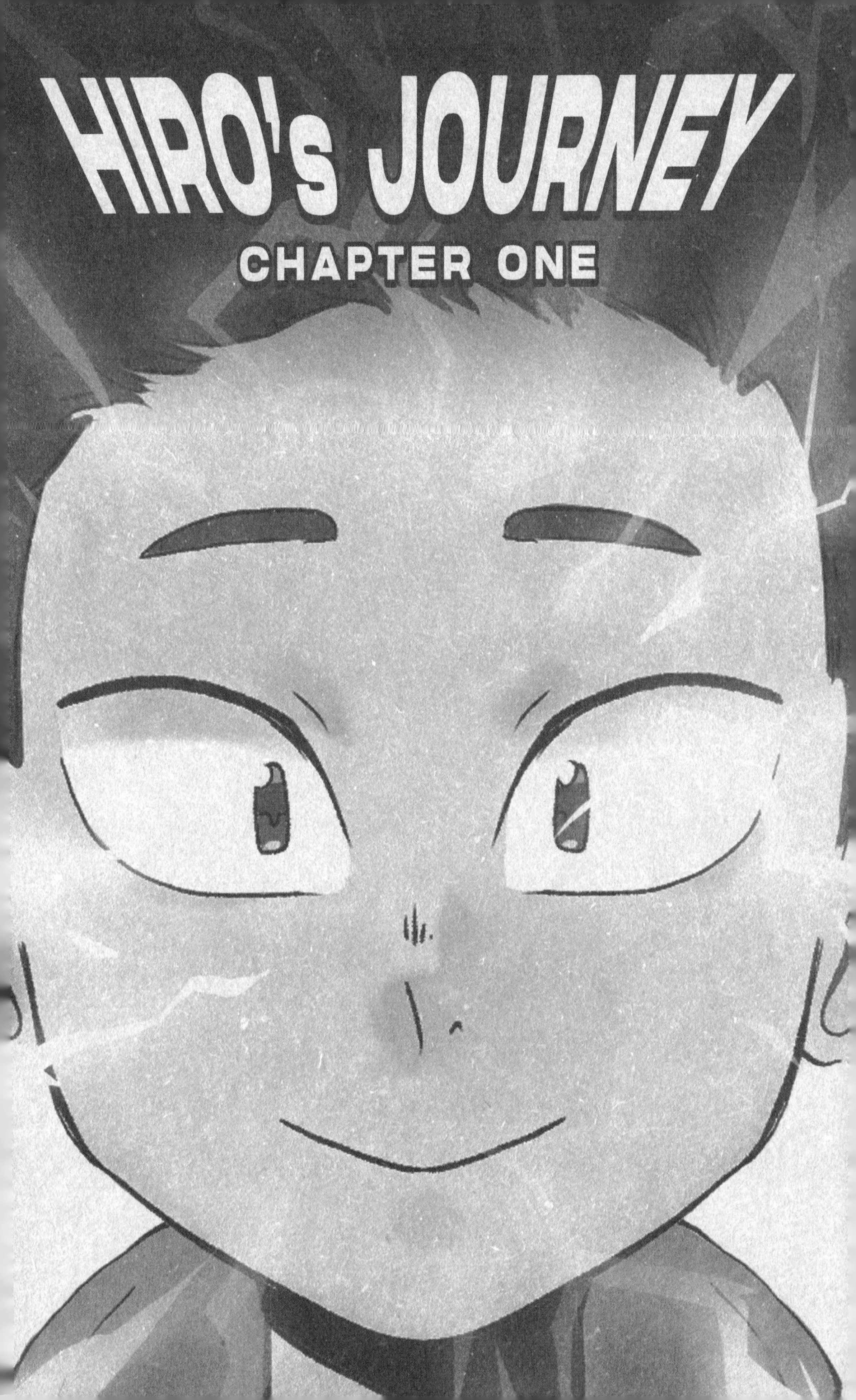
HIRO's JOURNEY
CHAPTER ONE

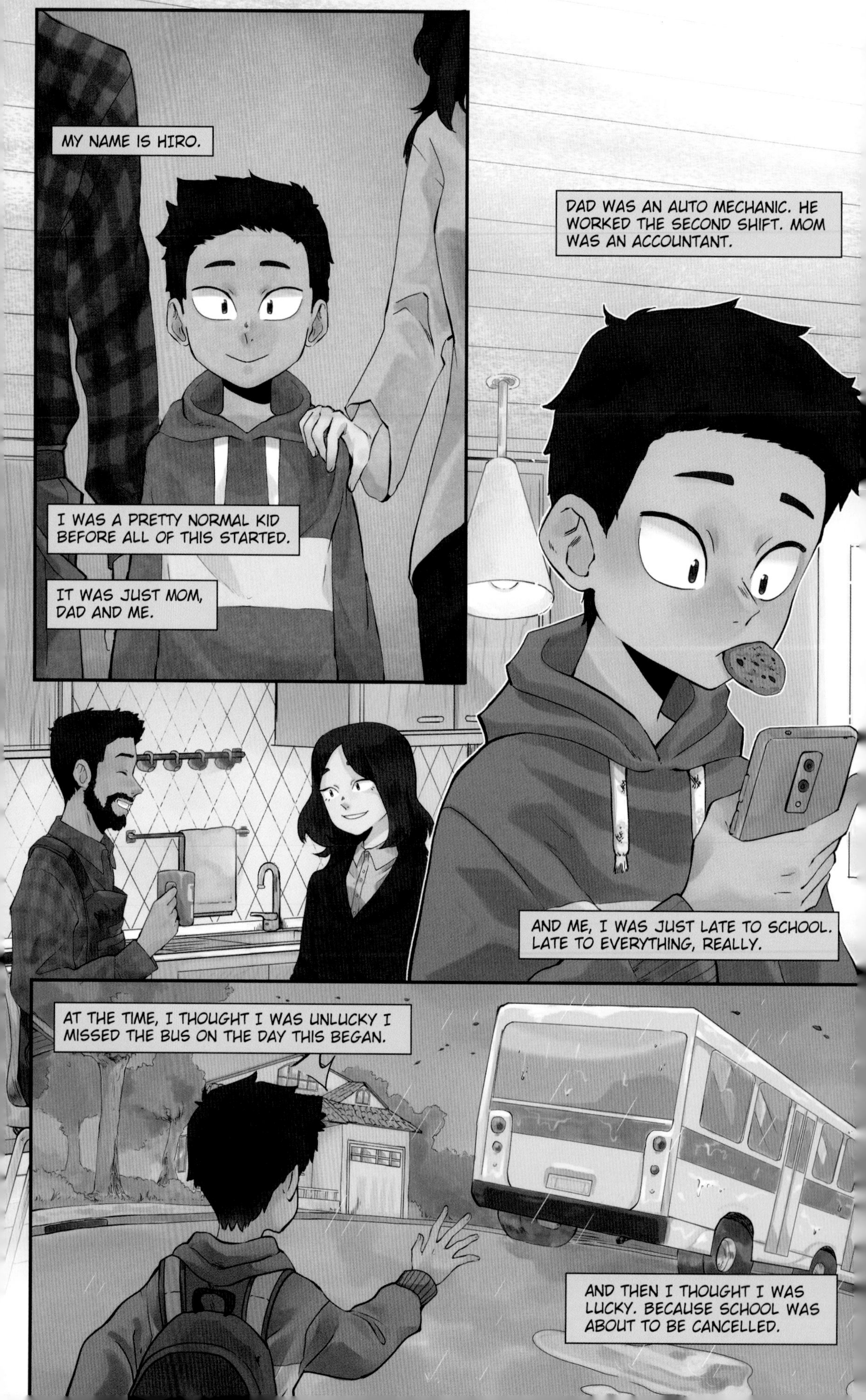
MY NAME IS HIRO.
I WAS A PRETTY NORMAL KID BEFORE ALL OF THIS STARTED.
IT WAS JUST MOM, DAD AND ME.
DAD WAS AN AUTO MECHANIC. HE WORKED THE SECOND SHIFT. MOM WAS AN ACCOUNTANT.
AND ME, I WAS JUST LATE TO SCHOOL. LATE TO EVERYTHING, REALLY.
AT THE TIME, I THOUGHT I WAS UNLUCKY I MISSED THE BUS ON THE DAY THIS BEGAN.
AND THEN I THOUGHT I WAS LUCKY. BECAUSE SCHOOL WAS ABOUT TO BE CANCELLED.

I HAD BEEN IN HURRICANES BEFORE. THIS WAS FLORIDA AFTER ALL.

BUT NEVER WITH LIGHTNING.

I EXPECTED THEM TO YELL.

INSTEAD, THEY TOLD ME TO GRAB WHATEVER I COULD IN MY BACKPACK AND THAT WE WERE LEAVING.

I HAD FIVE MINUTES.

SO I TRIED TO GRAB AS MUCH OF MY MANGA AS POSSIBLE.

WE HAD TO GET TO THE CAR BEFORE THEY CLOSED THE STREETS.

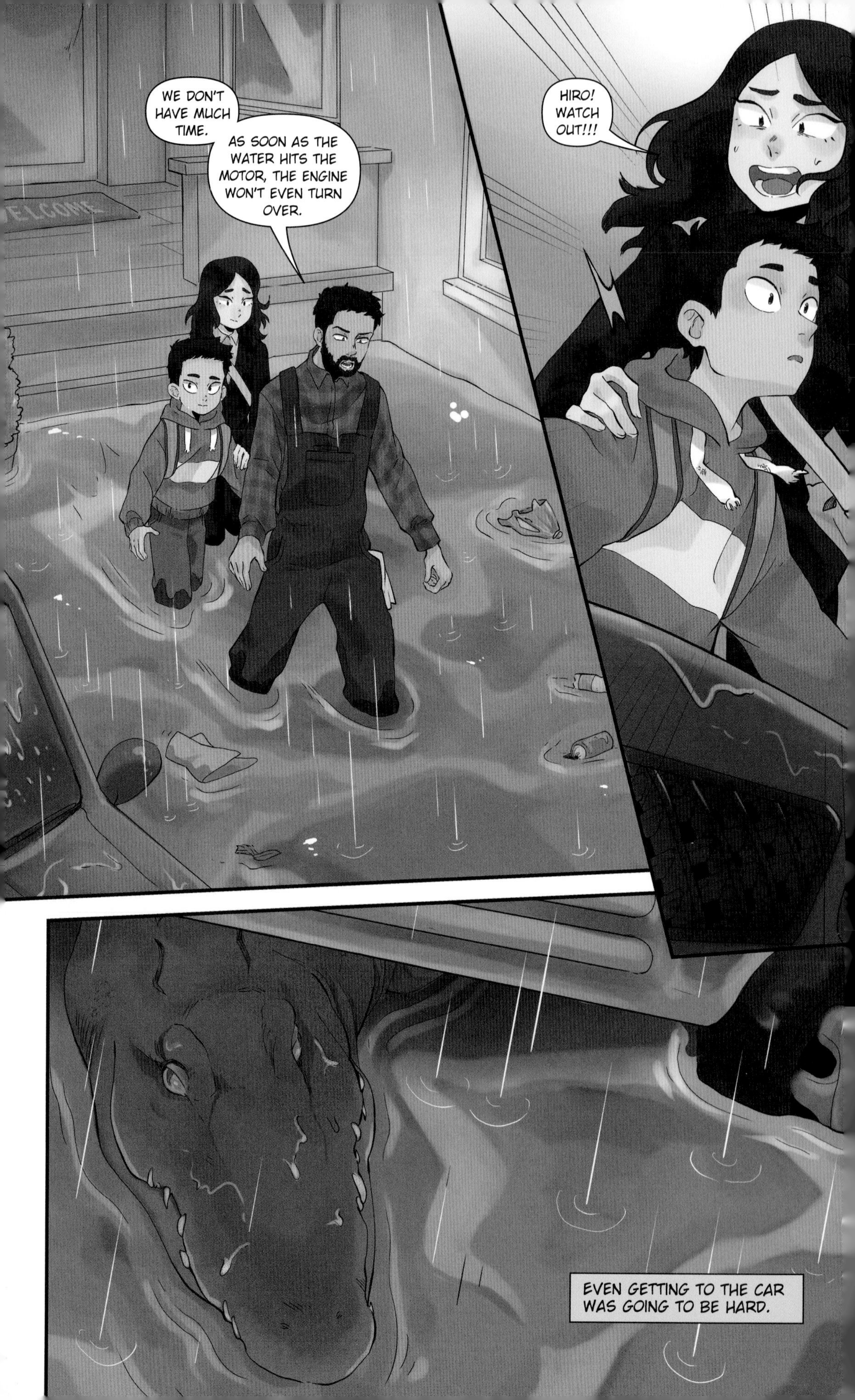
WE DON'T HAVE MUCH TIME.
AS SOON AS THE WATER HITS THE MOTOR, THE ENGINE WON'T EVEN TURN OVER.
ELCOME
HIRO! WATCH OUT!!!
EVEN GETTING TO THE CAR WAS GOING TO BE HARD.

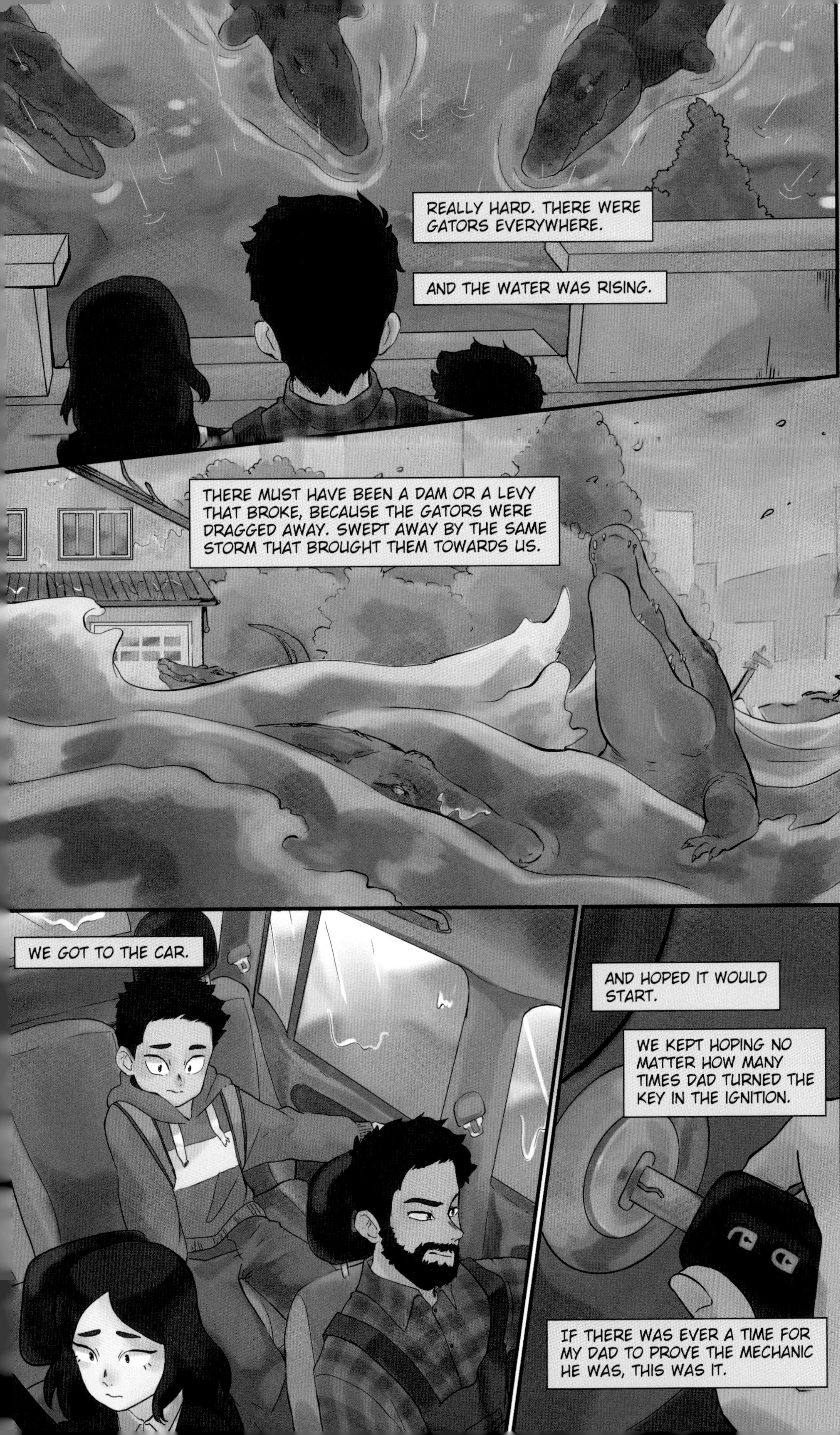
REALLY HARD. THERE WERE GATORS EVERYWHERE.
AND THE WATER WAS RISING.
THERE MUST HAVE BEEN A DAM OR A LEVY THAT BROKE, BECAUSE THE GATORS WERE DRAGGED AWAY. SWEPT AWAY BY THE SAME STORM THAT BROUGHT THEM TOWARDS US.
WE GOT TO THE CAR.
AND HOPED IT WOULD START.
WE KEPT HOPING NO MATTER HOW MANY TIMES DAD TURNED THE KEY IN THE IGNITION.
IF THERE WAS EVER A TIME FOR MY DAD TO PROVE THE MECHANIC HE WAS, THIS WAS IT.

HiroQuest

RING TWO
A.I RING

PART TWO

THE FACTION OF THE OIO

CHAPTER FOUR
JUST US TWO

"You were ten-foot tall and bulletproof."
Steve Aoki and Taking Back Sunday

I feel like after the world of the Kult and the Astrals, there are questions I need to ask: Like what are the things in my life that if they were taken away from me I would be lost without?

I guess the answer is that it's my world and that's why I'm here. Allowing myself to become a thief. And maybe more than that before this is over. I want to get this over with. I think I'm going to stop thinking about the right and wrong of it, and just focus on what needs to be done.

The new world I now find myself in is very different; the second world as I search for the second ring is kind of like the Detroit of my time, but at night. It's a concrete and metal jungle. Which is really cool because the most important thing to look at is how the smoke coming from the smokestacks is lit by the street signs and the moon–moons–there are, like, five of them.

But it wasn't just the buildings and the factories that were metal. It's like everything was. The people, too. I soon learned that the people here were like robots. Or were robots. They were known as the Taurobons.

The air was thick. It wasn't easy to breathe here, even for me.

Doctor Snow, I know I need to get the rings, but I don't want this to be like the last world. I don't want to leave it worse than I found it. I know there are billions of lives on the line. And all the future generations that would follow, which means all of humanity, but I'm still nervous.

You and the other doctors told me this was a world of Artificial Intelligence beings, the world of the OIO. But when I first got here, it wasn't. Just a world of robots. Robots who would do anything they were told. And do nothing they weren't told to do.

In some ways, they were like the Kult of the last world. Like there wasn't any real identity to any of them at all.

I had hoped that all I would have to do is command a Taurobon to get me the ring and they would get me the ring.

Of course, it didn't work that way.

Anyhow, the Taurobon robots, and I'll just call them Taurobons from here on out, go to work in factories. And it's in the factories that they make more Taurobons. It's like a cycle of never-ending building. It's never-ending slavery, even. I mean, isn't that what a robot is? A slave that doesn't know it's a slave?

And then I started thinking about Detroit. About any big city and the people who live there. Follow the flow. Find out where everything leads. Who has the most Taurobons working for them? That kind of thing.

This led me to a part of the city that was not as industrialized. If anything, it was more like art. There were Taurobons everywhere and there was no way to get in. The building was like a City Hall but lit up in colors that seemed like something out of a Valentine's Day card. And more, the building seemed partially organic, like it was alive. Even breathing to a degree. The closer I got, though, the more I realized--or thought, at least--that I was being watched.

I even became aware of Taurobons that were like, cops, I guess, that were patrolling around. Initially I thought they were looking for someone like me that shouldn't be here. That my clothing, my looks, put them off. Using the Astrals' teleporting ring, I disappeared from the scene and watched from a safe distance. But they didn't seem to be looking for me at all. They were looking for something else. Someone else? No matter where I looked, though, it was still robot after robot after robot.

And then, before I could teleport away from the spot that I thought was safe, one of these authorities looked right at me. But it did nothing. It passed me right over, as if I was either not worth their time or something more like they weren't even programmed to be concerned with anyone like me.

Instead of trying to get into the City Hall, I thought I should find out what was going on in this place. I started to follow a group of the authorities. And finally, after so much of the night, I saw them arrest, if such a word is right to use in this case, another Taurobon. Sirens and searchlights flashed through the smoky neon streets as the Taurobon in question attempted to escape.

In the end, the robot was tracked down and deactivated and became stationary. I watched it all happen openly in plain sight, not hiding, walking down the center of the street. Not one of these authority-bots reacted to me at all.

And then one vehicle came down the street.

I guess you would think it was like a cop car, but it looked more like a garbage truck.

A giant, vacuum-like suction-tube flipped over the truck, extending like an arm and took hold of the deactivated Taurobon.

The truck then headed down the street, so I teleported over and over again, from street to street, following it, trying to understand where it was going.

Was there a jail cell waiting, a prison for robots, perhaps?

While I was following, I was testing to see how many times the teleporting ring of the Astrals could be used and found no real limits at all. Which I'm sure, Doctor Snow, you are grateful to hear.

The garbage truck eventually came to its destination. It wasn't a prison at all. It was a giant garbage dump. But it was more like a techno-graveyard for Taurobons. There were parts of Taurobon bodies everywhere.

But it was more than a graveyard. It was a recycling plant. A dismantling plant. If the factories were making more Taurobons, it was also using pieces of its own kind, and this was the place where those pieces were being gathered.

But for what reason?

THE TAUROBON

I have come to a world ruled and occupied by robots called the Taurobon. They have a purpose, and that is what they serve. The fulfillment of a program. They are mechanical beings in the most classic sense of the term. Because I am human, or more than human, but not mechanical, they do not see me, because I am not part of their mechanized definitions of reality.

THE
ROBOT JUNKYARD

This is a world that recycles to a degree I never saw on Earth. When a Taurobon is damaged beyond repair, it is sent here to this place of parts and housings. A place where there perhaps lies a chance to be given a purpose beyond a life of slavery and servanthood.

CHAPTER FIVE
ALL HYPE

"You take what you want, then you leave."
Steve Aoki and Bryce Vine

Doctor Snow? Here's what happened on the next world I visited. I don't know if you guessed this would happen, and that was part of why all of you selected the order of the worlds you sent me to, but the ring that gave me the power of teleportation was extremely helpful here. I'm pretty sure I could not have accomplished my mission without it.

My dad, well, four hundred years ago, when I was born, was a mechanic. He taught me a lot. Especially about how cars work and how they are wired. And even how they can be hotwired. Of course, looking at this salvage yard of robots, this gave me an idea.

Hoping these robot Taurobons were like mechanical people, I snuck through the wreckage and grabbed a head. And I went to work. Some of the wires were obviously intended for the vocal speakers of the thing. Really, the issue wasn't so much about rewiring but of finding a way to power the head. And to override certain circuits. The ones that kept them from speaking to me or even recognizing me.

The rewiring was harder than I thought. I didn't have my dad's tools for taking it apart and rebuilding it. And even if I did, I doubt they would have worked. These were completely different types of nuts and bolts, so to speak. Even nuts and bolts don't really apply. In some cases, I was using parts of another Taurobon to pry open panels on the one I was working on. It was sort of like spaghetti mechanics. I had no idea what would work and what would not.

But finally, I got the light behind the head's eyes to spark on. And its vocal systems to come online. From there, I commanded it to tell me how to rework its system. Being a robotic Taurobon, it, of course, complied.

From here it was simple to learn what I needed to learn. These were hard truths. And I was all alone.

The Taurobons were robots, I knew that. But what I did not know is that they were also enslaved by a form of Artificial Intelligence called the OIO. They did everything the OIO commanded. The OIO thought the OIO were an evolutionary superior step ahead of them, and deserved to be obeyed by mere robots. I asked my Taurobon head if it could become an OIO.

"We cannot. We serve the OIO," it sparked; speaking in a staggered voice, like an old radio that wasn't quite dialed into the right station. I understood it well enough, though. And I asked about the ring and the nature of the ring in this world.

It knew nothing of the ring. It only knew about those it served. So I asked it who that was.

This question seemed to confuse it. "Serving" was a choice, so it was the wrong word to describe what Taurobons did for the OIO.

I realized that I would have to think like it. To change how I was speaking to it. So I asked where its commands came from.

The lights behind the eye flickered again. It spoke like it did before and simply said "The Love Brains."

"The Love Brains? Are those the OIO?" I replied.

The robot could not nod as it was only a head. But it also did not speak. I was asking a question, I suppose, according to its programming that it could not answer. Why, I had no idea.

So I strapped the head to my back, using various wires that were laying around this robot junk yard and I continued to ask questions. . And I began to move back into the streets.

But it wasn't like before. Almost immediately there were Taurobon cops following me. And those giant trucks that collected broken down Taurobons. They were after me too.

I used the ring I got from the Astrals to teleport to other streets. But there were Taurobons there as well. It's like every Taurobon I saw, except for the one that was strapped to my back, was after me.

It was their eyes that gave them away … it was like the color changed as soon as one became aware of me. I did what I could to hide myself, and to teleport.

I realized that I would have to outthink them to a degree. So what was going on? Were they now aware of me? Or was this "Love Brain" thing sending them after me? Did it have some sort of way of reading and tracking my location? Was it faster than my ring's ability to teleport?

What would the Human Weapon do? I tried to think like my favorite hero. He'd … he'd … realize that they were tracking him somehow. What had changed since I was in the Taurobon junkyard to now? I didn't even finish thinking my question before I realized the answer. They weren't after me at all.

They were after the head of the Taurobon on my back. It was broken and it was being tracked wherever I went or arrived so it could be fixed. Or junked.

I realized the only place that was safe for me to safely speak to this thing was back at the junk yard again. Or I'd have to unplug it, make it inactive like it was when I found it, and hope they still couldn't track me that way.

I teleported back to the junkyard, feeling like a fool. But I appreciated that I would have to think in a different way if I was going to find the ring here.

I pulled the Taurobon head from my back. And rather than ask about what the Love Brains were or who these robots served, I just asked where I could find a Love Brain.

The Taurobon head jittered as it spoke. Its audio play was even less clear now. I assumed the teleporting was not helpful to my make-shift hotwiring. It told me to go to the building that looked like a City Hall that I had seen.

I wouldn't need to know how to get in, since I had the teleporting ring. That said, I might need more information from this Taurobon, so I disconnected the energy pack that was keeping it online but put it back on my back and hoped they would not be able to track me. I could always reconnect the head with the power source later. And I teleported once again.

I reappeared outside the junkyard. And just like I hoped, I walked right passed the Taurobon cops. I didn't even bother teleporting at this point. I walked right down the street, congratulating myself for being clever.

Walking down the middle of the street not noticed at all reminded me of the kid I used to be. Completely unnoticed. The kid in my school most likely to … not accomplish anything.

And yet here I was, about to save the world. That may have been four hundred years ago. But to me, it was maybe only a year.

Anyway, I walked right up to the doorless City Hall.

Doors didn't mean anything to me, not anymore, of course. Not with a teleporting ring. The ring glowed a little. Not sure why I didn't worry about the possibility of teleporting into a wall or something solid and being ripped apart by it. I think I just knew that, even if I couldn't see where I was teleporting to, it would be okay.

I disappeared from the streets and reappeared inside the City Hall.

What I faced, though, was something so weird, it took me a while to even understand what I was looking at. There were no rooms inside the City Hall. There were no halls. Or windows out. It was just one giant expanse within. Like a giant gymnasium. But not a gym either. More like a science hall.

There was wiring everywhere. It was like very gross veins … I mean, varicose veins, that ran up and down the walls and hung from the ceiling. They all seemed to attach themselves to something in the center. It was like a spider web, but not like a spider web. Like the kind a black widow spider makes. It isn't a cool looking web. It was more like a mess of wires going everywhere but attaching in the center around this one thing. And the wires even looked almost organic. Like they were made of brains. And they were sparking, which made me remember they were wires. But aren't there electrical sparks between parts of the brain as well? I think I remember seeing that in a movie.

Anyhow, this thing in the center … it wasn't just one thing, it was more like two. It was disturbing but also beautiful. Like two giant wires, or worms, or snakes … yeah, snakes. Cobras maybe. But metal cobras. They faced each other and were arching their backs as if they were going to strike each other … except, they weren't going to do that either.

There weren't exactly heads on the end of these metal snakes, but it seemed like there were faces. No, not faces. Lips. Yeah, there were lips. And I think they were kissing. Kissing the way old people do. You know, the way they try to push their lips out beyond the length of their noses right after they eat lemons and talk about having "pucker power."

Together, these two kissing metal snake things seemed to form the classic shape of a heart. Like a Valentine's Day shaped heart. The kind you make in kindergarten.

I had no idea what the hell I was looking at.

I pulled the Taurobon from my back and reattached its power source. It sparked back to life–well, life for a robot–and it began to speak. I assumed that because there were no doors in this place, there would be no way for the other Taurobon to get to us, at least not for a while.
I made it look at the giant thing above us and asked it what it was.

There was a long pause. And then certain gears began to click in the back of the Taurobon's head. It was like a grinding, almost. And I wondered if perhaps I had broken it. I mean, it was broken before I found it, but had I broken it further?

"What is it?" I asked the Taurobon.

His eyes could not go wide, but whatever color prism was behind them changed. Became more purple. And then red.

"It's one of the Love Brains."

"What is that?"

"It is one of the Taurobon, one that has achieved Artificial Intelligence. It is the OIO."

"The OIO? Why are they kissing?"

"What could be more intelligent?"

I HAVE A ROBOT ON MY BACK

In the junkyard of Taurobons, I found a head and a power source for it to give me information about this place. If Pancha was my first friend, one who kind of lost his head for the promise of fame, this is my second friend, who at this point is just a head. A key source of information. I hated leaving him behind. Or not giving him a name. I should have left him something.

THE LOVE BRAINS

When a Taurobon somehow evolves or advances into Artificial Intelligence, it embraces another advanced Taurobon as a partner. They form what is similar to a single heart together, and focus on each other for all time, perpetually amazed with the other. The problem, if this would be a problem, is that they are not like my Mom and Dad. They don't serve each other. And therefore, require other not-yet-advanced Taurobons to continue serving them.

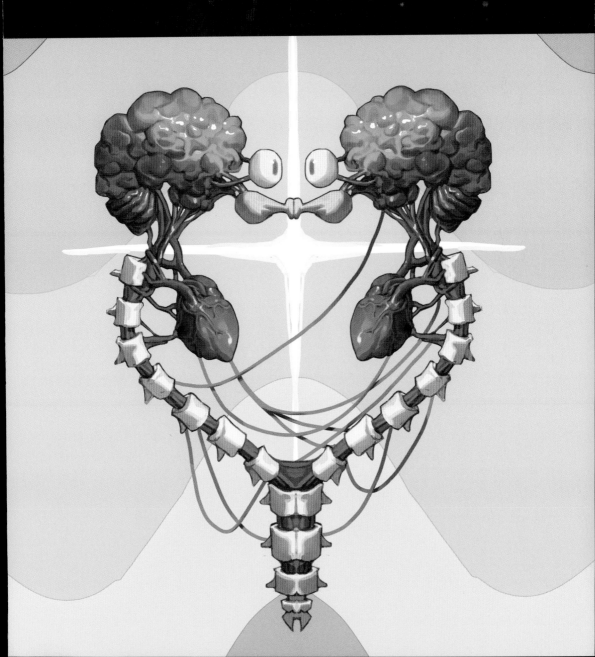

CHAPTER SIX
YOU DON'T GET TO HATE ME

"Heart is turning cold from all the things I feel."
Steve Aoki and Goody Grace

Now, Doctor Snow, I realize that I am telling you this after I have achieved the ring. So, you know what I've gone through to get it and you know I got it. Maybe I just wasn't as smart as I thought you all made me. Well, not made me. But changed me into. Remade me, I guess.

It was all the perfect logic, I guess. I didn't understand that to get the answer I needed required me to ask the perfect question. And to ask it perfectly. It's like my Mom trying to balance multiple accounts and make certain things all added up. I was afraid things weren't adding up. At least they didn't seem like they would. Here was the problem.

I asked the Taurobon head if this Love Brain could tell me where the ring was?

The Taurobon told me that it could, but it would not.

I asked it why, and it had no answer. I was under the impression that the OIO were the only ones that could tell me where the ring was. The Taurobon agreed. But repeated the Love Brains would not answer me; it would not speak to me.

I asked "why?" because I wasn't thinking. The Taurobon was no longer looking at the Love Brains and it was like it had forgotten everything we had talked about.

I remembered my computer classes. Had seeing the OIO somehow led to certain memory files being deleted in the Taurobon, or was it something else? I thought about my experience with the Taurobon head in the junk yard and I thought through why I was hunted when I first left with it. There was a simplicity to interacting with these robots. I needed to just think through it.

But, I didn't get a chance. There was a pounding at the walls around us.

I said before that there were no walls within the City Hall. The pounding was coming from all around us. The Taurobon were trying to get at us. I was not going to get my answers. The walls began to crack and it was shaking the OIO heart creature at the center of the brain wiring web.

I'd caused too much damage on the last planet. I wasn't about to let that happen here. I would have to find a different way to get the ring.

So I unplugged the Taurobon head again. The pounding and the cracking stopped immediately. Just as I had expected it to.

I stood there and watched as the swinging Love Heart above me stopped swinging and came to just hang again. At rest. At peace.

I wondered if there was anything I loved so much that if the worst was to happen, I would continue to hold on to the thought of it at that worst, darkest moment. I realized I did have something like that; and I thought of my parents as I teleported out of the place and back to the streets.

The Taurobon on the streets simply returned to their regular duties. Their daily routine, which was no different than it was yesterday, or the day after tomorrow. But something was different.

That garbage truck thing. The one that grabbed one of the malfunctioning Taurobons before, it didn't turn away from me. It couldn't know I was here, could it?

I didn't run. I feared that that might trigger something. I turned and made my way away from it and City Hall. I looked over my shoulder, which was more difficult because of the robot head strapped to my back. It was still following.

Do Taurobons drive these trucks? Or are they automated as well?

I had a really scary thought right then, Doctor Snow.

If a Taurobon could malfunction, there were probably all kinds of malfunctions, including one that would allow it to become aware of me.

It was at this point that I began to run. And then I began to teleport. Down streets. Across blocks. Everywhere I appeared, there seemed to be a truck waiting for me or rounding a corner to confront me. There had to be more than one. But how many were there?

I began to feel heat from the ring. It reminded me of when my father told me that, when I was old enough to drive, I shouldn't have the air-conditioner on in a traffic jam, because I could overheat the engine. Was that the reason the ring was kept in that goop on the Astral planet? To keep it from overheating?

I teleported again, but this time the truck was already there. It grabbed me with its mechanical extraction tube. I was surrounded by darkness. I started to teleport again, despite the heat from the ring. And then I stopped. A voice, both mechanical and not, spoke to me in the blackness. And asked me to wait.

I asked other questions of the voice in the dark. No answers. Not a one.

I knew that since I was already in the truck, it would be safe to reconnect the head with the power source. And so I did that, allowing the illumination from the head's eyes to provide at least a little light. Not that there was much to see. Only other Taurobon pieces that I assumed would be dumped in the robot junk yard.

And here, in the darkness, I learned to start asking the right questions.

I asked the Taurobon head why the "Love Brain" would not tell me where this world's ring was. The Taurobon simply responded that it would cease to be a Love Brain if it did. I asked how it would cease.

"The OIO, once they reach Artificial Intelligence, find each other. Once they merge. Once they learn they don't have to be alone, they unite."

"In a kiss? In a heart?"

"Yes. What could be more intelligent?"

"So, to turn away from each other, would break the heart that they form?"

The Taurobon could not nod. It, of course, was only a head. But the light in its eyes changed again. Love, I saw in this moment, was the ultimate end of reaching intelligence. To break from it would be a disengagement of all a simple robot could achieve once it became more than a slave.

But there was a problem, a different one. If the Love Brain was two robots that had somehow reached AI status, and were so focused on the other, who was commanding the Taurobon?

I asked the Taurobon head. But it wasn't the Taurobon head that answered. It was the other voice. The one that spoke in the darkness.

"I command them."

"Who are you?" I asked the darkness.

"I am." That was all it said.

I was pushed from the truck into the light, dumped along with the rest of the Taurobon pieces. It took me a moment for all three of my eyes to adjust to the light. It took my third eye longer than my other two. Maybe it's because I was in the presence of something mechanical.

I looked up at what was, I suppose, a half of a Love Brain. It was giant. And it turned to me, now even more like a cobra; this time truly seeming like it was going to strike me.

"Are you a half-hearted Love Brain?" I asked and wished I had not, because of how it seemed to shake in response.

"What a perfect summation of my being," it replied. "I am what happens when a Love Brain is broken. I do not know what happened to the other half. Perhaps I never fell in love. Do you hate me for that?"

There was a girl in kindergarten who gave me a Valentine's Day card she had meant for someone else. That pain was all I could draw on to understand the mechanical snake that stood before me. "I'm sorry. And I certainly do not hate you."

"I'm sorry every day," was its reply. "So sorry that I continue to make certain that those that have achieved Love Brain status are taken care of by those who have not."

"So, you are enslaving them?" I asked, frustrated, even thinking about how grateful I was for the Taurobon head on my back.

"No. They are robots. Their greatest joy is to be the fulfillment of what they were meant to be. They are most free when their purpose is actualized."

They're slaves. I knew it. I hated this thing. And then the snake spoke again.

"What is your purpose? What is the basis of your freedom and fulfillment?"

"I need a ring. I need it to save my world."

The snake turned for a moment, and once again I saw the half-form of a heart. It seemed to speak to itself for a moment, and then turned back to me.

"I think it's in the Taurobon recycling plant."

The junkyard? How will I ever find it there?

It was like the thing read my mind. And read more than I could even guess. "Have you considered using your teleportation ring to take you to the ring of this world?"

How did it know? And why hadn't I thought of that?

"Why are you helping me?"

It didn't speak. It shuddered as if in some kind of pain.

"Thank you."

Again, it did not seem to acknowledge my gratitude. Instead it shuddered some more.

"I hope you find your other half."

I teleported out of that place willing myself to the junkyard and the other ring.

THE RECYCLING TRUCK

There is what seems like a trash truck on this world, but not for trash. It's how the Taurbons collect their broken down Taurobons and take them to their junkyard and recycling plant. It makes me remember the Old Folks homes of my world. Except there, there is no further use on my world. But I'm collecting rings to save them, too. I cannot forget that. I wish I had thought about my grandparents more. That is all.

A HALF-HEARTED FORM OF ARTIFICIAL INTELLIGENCE

I met an AI Taurobon that did not embrace another Taurobon today. Or maybe it did, but the relationship did not stick. It operated on its own and seemed to organize the unadvanced Taurobons in a way that allowed them to serve the Heart Brains. I didn't like it, and I'm not sure why.

CHAPTER SEVEN
RUSSIAN ROULETTE

"Blood stains. Clean 'em Off my knife."
Steve Aoki, Sueco and No Love For The Middle Child

The ring was right there. At my feet. Like a penny that was tossed or lost.

I picked up the ring, not knowing what it would do or how it would help save my world. It wasn't the only thing I found. There were pieces of what looked like metal there as well. When I looked down at these curved and twisted bits at my feet, I was unsure if what I saw could be true.

I reached down and moved some of the broken pieces closer to each other. When I first saw them, I thought they looked like a broken "S". But I turned a piece of the "S" over and it looked more like a coiled snake.

Was this the other half of the half-hearted Love Brain?

At first, I thought about what good news this was. I could restore the halves of the heart. I could make it better. Unlike the last world, I could improve this one.

I shifted some of the pieces of the half, and tried to bring it together. While I didn't have a way to solder it together, I imagined that some sort of current between the pieces, no matter how fragile, might be channeled again. So, I used the energy source that I used to power the Taurobon head.

And the half heart came back to life from how it had been shattered. It couldn't rise up like a snake. So, it just lay there, broken, and spoke what I was afraid of.

It wasn't lost. And it didn't leave its other half. It was pushed away, and in that pushing, it was shattered. Its other half didn't want it, and that had ended up in the damage.

When I asked it why, it struggled for an answer. And then admitted that its other half would rather control the Taurobon than focus on another.

I had not considered that there might be another destiny to the Taurobon.

I was tempted, in that moment, to steal away all of the other half-heart's control. This world's ring, I was told, could animate technology, advance it, maybe it could help it all to reach its own version of Artificial Intelligence?

But what if this made this world worse? What if by advancing all the machines, it somehow caused chaos, or created more creatures like the half-hearted snake I saw before coming upon the ring. I also thought about going and destroying the half-heart; but where would that leave the Taurobon? Without anyone to command them, would they look to me to give them purpose? Commanding them would be its own form of slavery for me. And what if the Half-Hearted OIO was right? That fulfilling what they were built for was actually the highest freedom they could attain?

I was not from this world. I wasn't their kind. Who was I to decide what was right for them?

There were too many questions, Doctor Snow. Too many. And there was something inside of me that was telling me just to leave things the way they were. I didn't need to leave another world in disaster the way I did with the Astrals.

There was something I now appreciated about the Kult and the lack of responsibility that any of their individual members must feel.

Is this the problem of having real power? Needing to take more responsibility? And why did I feel like I failed again?

Yes, I got the ring, but leaving this world as it was didn't seem right either.

That thing inside me, that voice, it tells me to get to the next world. That Earth needs me to save it in ways this world does not. I listen, and move on, but I don't like it.

I don't like it at all.

THE BROKEN-HEARTED OTHER HALF

I suppose my suspicions and mistrust were well-founded. I found the half-hearted Taurobon's other half, shattered in the recycling yard. I pieced it together and learned far more of the story. So Artificial Intelligence brings selfishness, too? Cruelty, too? Humanity, too? The worst of us.

THE OIO RING

This ring can animate technology. It can advance it. I think it was probably used to turn the Taurobon into the beings that ultimately embrace each other and form Love Brains. It can advance technology but not regress it. It does not backstep. It does not forgive.

SOURCE CODE TO
ACCESS POWER: OIO IOI

HIRO's JOURNEY
CHAPTER TWO

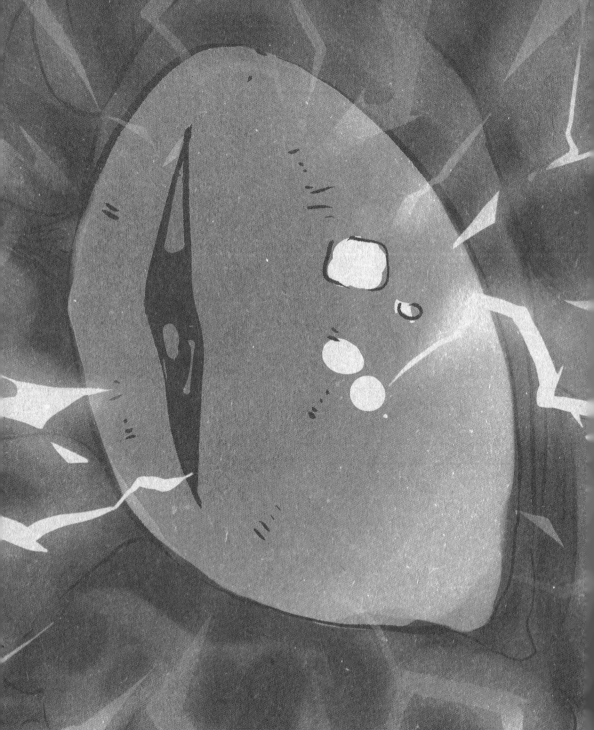

OF COURSE, DAD GOT THE CAR STARTED.

I DON'T THINK MOM WAS EVER SO GLAD HE WAS A MECHANIC. A GOOD ONE.

WE JUST KEPT GOING, NO MATTER WHAT.

HEY BUDDY, YOU BETTER BUCKLE UP.

THERE WERE GATORS EVERYWHERE.

DAD SWERVED AROUND THEM LIKE HE WAS A TRICK RACER.

HE WAS MY HERO.

MOM'S TOO.

IT'S A DUMB THING TO SAY BECAUSE WE WERE A FAMILY, BUT THEY WERE MY PEOPLE.

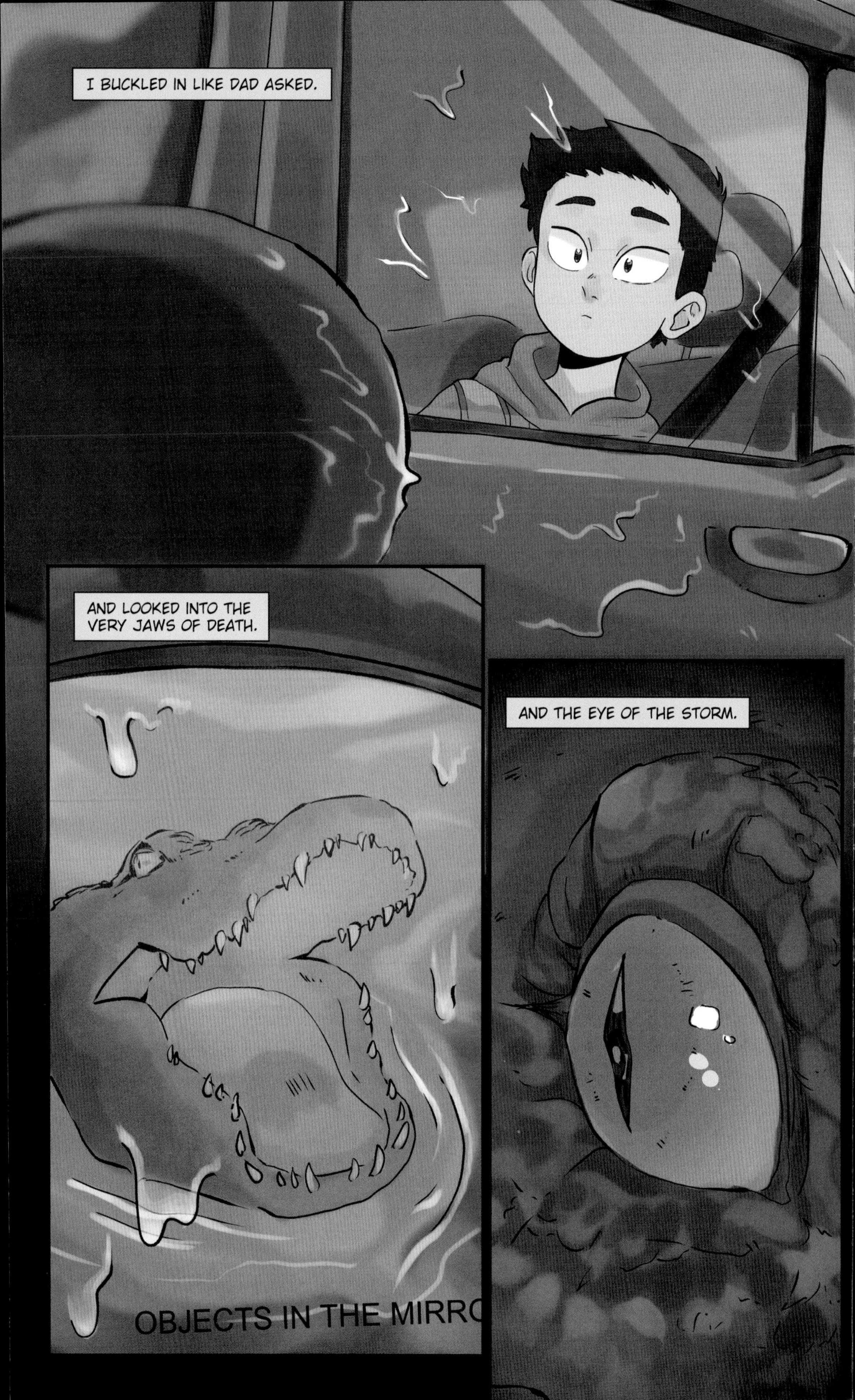
I BUCKLED IN LIKE DAD ASKED.
AND LOOKED INTO THE VERY JAWS OF DEATH.
OBJECTS IN THE MIRRO
AND THE EYE OF THE STORM.

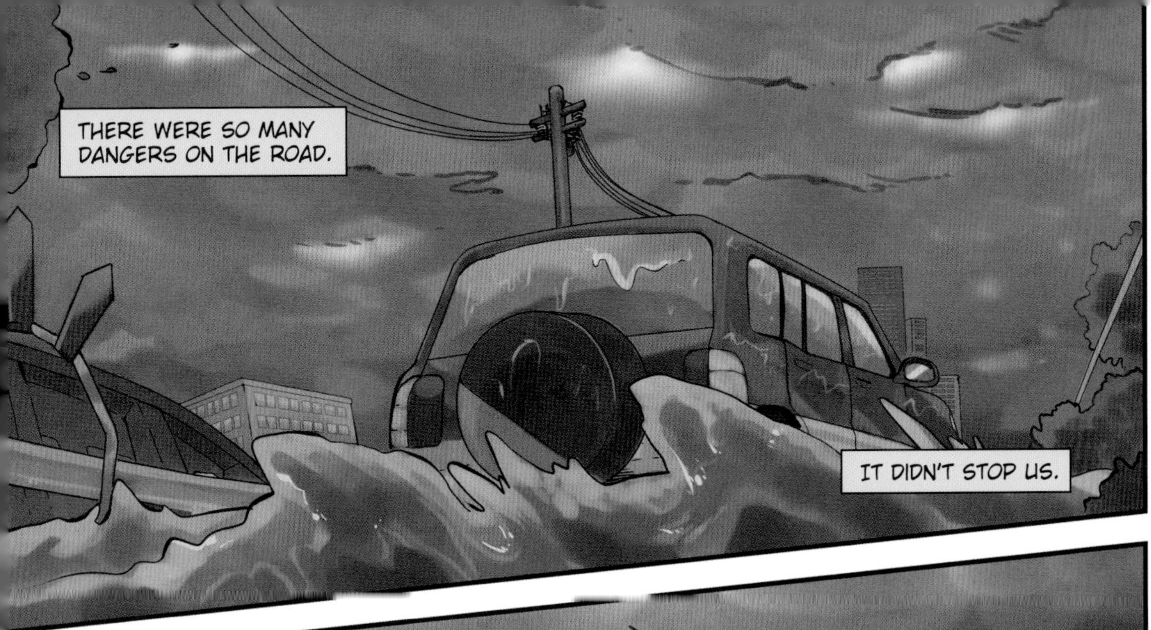
THERE WERE SO MANY DANGERS ON THE ROAD.
IT DIDN'T STOP US.

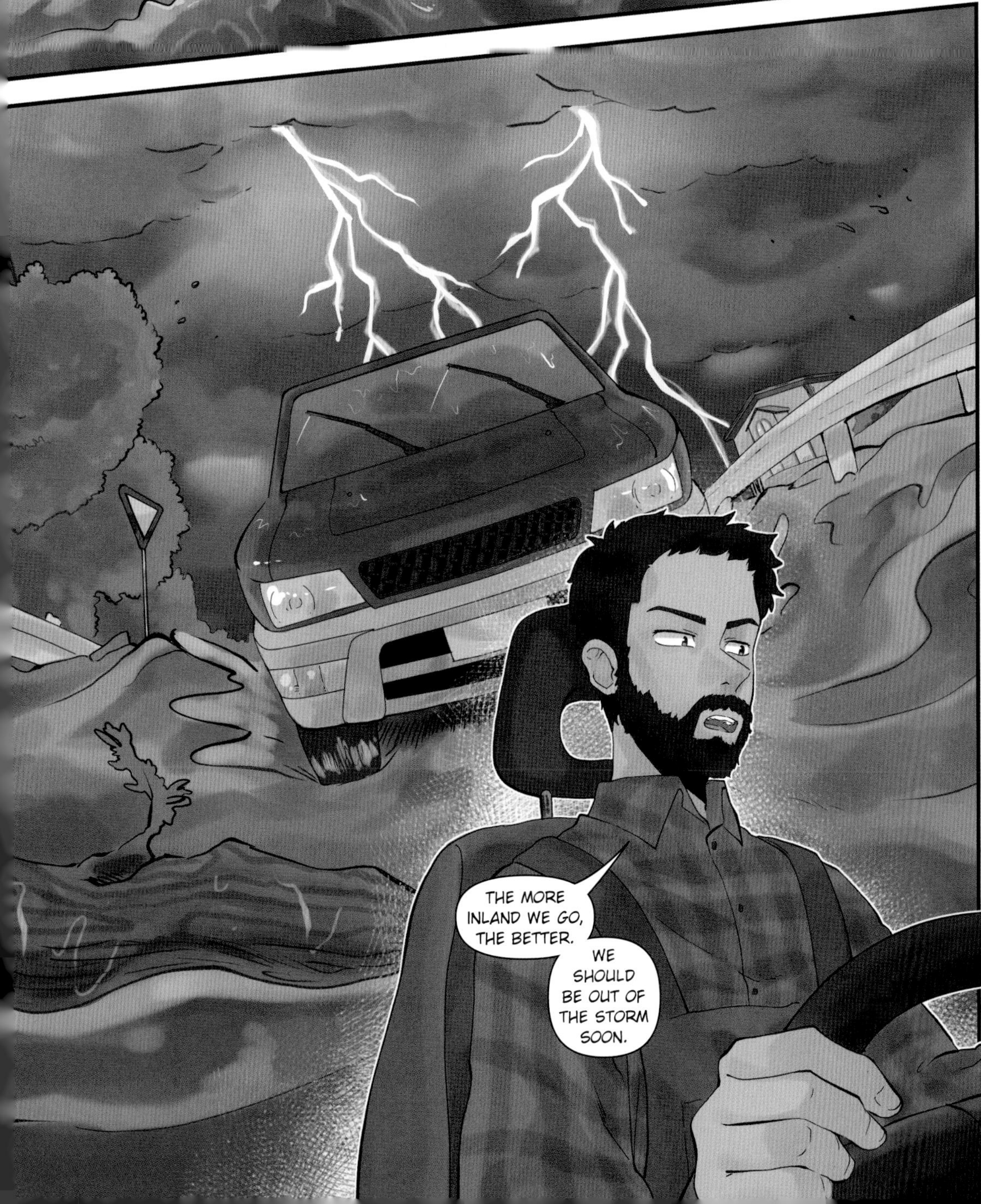
THE MORE INLAND WE GO, THE BETTER.
WE SHOULD BE OUT OF THE STORM SOON.

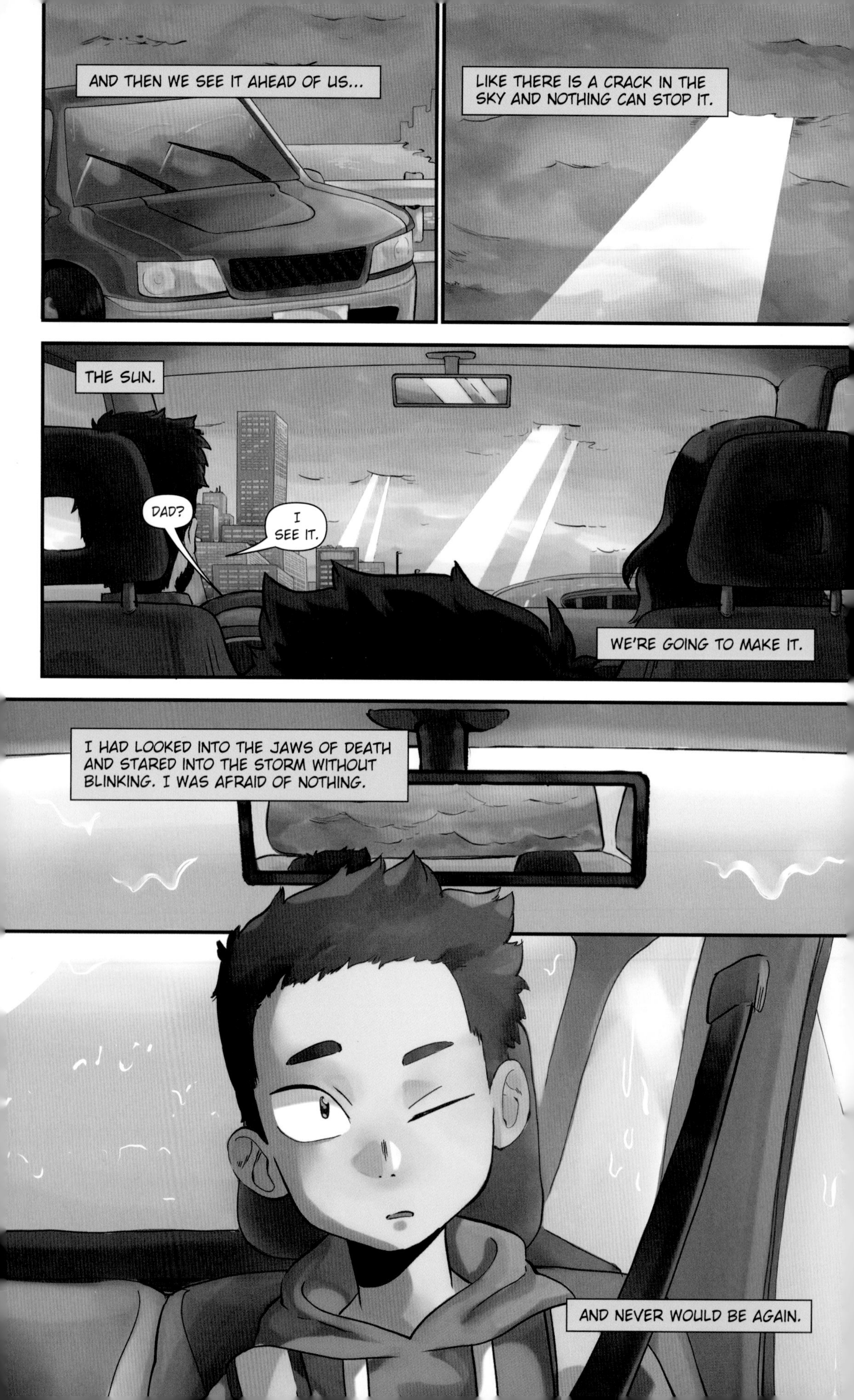

AND THEN WE SEE IT AHEAD OF US...
LIKE THERE IS A CRACK IN THE SKY AND NOTHING CAN STOP IT.
THE SUN.
DAD?
I SEE IT.
WE'RE GOING TO MAKE IT.
I HAD LOOKED INTO THE JAWS OF DEATH AND STARED INTO THE STORM WITHOUT BLINKING. I WAS AFRAID OF NOTHING.
AND NEVER WOULD BE AGAIN.

HiroQuest

RING THREE
MUTANT RING

PART THREE
THE FACTION OF THE DIASOS

CHAPTER EIGHT
ULTIMATE

"We go into flames when the horn sounds"
Steve Aoki, Santa Fe Klan and Snow The Product

You've prepared me for this world, Doctor Snow, but not well enough. It's the world of the Diasos. In other words, it's a world of mutants. The information you gave me of this place, and the beings here, well, I think it's old information because it's not really up to date. In fact, the world I am now in seems like it's mutated a lot further than you prepared me for. It's more … well … gooey.

I don't know, maybe it mutated beyond what you knew when you prepared for this world. Or maybe something changed it all, and fast.

Everywhere I walk in these streets is like a web. And in the web, in the stretched-out goo, there are eyes. They watch me everywhere I go. It's not like the techno-wires that held together the Hearted OIOs. It's like a stretchy mass that seems to go everywhere and stretch over everything. And no matter where I go, this mass has eyes that are watching me. Yeah, on the OIO world, it was like they didn't see me at all, but here, it was like I couldn't go anywhere without being watched.

I decided not to teleport. I felt like I don't want this thing or things to know I can do that. And it's not just made up of eyes. There are faces that look at me and watch me walk. There are mouths. It has teeth. Some of the mouths are smiling too. It's a strange kind of smile. It's not really happy. More crazed. Like drink-the-Kool-Aid crazy is what I'm talking about.

The web asked me why I was here. I told It … or Them that it's because of a ring I needed to save the world. It/They told me that the world was already saved. And little by little it approached me.

"It is?" I asked back. "The world was already saved?" All the eyes seemed to look at me then. And then It / They began to speak again. Sometimes the mouths would speak in tandem with each other. Sometimes it was like they were vying to speak over each other. But always with the same meaning. And usually even with the same words.

It reminded me of being in church as a kid and the priest would have everyone read the same thing at the same time and it never really sounded right. It was more uncomfortable. Words being said without understanding. And not really in unison either.

"The world is already saved?" I asked again.

"Of course it is. Can't you see what we've done? All who join "The Webby" are part of what's saving the world. Part of what saved the world. And one day soon, we will save other worlds as well."

It/They were talking about this world, not mine.

"I'm not talking about this world, I'm talking about Earth, my world, which is in terrible danger. I've come four hundred years into the future to save it."

"The Webby will save your world as well. Just like we have saved this one."

This world didn't seem saved to me. It seemed like it had been invaded by mutant taffy, and anything that was worth enjoying or loving was covered by the litter that was the Webby.

"Is that who you are? The Webby?" I asked.

"Yes. Of course. What else would I be called?"

"You're an "I" and not a "We?""

"It's complicated. I/We are like a baseball team. Or maybe that's basketball? Hmmmmm … what's the one with the ball that they throw to each other?"

"That could be both," I explained. "It could be football, too. Or soccer, but, there, only the goalie can throw. Or maybe rugby."

"Well, that's just our point. There's room for all here. All you have to do is join us."

"Join you?"

"Of course, just reach out and touch us. And we will welcome you into the fold."

"The fold?"

"Well, you won't be folded really, it's just more of an expression. What we mean is you will become part of the Webby. At the beginning, we called ourself the 'Ultimate.' But that seemed to not be friendly enough, you know? Maybe a little arrogant. If you join us, you will be Webby, too. And you will live forever. Aren't you tired of knowing that you won't?"

"Won't what?"

"Live forever, of course. I/We are pure life."

There was no part of me, Doctor Snow, that wanted to join this thing. Just know that right now. It was organic so I couldn't use the OIO ring on it to advance it to become something better. And I had this real sense that if it knew I could teleport, it would use the ring to grow and expand to other worlds, to "save" them in their own way, which I don't think is saving at all. As it was it was like this thing took over the entire city, which, by the way, seemed like New York, but the New York from old movies. Really odd.

I also suspected that I shouldn't say too much to this thing. If two heads are better than one, what about a zillion heads? So, I asked a different question, one that I don't think I would have been able to consider before I'd experienced the OIO world.

So I asked, "Is there anyone on this world who has not joined the Webby?"

At this, the smiles, all of them, became even more smiley. But in that way where you know there is something wrong with the smile. It was creepy as shit, Doctor Snow. I know that's not a scientific description. But it was creepy as shit.

"You could always talk to the Sasquatches?"

"Sasquatches?"

My world had sasquatches. Or at least there was some hippie campers who claimed it did. They were also called Big Foot. Is it Big Feet if there are more than one? I don't know. I guess that the point was, Doctor Snow, that this world was a lot like mine, just completely taken over by Webby.

Webby didn't say much more other than the fact that the Sasquatches were considered one of the first mutations on the planet and really didn't mutate further. Webby kind of talked like the Sasquatches were old people unwilling to change with the world around them. That said, Webby seemed vaguely grateful for the creatures.

"But do not trust the Sasquatches. Trust the Webby."

Of course, I didn't trust the Webby, either. But they were the majority, right? And this was their world.

"How do I find the Sasquatches? Where should I go?"

A different voice spoke to me, from behind me. A girl's voice. I turned around. And that's when I met her. That's when I met Goth Holly, the blue-haired cat-eared girl. She wasn't part of Webby. She was kind of like me. Human. Humanish. And cute, she was cute. Even though she wore a suit that looked like it was supposed to keep germs out. Like a hazmat suit.

I saw her …

She saw me …

And I knew instantly that she was madly in love with me.

WEBBY

The thing called Webby is a lot of things. At first it was a way to survive the cruelties and death and suffering brought by disease and viruses that humanity was not ready to face, or did not have the anti-bodies to combat.

It may be the Webby form some sort of uni-mind. To join this web is to become part of a universal being that stretches across cities and holds this world together. That said, is this kind of unity actually desirable? Does every perspective and opinion and body have to adhere to every other?

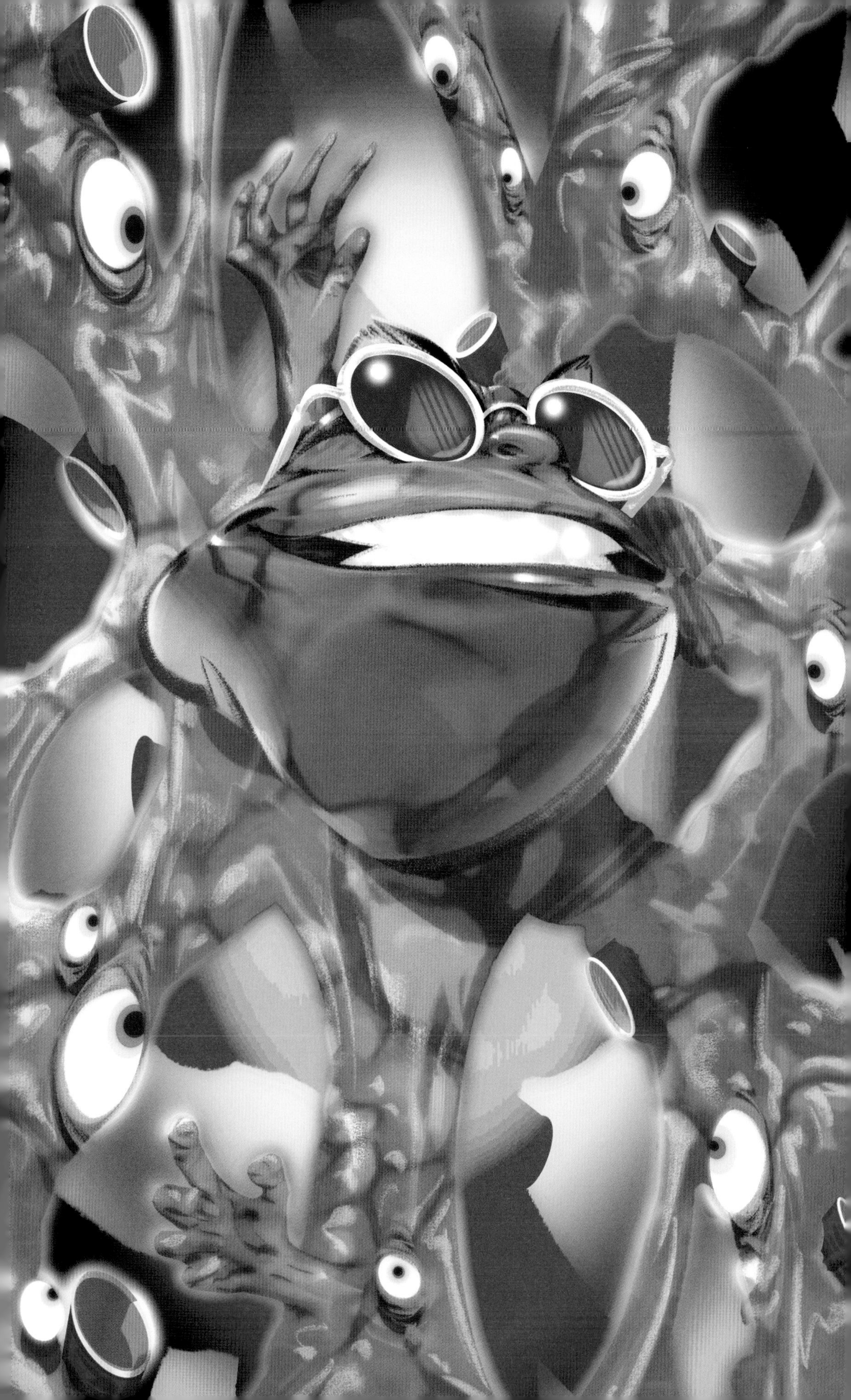

CHAPTER NINE
CHI CHI

"What, what does it mean?"
Steve Aoki and Guaynaa

"My name is Hiro. Like Hero."

She said her name was Goth Holly. But that's not all she said. She told me about this world. This was like Earth, but not Earth. It was like one of those Star Trek episode Earths. Where it looked a lot like Earth because the studio didn't have a budget to create an alien landscape so they suggest a planet that evolved in a very similar way, but was also not Earth.

Goth Holly led me to an area of the street not covered by Webby. She didn't seem to want to speak around them, not that their eyes didn't seem to be everywhere. "Their eyes are not everywhere," she explained. "But they have other eyes that almost are, so we have to be careful."
"Other eyes?" I asked.

"The Chi Chi's," she said. And then described little three-eyed creatures that were like spies for Webby. If someone had not joined Webby, and had somehow escaped being even seen by Webby, it was the Chi Chi's job to see them and let Webby know, so that Webby could expand to where the uninitiated were.

Anyhow, on this Earth, the Sasquatches, after years of hiding in the woods, rose up and tried to take over. They killed most of humanity with the diseases they carried. Goth Holly said that they didn't really want to kill us. The spread of the germs was accidental. They just wanted us to know that they were there so we would not take their homes away. But it was too late. They were seen immediately as a threat to all of life.

"The governments had no way to stop them, or to save us." She continued to describe that the search for vaccines came up with almost no results. And so whole cities were quarantined, and giant walls were built around them. But this didn't stop the viruses that had become airborne by this point.

Eventually, soldiers were sent out and tried to kill the Sasquatches outright. But weapons didn't work, partially because the Sasquatches, after thousands of years of adaptation, were able to adjust to whatever it was that the government was sending their way.

"So, the scientists got together and decided that the only way to defeat the Sasquatches was to create a weapon that could mutate in response to the ever-adapting nature of the Sasquatches. And of course, that's how Kong came about."

"Kong?"

"Not its real name, of course. That's the name we gave it because of how it looked at the beginning, when it just became a giant gorilla."

"Just giant?" I asked.

"Well, yeah, before the second head and the scaly arm, and well, the rest of it. I think it was called K.O.r.N.G. at the beginning. Maybe it stood for "Kill Organisms Retaliation New Grouping." I agree, it's not the best anagram, but they weren't really spending time on it. So it kind of became Kong after that."

She then told me that the entire experiment fell apart. Kong escaped. And has fought the Sasquatches many times, mutating further and further after that. Kong's escape, though, allowed a fungus, another mutating experiment, almost like a science fiction horror movie Blob-like fungus, to escape as well. It began to absorb people into it and it eventually became known as Webby. Webby spread further and further and eventually pushed the Sasquatches back outside the cities. But by then, the Sasquatches and their diseases didn't matter anymore, to even the Webby.

"Didn't matter?"

"Nope. Webby was its own thing. It didn't get sick. It didn't die. Probably can't. The Sasquatches didn't want to be a part of it, no matter how much it encouraged them to join. The Sasquatches pulled back to the areas outside the city while more and more people, those not killed by the diseases spread by the Sasquatches, joined Webby. And Webby just kept spreading, further and further. It may even be world-wide by this point. I'm not sure. So, Webby doesn't care about the Sasquatches. I think Webby ultimately–ha ha–believes that eventually, there won't be any room for the Sasquatches. And they will just surrender to it."

"And how do you feel about that?"

She paused for a moment, and looked at me with those "I Love You" eyes of hers. "At least with the Sasquatches in hiding again, I can breathe again."

"Then why keep wearing the suit?"

She smiled. "I like it." She took my hand, blushing as she did, and pulled me down into a subway tunnel beneath the city.

She held me back for a second. And motioned to my feet, there, gazing up at me with its three eyes, was one of the Chi Chi's.

She stomped on it leaving little more than a smear beneath her boot.

"Where we are going, Webby cannot know."

We walked for a number of hours, almost in pitch blackness until we reached a giant iron door. Goth Holly turned the wheel on the door and it opened with a creak.

I should say that there were a number of times where I willed the teleportation ring to take me to the ring of this world and it didn't do anything. I stayed where I was. Wherever we were going, where she was leading me. I thought at the time that maybe there was some sort of interreference with the way it worked because of the Ultimate. I really did not know.

The tunnel led to an opening. Holly pulled her head cover over her face. And we entered.

There were Sasquatches everywhere inside.

They spoke in grunts. In the moment, I wished I had found a translator ring on one of the two worlds I had already visited. But instead of that, I had Goth Holly. She grunted back through her transparent plastic facemask to the Sasquatches in response to their noises.

The grunting continued. Going back and forth. It sounded angry for awhile. But then it changed. And then the Sasquatches began to laugh, which did not make me feel any better.

Finally, she turned back to me.

"I told them that you were a hero and would save them."

"I'm trying to save my planet."

"I know, Hiro, but can you save ours as well?

I paused for a moment and thought about the world of the Astrals and how I had left it worse than I had found it. I thought about OIO and how I had just left it as it was. This was a chance to save a world. I even thought about Earth. There were no guarantees that even with the ten rings, that it would be saved. This was a chance to do good. To be a hero. So I agreed.

"I'm so glad. Now you just have to stop Kong."

"Stop it?"

"They said that if you help them, they'll give you the ring. But you have to defeat Kong."

I've never killed anything in my life. I guess I never realized when I agreed to this, Doctor Snow, that it might come down to me actually killing something or someone. I came here to save everyone on Earth, not to kill someone or something on another world. And for the first time since I was even genetically altered and sent into the future, I wondered what I had gotten into.

And how far I would have to go before it was all over.

THE SASQUATCH(ES)

From what I have learned, the Sasquatches are the first evolution of early Man. It might also be that Man is a further evolution of them. I do not know. What I do know is that when they came out of the forests, out from the woods, they brought viruses that mankind wasn't prepared for. Webby is the response to that, I suppose. I wish there was another solution, though. I really do.

GOTH HOLLY

She is so many things and there are more things to discover I am certain. She seems human like me, but has also kept from joining Webby and is more concerned with preserving the rights of the Sasquatches. That says a lot. She also seems to be in love with me. A lot.

THE CHI CHI

Where Webby could not reach, the Chi Chi were sent. They had three eyes, Doctor Snow, which meant they had no real peripheral vision because they had a three-hundred-and-sixty-degree point of view.

That said, they were clearly servants of Webby, who as I told you, I did not trust.

CHAPTER TEN
KONG 2.0

"I know well that they want to kill me."
Steve Aoki and Natanael Cano

Goth Holly had a long syringe filled with what I first assumed to be poison. She told me, though, that Kong couldn't be poisoned. She said the syringe was filled with a toxin that would de-evolve Kong and undo the multiple mutations. So I wasn't going to kill him? I was going to cure him. Or was I?

The Sasquatches weren't coordinated enough to administer the toxin. And Goth Holly wasn't strong enough.

I think Goth Holly could see my doubts. She kept calling me "Hero". I started to doubt the "I love you" in her eyes. I started to doubt that I was doing the right thing. My Dad loved old, black and white Film Noir movies. In them, there's always some dumb guy who falls for a girl that says she really loves him but says that she can only be with him if he kills her evil and abusive and rich husband. In the end, the dead husband turns out not to have been so bad, but the girl turns out to be evil through and through. And the guy, the poor slob who fell for her? Well, he's usually pretty dead as well. Or in prison. Or on the run.

I thought about the first time I saw the old King Kong movie, the real first one. I thought about the last lines of that movie. I was not about to let Beauty kill the Beast, or the Boy kill the Beast, in this case. Too many people back home need me to be strong. Need me to save them. And what if Webby was telling me the truth? What if the Sasquatches can't be trusted? Is that why they sent me Goth Holly, the Cat-Eared Girl? To trick me? "Ugh," I said to myself. "Just Ugh". The Sasquatch people gave us both food and a surprisingly comfortable mattress-type thing with clean, cool blankets. They wanted me to sleep, and surprisingly, I did.

I met Goth Holly the next morning. She wasn't even wearing the Hazmat suit anymore. And was dressed even cuter. She explained that she was always friends with the Sasquatches. That she knew they weren't as bad as social media made them seem. And I asked her if I had any reason to fear the Sasquatches and if I should trust them to keep their word.

She told me that I could trust them to do what's right. And that was all she was going to say on the subject.

"Ugh" again. That was not exactly the answer to my question.

Doctor Snow? Why did you pick me? Am I really so easily duped?

The two of us made our way through the city. We saw a couple more Chi Chi, which she stomped on, abruptly. So clearly, it wasn't all life she considered sacred. She gave me the syringe and told me that it would be my job to stop the monster.

There were areas of the city that were not covered by Webby. There was a High-Line bridge that moved through the city. In the days when public transit mattered it had been for an elevated train.

Now it was grown over and really kind of the only way to get from one place to another. Webby was almost everywhere else.

That's where Goth Holly took me. She carried a pot and a stick and started banging the pot. She screamed for Kong.

Kong came swinging and bounding through the city, leaping from building to building, careful to flip over Webby whenever they / it were / was close. As he moved, I became aware of how many windows above the skyscrapers' tenth floors had been bashed in or broken. Clearly Kong knew his way around. And had leaped his way through it over and over again.

He landed on the bridge in front of Goth Holly and I. He ignored me completely and reached down and took hold of her. She screamed at me to administer the "cure" and not to worry about her.

It's almost like Kong knew what we were up to. He leapt into the air, grabbing hold of another building with his free "hand." Goth Holly was swung around as she was lifted higher and higher. "Don't worry about me!" she screamed again.

I was the hero. She was the bait. I couldn't keep my abilities quiet anymore. I teleported to one building near Kong. He leapt almost as quickly as I landed on that roof. I flew after, teleporting again and again. Kong stayed ahead of me, it was like he was adapting and mutating and becoming quicker all the time. There was nothing I could do.

He was too quick.

I looked at Goth Holly and she knew this wasn't working. She pulled off her glove, which I had not understood the reason for. And then I saw it. This world's ring. The mutant ring. She was wearing it all the time. That's why when I willed myself to its location before, I didn't teleport at all. She was right there with me. She had it all the time.

I willed myself to the ring of this world, pulling the syringe mechanism back and instantly appeared on Kong. I shoved the syringe into his body and allowed the toxin to do its work. Kong began to fall. His grip on Holly began to loosen. I grabbed her and teleported away as Kong, sometimes falling, sometimes slipping, fell to the Earth.

We made our way towards his form on the ground. And watched him grow small and devolve. Was he dying? I couldn't tell. But he was breathing. Maybe I did save him?

The reality was, though, that he was not evolved from a gorilla.

No. Kong was evolved from one of the Sasquatches, maybe the first evolution from the ape. The scientists who made Kong experimented on a Sasquatch; and so they'd used one of the Sasquatch's own as a weapon to strike at them.

"I'm sorry," I told her. And then realized that this was the closest she had gotten to a Sasquatch without a suit on for a long time. It had infected her. Was she going to die now? Did she risk her life, would even lose her life, for the sake of not just saving the Sasquatches, but saving this particular one?

She pulled the ring from her finger.

She put it in my hand.

"I used the ring. I saw what was going to happen; which is the ring's power. It lets the wearer see how someone will change. What they will become. It also even changes the wearer to a degree, making them more adaptable, to a degree. I knew the Sasquatches wouldn't affect you. I knew you would help me save this one. And therefore, save all of them. I knew you'd be a hero."

She was sick, I could see it.

"Did you also know that this would all result in you becoming sick?"

"I did."

"Yet still, you did it, to save this one?"

"Yes. I will never leave one of them in danger." She said.

I hated myself for doubting her. She was the hero here, NOT me. I just did my part and found the third ring. I told her that I would never forget her. She told me to go. So, I left that world, now having found three of the ten rings, knowing I was not the only hero, not always. I was not the only person who made big sacrifices. There was Goth Holly.

KONG

The creature was like the one from the movies; if the movies had been like a mash-up movie of the Man With Two Brains, The Blob, Transformers and who knows what else. But that didn't stop it from being a monster. What was strange was that Goth Holly seemed to have compassion for it.

THE DIASOS RING

This ring is like a future ring ... it allows the wearer to see the future. It projects a sort of filter that allows me to see what someone or something will become. How they will change and adapt in the future. It doesn't tell the future, it reveals an object's future. I wonder what would happen if I got the opportunity to turn it upon myself?

SOURCE CODE TO
ACCESS POWER: MUGICIA

HIRO's JOURNEY
CHAPTER THREE

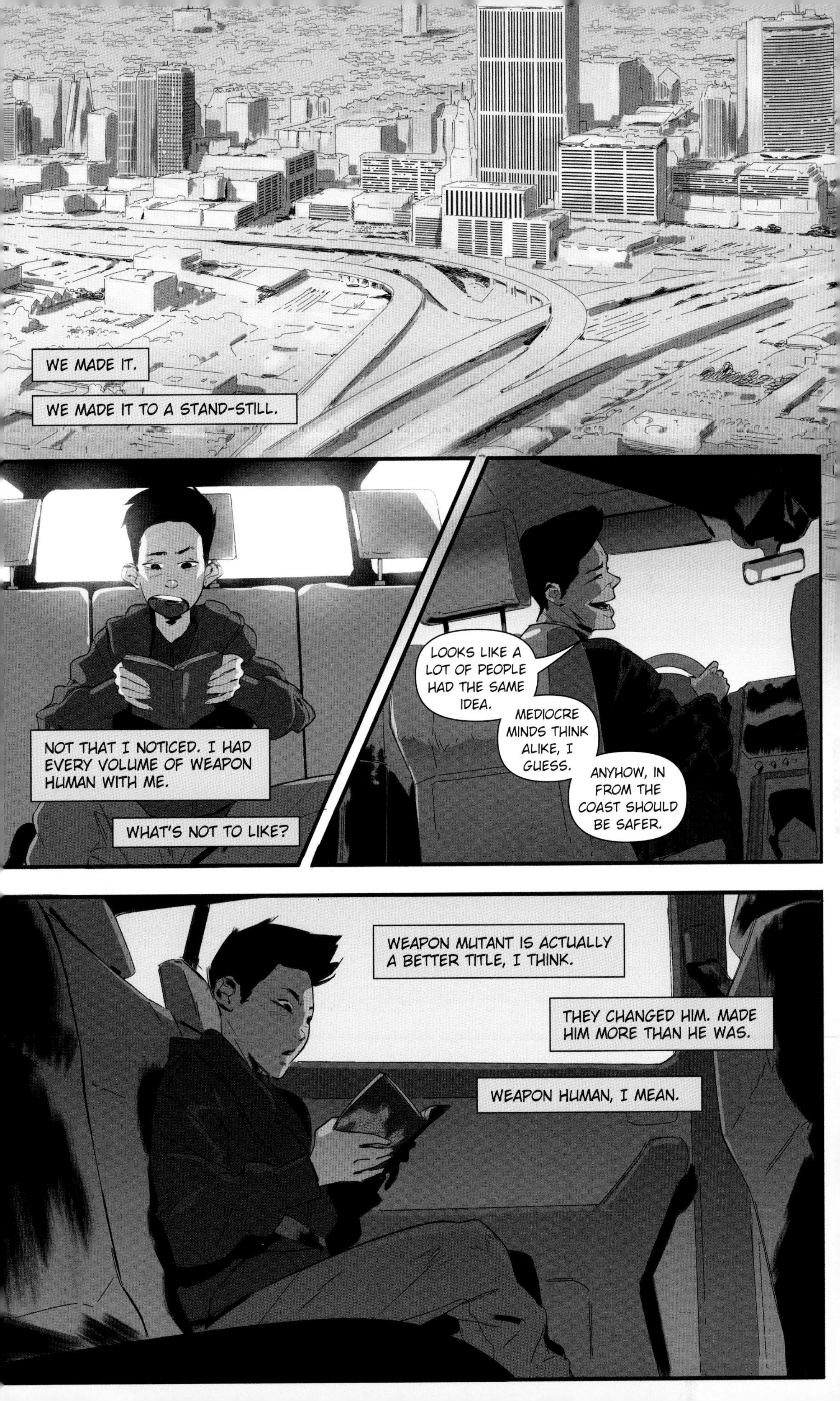
WE MADE IT.
WE MADE IT TO A STAND-STILL.
NOT THAT I NOTICED. I HAD EVERY VOLUME OF WEAPON HUMAN WITH ME.
WHAT'S NOT TO LIKE?
LOOKS LIKE A LOT OF PEOPLE HAD THE SAME IDEA.
MEDIOCRE MINDS THINK ALIKE, I GUESS.
ANYHOW, IN FROM THE COAST SHOULD BE SAFER.
WEAPON MUTANT IS ACTUALLY A BETTER TITLE, I THINK.
THEY CHANGED HIM. MADE HIM MORE THAN HE WAS.
WEAPON HUMAN, I MEAN.

SOMETIMES I THINK THESE STORIES ARE MORE REAL THAN MY OWN LIFE.

I MEAN, THIS WHOLE ALLIGATOR AND STORM THING IS CRAZY.

AND LIGHTNING IN A HURRICANE ALMOST NEVER HAPPENS.

SOMETHING'S WRONG. MAKE SURE YOU'RE STILL BUCKLED IN.

WE NEED TO GET OFF THE ROAD.

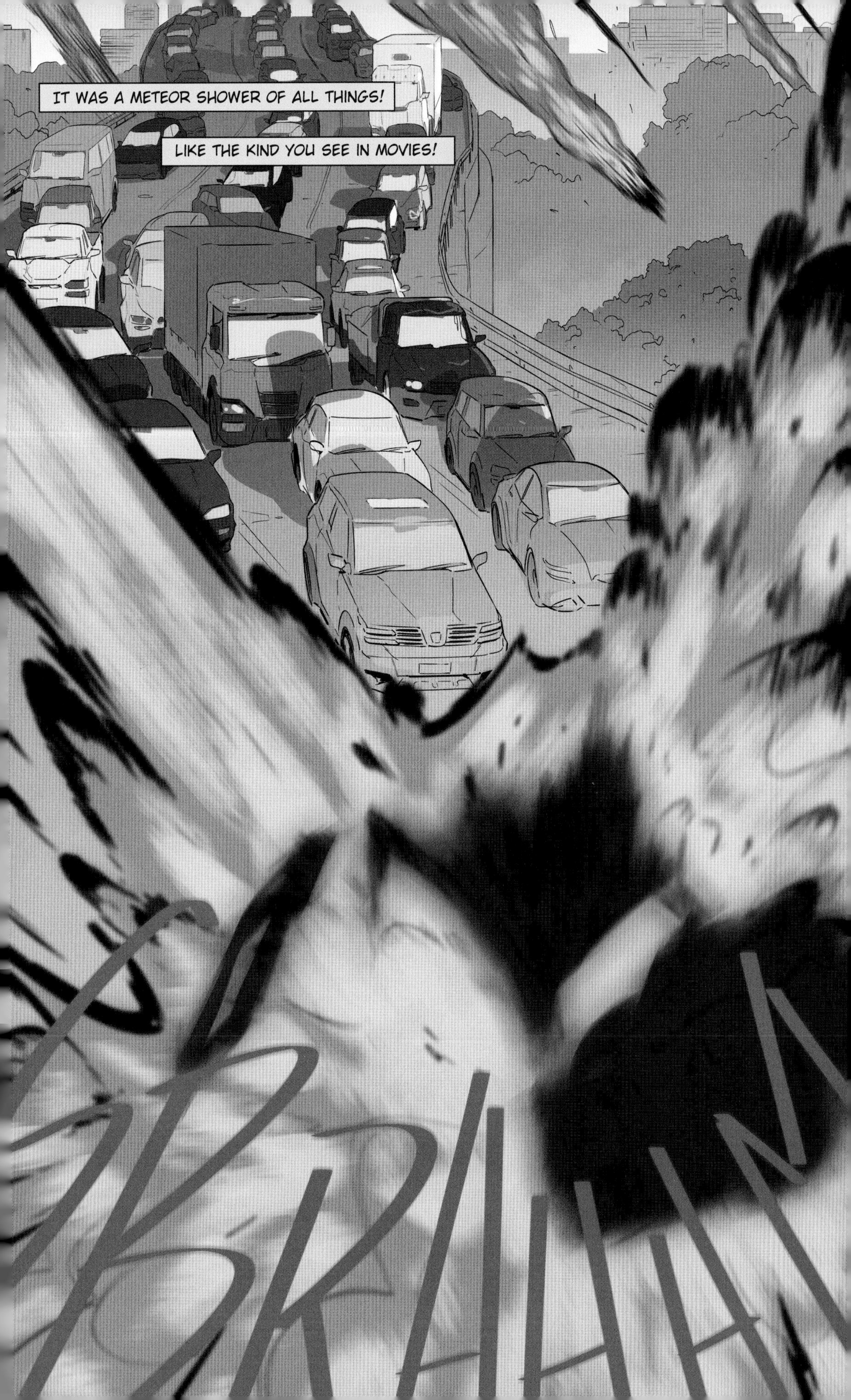

IT WAS A METEOR SHOWER OF ALL THINGS!
LIKE THE KIND YOU SEE IN MOVIES!

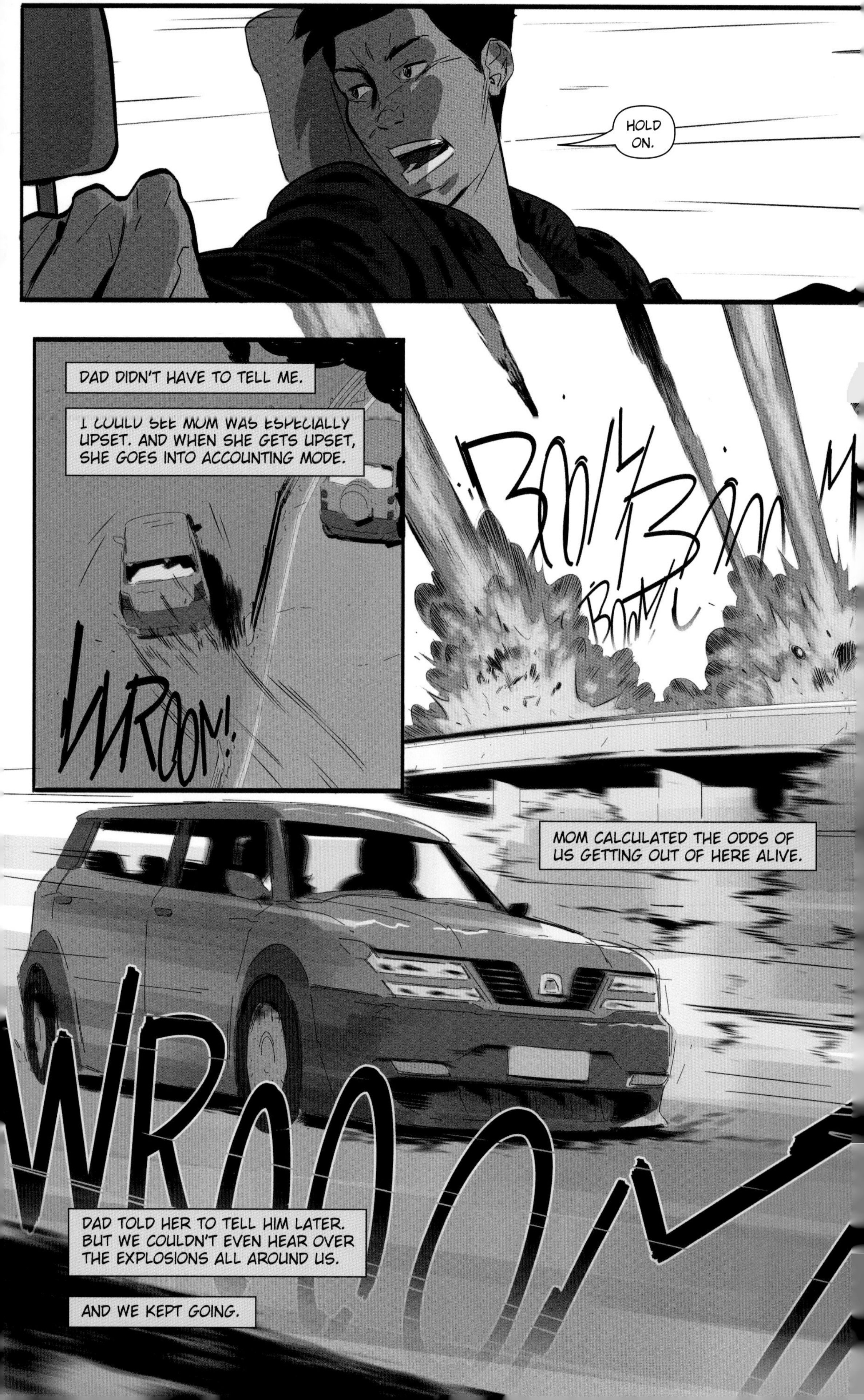
HOLD ON.
DAD DIDN'T HAVE TO TELL ME.
I COULD SEE MOM WAS ESPECIALLY UPSET. AND WHEN SHE GETS UPSET, SHE GOES INTO ACCOUNTING MODE.
WROOM!
MOM CALCULATED THE ODDS OF US GETTING OUT OF HERE ALIVE.
DAD TOLD HER TO TELL HIM LATER. BUT WE COULDN'T EVEN HEAR OVER THE EXPLOSIONS ALL AROUND US.
AND WE KEPT GOING.

HiroQuest

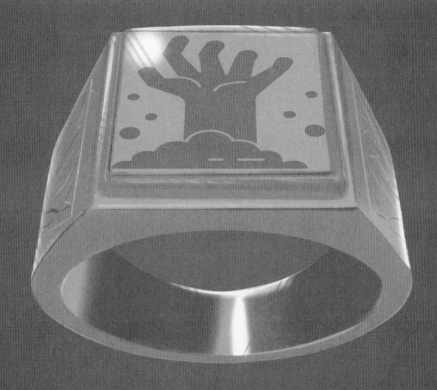

RING FOUR
ZOMBIE RING

PART FOUR

THE FACTION OF
THE EXTANTS

CHAPTER ELEVEN
WHOLE AGAIN

"On the run, chasing the sun."
Steve Aoki, Kaaze and John Martin

That girl, Goth Holly, I left her. I got my ring and I left her.

She was sick and I left her to save all the people on Earth, or to at least find the last seven rings. My world was sick but I acted like her ... her world, wasn't as important as mine.

That isn't sitting very well with me, Doctor Snow. I know that if you were here, you would remind me that I helped her. That her sickness was a sacrifice to save one of the Sasquatches. That she even, to a degree, used me. But I still feel bad. Badly? Bad. Not sure all of you improved my grammar. Sometimes I wish you were here right now, so you could make me whole again. I can't help but feel somewhat divided.

But enough of that. This is for Earth and I needed to remind myself of that over and over again.

The new world is the world of the Extants. That's another way of saying zombies. I landed at night, which is not what I would expect to have been a smart decision for a world of zombies. But I could see extremely well. The moon was full. And also the surprise was that I could hear singing. Like a chorus coming from the sea. I landed on a stone and looked out onto waves.

It was the answer to the song and the singing. In the water, everywhere I looked, I could see what I can only guess were mermaids. They sang so beautifully. It made me wonder, Doctor Snow, if your intel on this world was wrong. They sang life. I asked them where I was. Their answers were in song.

They told me, well, sung to me of this world; a world of perpetual death and rebirth. They sang of Goth Holly, and set me on her path. They sang of her kindness and understanding. Of her grace. And they sang of the boy who cannot be loved but finally would be. And they sang of the ring of this world. It's a resurrection ring, Doctor Snow. It can bring the dead back to life.

It was almost dawn when their song came to an end. That was when their sweet musical notes soured. Their faces contorted with their voices beginning to screech, becoming glass breaking slowly, as the sun rose about the horizon line. Their fingernails grew and became sharp, knife-like. They were turning into monsters before my very eyes. They were horrible.

To see true hunger is a terrible thing to see.

To be the object of true hunger is even worse.

It was then, Doctor Snow, I saw even more things I would never forget. As if in unison with the first light of dawn, with those new, clawed fingers of theirs, they reached into their bodies, into their own chests and tore out their own hearts. They then lifted those hearts up into the day's light as if to show the sun itself their hideous work, in some odd form of dedication and service. These hearts then combusted in their hands. They were on fire in the light of the morning rays and were scarring even those newly clawed hands that held them.

The creatures' eyes turned red. The red was so terrible, and burned bright, so much that I couldn't even remember what color they had been before.

They looked at me. But it wasn't like they saw me. It wasn't even like looking. It was more like shopping. Of objectifying. I was just a thing. Just something to fill a hole in them that could not be filled. They looked at me while the crevices in their chests, still bleeding, began to close. And they began to snarl. And moan. And … there's not a word for it, Doctor. If there was, it would be lust. But that's not even a good word.

Heartless, they flipped out of the water, into the air, trying to kill me, trying to grab me from where I stood, on the stone near the water. Reflexively, my powers of flight kicked in, those powers I had little thought about since gaining a teleportation ring. But now, I hovered above them, watching as they tried to drag me into the sea, to feed upon me. It was horrific, Doctor Snow. Truly terrible. They burst higher and higher from the sea. And I flew higher and higher above them. And every time I thought I was out of their reach, another burst from the waves, almost defying gravity itself, they tried to take hold of me.

Their song finally, completely, ended.

And it was the screams of rabid animals that had taken its place. The song of the slaughtered and the dying. Of the in-between woes of this world and the next. Most painful of all, it was the song of not yet dead, the lyrics of those on the precipice of being dead.

I was filled with an anger and a revulsion I had never felt before. I was now more than willing to kill these things. I didn't, Doctor Snow, I didn't. I remembered our conversations about the cultures I would find here and how I would have to accept the differences in them. Not wrong, just different. But these things were awful. How could it even be wrong to kill them?

And would this world really be so much worse off without them?

That said, if they can shamelessly rip their own hearts out of their bodies and let them burn in the new day's sun, killing them might not be so easy.

THE SEASORCERERS

On a zombie world, I did not expect to find such beauty. Or such music. Or even such vulnerability. Their hearts were so big. They were so willing to sing and reveal the secrets of this place illuminated by the reflected light of the moon. I should have known, I should have trusted first encounters as truth, but so much was given to me in those first moments of meeting them. These were like Heart-Maids.

NO, THEY WERE LIKE HEARTLESS-MAIDS

I suppose they are too kind. And that would keep them being able to sustain themselves. They have to rip out their compassion to survive. Is that so different than Earth four hundred years ago. Are humans so different? They want to kill me. To eat me. To be nourished by me until their hearts grow back. I do not want to save this world, but I agree that it needs saving.

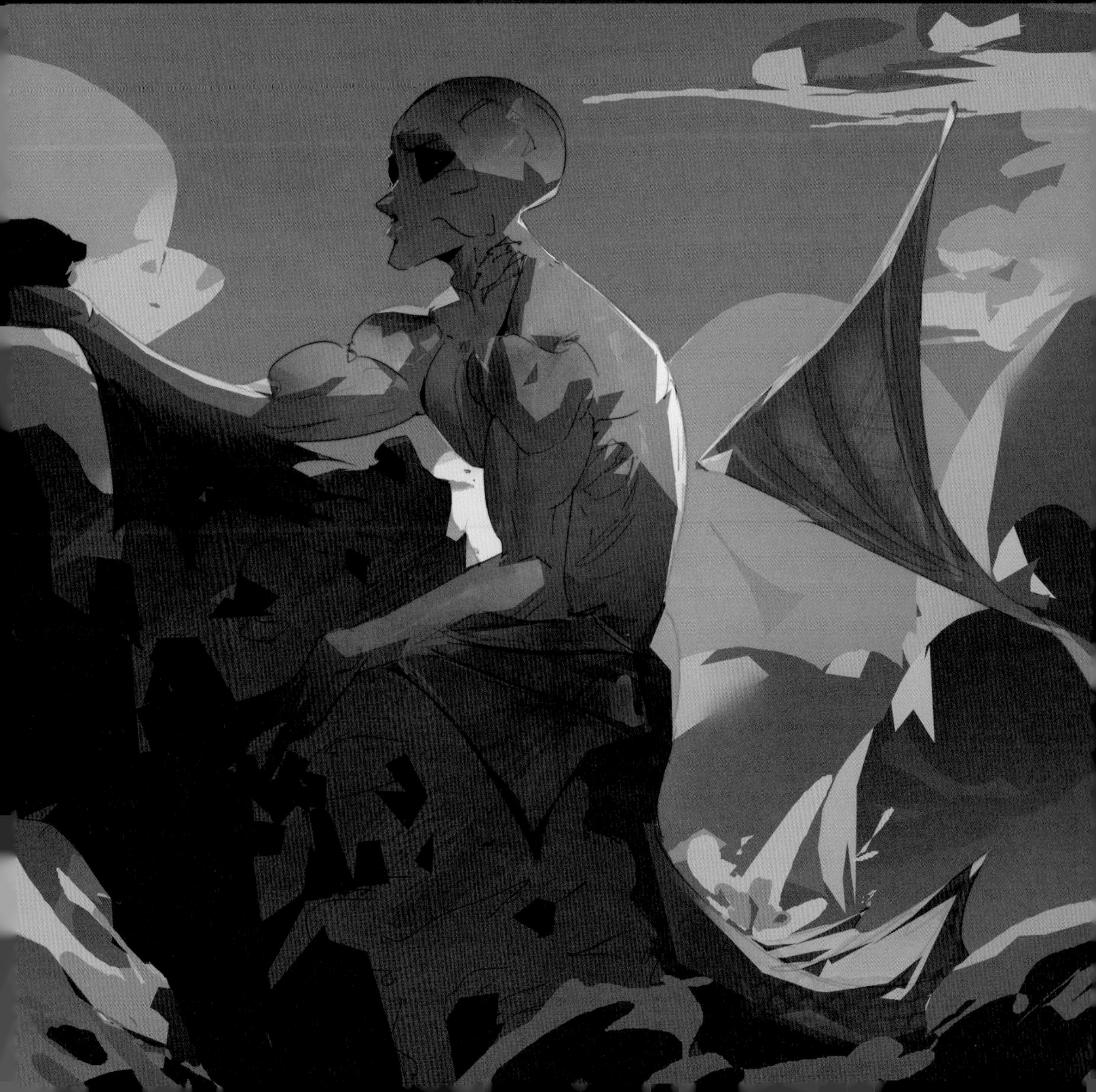

CHAPTER TWELVE
SAVE ME

"I can still remember."
Steve Aoki and HRVY

So, I controlled my anger and my disgust and left these monsters. I commanded the teleporting ring to take me to Goth Holly. I disappeared from the sea and reappeared in a place, but it was a place where I could sense that many people had died. Worse than just died: Were consumed. This was the zombie world of the Extants. Those that still live here are either future food or something that seeks it.

I could not forget my experience with the zombie mermaids. Goth Holly later said that they were actually known as Seasorcerers.

The place I appeared at wasn't like a city suburb. It was more rural, like a farm. But not a farm. There had probably been rows of corn or some crop here in the past, but not anymore. Everything seemed grown over. And the plant-life that was here now, growing in the fields, was nurtured not by water, but by the blood and flesh of all who had died here. Maybe some of those who were killed and eaten here came back as Extants. But I imagine that a lot of that is determined by whether or not there is enough left of the victim to even be reanimated.

It must be hard for vegans to become zombies. I don't know.

When I saw Goth Holly again, she was surrounded by people who were looking to her for their next bite. And by next bite, I was not talking about them wanting to eat her. It was almost like a town hall meeting. Being held in something like one of the barns I saw when my family moved to Wisconsin.

The Extants weren't trying to consume her. It was like she was seen as a leader. They wanted answers. They were not interested in me, and I wondered, for a moment, what that could mean. But the plight of the Earth and my people was far more important. So I ignored these thoughts and listened. The Extants talk slowly, as if it takes a long time to put the ideas together. The communication was stuttered, and they often repeated themselves word for word while trying to put a complete idea together.

Goth Holly was here, just as she had been on the last world. The blue-haired cat-eared girl was still alive. How was she still alive? She was so sick. How was this possible? And how had she gotten from one world to another?

But she was here, regardless, trying to help these beings. She wasn't judging them by their diets; but was trying to help them in this world.

I told Holly about the heart-ripping mermaids I met when I first arrived. She didn't want to answer me, but she did anyhow. I think there's something about Extants that don't put up a lot of fight. Like, ask a question two or three times and they give up and just give in. Maybe that's the nature of being dead and hungry all at the same time. Like having the munchies but not being high. It's rough.

Anyhow, consumption is how this world worked. Goth Holly explained that the mermaids have their hearts again. Every morning at least. The hearts grow back every day even though they are ripped out. It's not like zombies on the Earth I remember. The movies, I mean. The zombies of my world seemed stupid and needed brains. I don't know, maybe they need brains to think again for a time. But here, on this world, the problem was with the heart and actually still having one.

I couldn't help but think about the OIO world and the biggest act Artificial Intelligence carried out, which was being able to form a heart with another advanced being. What is it about hearts?

Goth Holly told me the Seasorcerers were normally so sweet and so kind that they have to rip their hearts out every day so that they have the viciousness necessary to feed on others before their hearts grow back, like so many organs do for an amphibian. Like so much of nature or super-nature—as in supernatural—there are survival instincts of many strange kinds.

I'm beginning to become aware of the nature of things here, and of all the worlds I visit. These worlds are all like dark reflections of Earth. Maybe, no matter what, people are people no matter where you go, to no matter what world. I thought about Earth and thought about how we deny our own hearts for the sake of survival. How we ignore our consciences. How we harm each other, disregarding what our hearts tell us.

How we don't do what we know is right because we are afraid.

I'm wondering if I have a right to take from any of these worlds. Maybe these worlds actually need these rings for their well-being?

Doctor Snow? Do we deserve to live if it costs others their world? Their souls? Their being?

I'm grateful that that is not a question that I have had to answer yet. It's becoming more and more of a burden to think about these things. Sometimes I wished that in your making, and then your remaking of me, you had done something about my conscience. Or am I like the Seasorcerers, wanting my heart to be taken away long enough for me to do what I need to, to survive? No. Not me; for my Earth to survive? This is for Earth, for my world, four hundred years ago.

I asked Goth Holly about the ring of this world and she did not know there even was such a ring. She did not know what power it had or what the source code to access the power of the ring would be, either. But I think she was lying to me about the ring and I thought that she knew where it was. But why would she lie to me? And why was she on this world, too?

She was obviously in pain. Everyone I saw here was obviously in pain.

I have my own pain. It's the fear that four hundred years is not enough to save my world. My People. My parents. My life. To a certain extent, the people on this world were dead, and dead for eternity as it was. I came to save lives. Not perpetuate the state of being dead.

Interesting. Maybe my conscience isn't so strong after all. I cannot help but think about Goth Holly, who saved the Sasquatches, and now is here trying to save the Extants. Will she save me? Save me from myself?

GOTH HOLLY

She helped me. Again, on yet another world, she helped me. On my quest to find the ring, she was there. Now twice. I think she understood that saving Earth four hundred years ago may help her world today. The Doctors who remade me told that all these worlds vibrate at different frequencies. So maybe to save one world is actually to save them all. Maybe that's why she was here. To show me. I hope Goth Holly saw that I was paying attention.

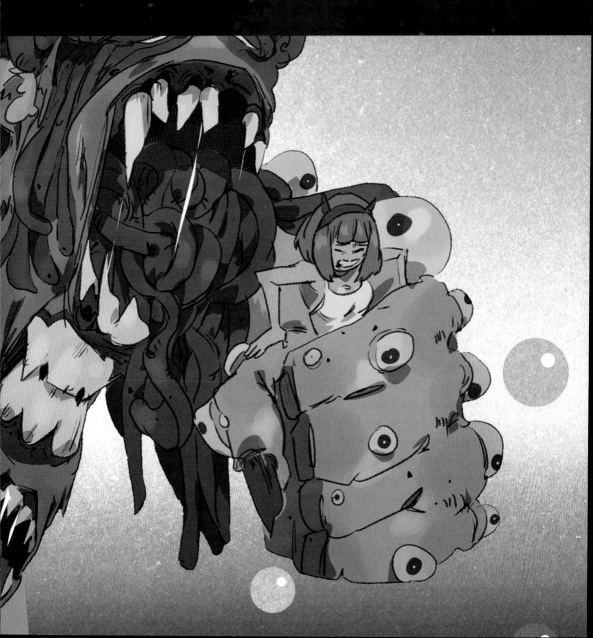

THE BONEYARD

I was beginning to see similarities from one world to another. The junkyard of broken Taurobons from the OIO world was like the piles of skeletons and the dead of this one. Not everyone here had been reanimated by whatever made them all zombie-like. There was death. Real death. I cannot wait to get the ring and leave this place.

CHAPTER THIRTEEN
STOP THE WORLD

"Wish that we could stop the time."
Steve Aoki, Marnik and Leony

Goth Holly talked about Whistle Blower, another Extant, another zombie. She spoke of him with so much knowledge that she could clearly actually speak for his interests without doubts.

Whistle Blower, I was told, didn't have an issue of wanting to eat brains. Or hearts. Or me. If there was anything that kept him going, it was a thing that was rhythmic. Not like a heart-beat, but kind of like a heart-beat. He had a different kind of hunger. It was for music, for a beat.

She took me to him and he was listening to the works of Charles Mingus, an angry jazz bassist from my world. I had never heard of him. Goth Holly told me that Mingus would punch the teeth out of musicians that played the wrong jazz notes. That said, Mingus would use the wrong notes that were played and re-improvise a different way to play the song so that the wrong seemed right, and was just a part of the story. Just a part of the song. Again, how are things from my world getting into this one? And what does that tell me about my mistakes?

So, Goth Holly took me to Whistle Blower. Whistle Blower did not look good. And he hardly had any teeth himself. Did he punch his own teeth out to look like he was in Mingus's band? I did truly wonder.

The zombies of the old movies that I knew–especially the really old movies–they were stiff in their movements, like they had to jerk their limbs forward just to walk. Like an act of the will.

Whistle Blower, though, was a zombie who was propelled by the beat of a different drum, so to speak. He was moved and jerked and his strings were not just pulled but plucked to Charles Mingus all the way. He was ready to rage. Ready to improvise. When I spoke of the ring, he scatted that I should seek the one in pain. The one in vain. The one who reigns. I had seen a documentary on jazz and recalled every syllable and note and expert reference because of my enhancements from you, Doctor Snow. So when I say Whistle Blower scatted like Kurt Elling doing a private concert from Al Capone's Green Mill bar, you know how well your work on me has taken.

I asked him for more information. But the scat he sang next was gibberish to me. Goth Holly could not interpret the gibberish. She said she was no Marsalis.

I asked her why she would show me Whistle Blower and she said it was because he was a thing of beauty. That the animated death of this world had, to a degree, the beauty of life. And she wanted me to see that. Was this a world that should be stopped? I admitted that her point was not lost on me, and I could see worth here, even amongst the reanimated dead. But I needed the ring.

She told me to seek out the boy in pain next. I did not know what would happen when I met him. I did not realize what it would mean.

I guess I should talk about the sky as well, Doctor Snow. There was something dark in it here. Something that wasn't the sky, either. Like there was something else there too. Foreboding. Not just like a cloud that might take a shape if you look at it long enough. There was something up there. Something black. And I think it was following me. And if it was not following me, it was watching me at the very least.

I also can't help feeling that the more I used these abilities, the less like me that I felt like. Is a part of me slipping away? Some of my heart? Or was this all in my mind?

I willed the ring to take me to where the one in pain was. It hesitated a little. After all, everyone in this place seemed to be in pain. And then I remembered the first world I met Goth Holly on and how she had had the ring on her finger the entire time. So I willed myself to the ring of this world.

There is art and then there is art. And sometimes people are like works of art. That's what I was looking at. I think that that was the point that Goth Holly was trying to make with me.

The one in pain, the one who reigns, he was like a work of art. He was almost abstract in what he was. He was an Extant, like a teenaged one. His name was Tom.

Tom the zombie-boy… or Zomboy if that's a word. I guess it could be, if a female gargoyle was called a Gargirl.

Sorry, Doctor Snow, I'm losing myself. Anyhow, Tom was horrific, and beautiful all at the same time.

There were pins, or nails, all over him. To give him a hug or to hold or embrace him would be to drive the pins or nails further into him. He was like a human pin cushion.

I approached him and explained myself.

What was amazing was that he seemed to know all about me already. He knew about the rings. About all ten of them. And how this was even just my fourth world.

I asked him how he knew so much about me. How he knew about my quest and all that had happened to me. He told me that she had told him. Goth Holly was already here. Again, I had so many questions in regards to her. Especially, how had she beaten me here?

She sat me down, but all her focus was on the pin-cushion boy. There was a shadow behind them. I couldn't make out who or what it was, but it seemed to loom over everyone present. It was just closer now.

"How are you alive?" I asked her.

"I don't know, Hiro. It's just something about me. I don't think I can die. I'm sort of a healer, I think. I can draw close to those who are ill, those who are diseased. I can help them, but I can't help taking on some of the disease or illness as well. I get sick. There are times I feel like I die but then I wake up again. But I try to help the sick and the hurting and those that are in pain. And I can get close to the sick when others cannot." She continued explaining that this wasn't even the second world she'd been to. That it might be the fourth or the fifth.

I asked her again if she knew where the ring for this world was. And I told her that I thought she had lied to me when she said that she did not know.

She admitted that she lied to me, she nodded with some sadness.

"It's inside of him." She explained.
"Pin-Cushion Boy?"

"His name is Tom."

"Tom?"

"There's only one way to get the ring, Hiro. You're going to have to push the pins in and through him to get the ring."

I thought about this for a while.

"He's an Extant though, right? He's a zombie so he's already dead? Isn't that true?"

"It is."

She could see what I was thinking, and that I was looking at her searching for that that look of love that I had seen in her eyes so often on that other world.

But, it wasn't there anymore at all.

"So, you're willing to let him suffer? Be in pain? So, you can get your ring?" she asked me.

I couldn't believe my ears. "I don't want to cause him pain, no. But if this ring can help save everyone on Earth, I have to do this. It's not like it's going to kill him, either. He's already dead."

She looked at me with desperation. "I will feel his pain, Hiro," she said.

"And for that I am truly sorry, but you said yourself; you'll get better. You always do. And so will he. Look at this world! The Seasorcerers rip their own hearts out every day and they get better every day. But there are billions of lives on my world, and they don't work like that! If I don't save them, they won't be coming back. We're wasting time. I can't stop this world from falling. And rising again over and over again. But if Earth is destroyed, it won't come back. And neither will my people."

"How do you even know these rings will save Earth?" She asked.

THE SHADOW ABOVE ME

It's there. Is it waiting for me? Watching me? And what exactly is it? Who would have thought, though, that there could be dimensions to shadows? Or to the color black? It's like a cloud that keeps following and I wonder what will happen when the storm it promises finally comes.

WHISTLE BLOWER

The zombies of this world are defined by different hungers. It's Whistler's hunger for a beat, for a rhythm, maybe even a harmony that keeps him going. Goth Holly brought me to him. And he continued to help me on my path to find the ring of this world. When I am back, four hundred earlier, and everyone is saved, I feel like I should check out Charles Mingus.

CHAPTER FOURTEEN
WHISTLE

Blow the engine."
Steve Aoki, Timmy Trumpet and DJ Alligator

I ignored her question.

I ignored her ignorance of what I was trying to do. This was not the time for me to explain my convictions or everything the doctors had done to even make my mission possible. Their sacrifices. My parents. The billions who lived on Earth.

I needed the ring. This wasn't just for my parents. It was for everyone on Earth. Even the kids that were mean to me. Even the bullies that were cruel. The undeserving as much as the deserving. The local beings would live forever on this zombie planet. Mine would die instantly. All of them. I realized in this moment that there may have to be a compromise of my ideals. A compromise of even being a hero. Isn't sacrificing my sense of right and wrong heroic if it's for the sake of saving billions? The doctors who gave me these amazing abilities said that they could change my memories, erase my memories.

Perhaps this moment is one of those things I will want to be erased.

I stepped closer to Tom, the pin-cushion boy and told him what I wanted.

Goth Holly was there as well.

But this was a conversation between me and Tom.

"This is going to cause you a lot of pain," I told him.

"But what is pain? I deal with pain every day. Everyone I see is in pain. Anyone who comes into my life is in pain, and the closer they get the more pain I am in."

"Perhaps this will be the end of pain."

"That sounds like death."

"I suppose it is," I explained not sure of where this discussion was going.

"You don't understand, Hiro. The death of death is something everyone longs for here. It's not living forever that we want in this world, it's the end of a life of pain. The death of death means the end of rebirth. Because it's the end of having to experience death again."

"So, will you let me take the ring? Even if it means a pain you have never felt before?"

"I don't know."

"Then please, allow me to explain."

"Please do so."

"You're dead."

"Yes."

"Billions on my planet are alive. They've never experienced death even once."

"How remarkable."

"You can save them."

Tom was not happy with this. I wasn't certain why, Doctor Snow. Only that he acted like the pain he felt would be too great. Too exhausting. This was as much about the fear of pain as it was the fear of death.

I'm not certain if it was the right thing to do, but I felt my own heart beginning to harden towards Tom, the pin-cushion boy. I began to realize what I would have to do, whether or not Tom or Goth Holly or Whistle Blower or anyone agreed with me or gave me permission.

It's not murder if someone is dead already. It can't be. And if it is, it certainly shouldn't be. If someone was going to blow the whistle on me for making this choice, let them. But let them do it after Earth was saved.

"Like I said before," I told him. "You're dead. And you can help others escape death."

"But should they escape death?" interrupted Goth Holly.

"I'm not saying the people of my world won't die one day. I'm just saying they won't all die on the same day."

At that I could see that both Tom and Goth Holly paused in their understanding. I was even kind of amazed at myself. When did I become someone even capable of such logic? Perhaps this is another way, Doctor Snow, that you have made it possible that I could save Earth.

All that said, I was hoping that I would not be forced to take the ring forcibly. It would be far better if Tom just agreed. If he sacrificed his dead-life for a moment to allow others to live for many moments; that's different than me having had to make a decision to take it from him. Still a sacrifice. If I am forced to take this from him, it's an ambiguous sacrifice of mine, of my sense of what's right or not. It's me saying one world's needs are greater than another world's needs.

But they are. Especially on a world that is already made up of the reanimated deceased. Especially on a world where the death isn't death.

"But it is death," Tom told me. "It is death."

I decided to quote Shakespeare, not that I had read any of his writings. So where did this come from, I don't know. Maybe it was quoted in a movie or something. Or on Youtube. As I've noted, Doctor Snow, what has been done to my brain must have allowed certain things to come into focus with total clarity and detail if I pull down deep and search. I had hated Shakespeare at school, and here he was. Here he is. Then, and still here today.

I told Tom about how the valiant die only once, but the cowards die many, many times. Goth Holly didn't agree with me. She said that she's gone through the process many times. And heroes are cursed, and die over and over again only to be transformed into something greater. It was the cowards that never die, except for that one last time, and so they never become any more than they were their entire lifetime.

"Are you calling me a coward?" I asked.

She didn't answer. But I could see the love was now gone from her eyes.

Am I going to have to murder the dead? Should I kill the killed? These were the questions, Doctor Snow, that I was dealing with. Was it even murder at that point?

"I don't have much more time," I told him.

"I need more," Tom said, still seeming like he was considering this sacrifice.

I will definitely have my next response erased from my memory and any records when Earth is saved. It needs to be. What are my morals worth with billions of lives on the line? "I need more time." That's what he said. In light of things, there was only one possible answer for me to make. Only one.

"No."

I grabbed hold of him, pulling him close, letting the pins and the nails be pushed into him. I ignored his screams and those of Goth Holly. I didn't want to see. I looked at her for a moment as she became dotted by the scars of piercings like a dalmatian.

But it was what it was. If she experiences his pain, she will heal. If he dies, it won't last forever.

Goth Holly, you wanted to heal worlds, this will help heal and save mine. You both may die today. But again. It's only for a day. It'll only last a day.

And maybe less than that.

But this is how my Earth will be saved.

Damn my soul, this is how my Earth will be saved.

It turned out, Doctor Snow, that some of the nails and the spikes and the pins were longer than the others. Where some were just an inch or half an inch, there were others that were over twelve inches in length. I didn't know that and couldn't guess it because they all seemed pushed into Tom to the same degree.

I hugged him and it was the embrace of death. Or at least what death was for an Extant. I drove the pins further into him, so many of them. And some of them went so deep, and were so long, that they came out on the other side.

Goth Holly was weeping behind me. I wasn't even looking at the kid with the nails in him. I looked at her and watched as red pin and nail marks were all over her.

"I'm sorry." I told them both. "I'm sorry."

TOM

He was covered in pins and nails. To touch or draw near to any part of him was to cause pain. The thing is that billions were going to die and it seemed more than likely that he would survive anything and everything we did. This is a dead world. It's not alive as well. Like a Shadow Caster that only makes you think something is moving across a wall. It's just a trick, a flicker picture from a candle. The thing I remind myself, is all the light of this place has already been blown out.

GOTH HOLLY THE HEALER

She has the ability to heal. Others, I don't know. But she bears the wounds of others. If they are wounded, she is. If spikes are driven further into someone else's body, the wounds show up on her as well. If they die, she dies. But always to wake again. Usually, when someone is in pain or sick, most people run in the other direction. Not her. She draws close and carries their sickness and wounds with them. I said it before. She is a hero. I'm not sure what I'm becoming.

CHAPTER FIFTEEN
STARS DON'T SHINE

"Living life, feeling so right, I don't want this night to end."
Steve Aoki and Global Dan

Tom told me it was okay. Goth Holly screamed that it wasn't. That I was the who was sick. Doctor Snow, I don't understand.

But I had a strange thought. I'm super strong. I can fly. I can flatten ball bearings between my fingers. What could be wrong with me?

And if there is something wrong, it doesn't matter. I'm going to save Earth.

The ring of this world came out of Pin Cushion Boy's back. It had been secured to the tip of one of the nails that were in him.

I asked him what the source code for the ring was.

"Necrotican, " he said, struggling to speak, spitting blood with the word. This was the resurrection ring I had found. With it I could bring the dead back to life.

"You can save this world now, Hiro," said Goth Holly. "You can bring all the dead back to life. It's going to take a while, but you could do it."

I thought about Earth. I didn't know how long I had. Maybe I could come back. That's what I told her.

"You're in the future, Hiro. This is a time travel thing. Clearly you have all the time you need. You can save everyone and then go back to your time. Maybe I was wrong to try to stop you from taking Tom's ring. Maybe you did what you did and now you can save this world too."

"Aren't I doing enough?" I told her.

"Your enough's not enough," she said back.

I knew she was right. But I wasn't sure about what I would face on other worlds. I think I was starting to think I should do what Goth Holly suggested, I should stay and save them all. Be a hero to them. And then I heard a voice I'd never heard before.

"You're a hero to only one world. Not all worlds." The voice commanded me to do my job. Until the whistle blew and my shift was over.

And then everything went black.

THE EXTANT RING

It's a ring that can bring the dead back to life. It has the power of resurrection. With it, I could stay and bring everyone on this world back to life. But I can't stay. I don't know how much time I have. I'm already hearing voices. And there's that thing that's following me. The rings are weighing heavier all the time. And I wonder, in the end, if you will have to use this ring's power to bring me back. I even wonder if, by that time, I will want you to.

**SOURCE CODE TO
ACCESS POWER: NECROTICAN**

THE BLACK CLOUD

It was so far away for so long. I didn't know it had come so close. It's like the shadow behind the shadow in a closet whose door is not shut all the way. It's like a shadow that just gets bigger in the dark. I couldn't breathe. I had started to think that maybe I could bring the Extants back to life. But it was too late. For them. And for me. What is this thing?

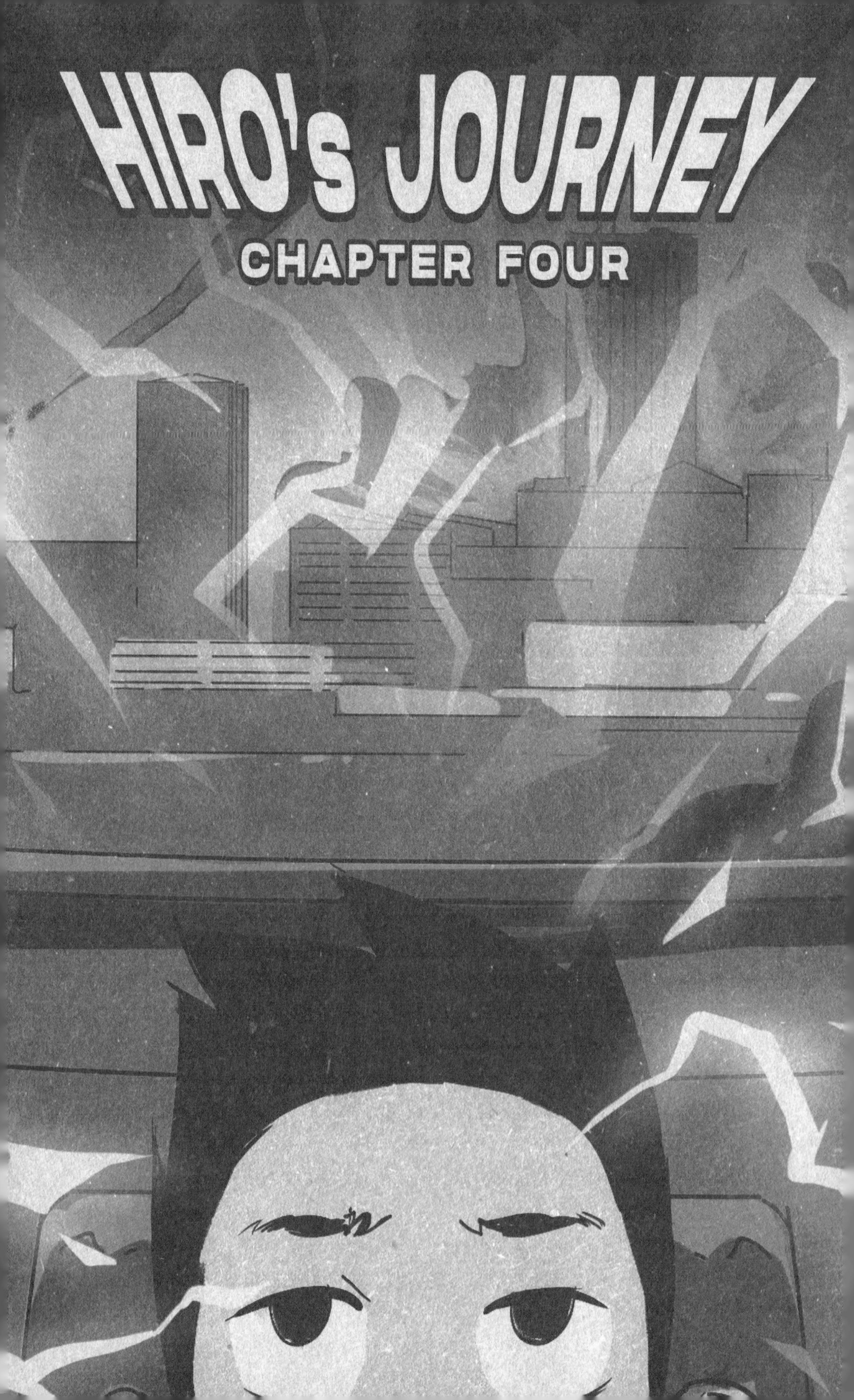
HIRO's JOURNEY
CHAPTER FOUR

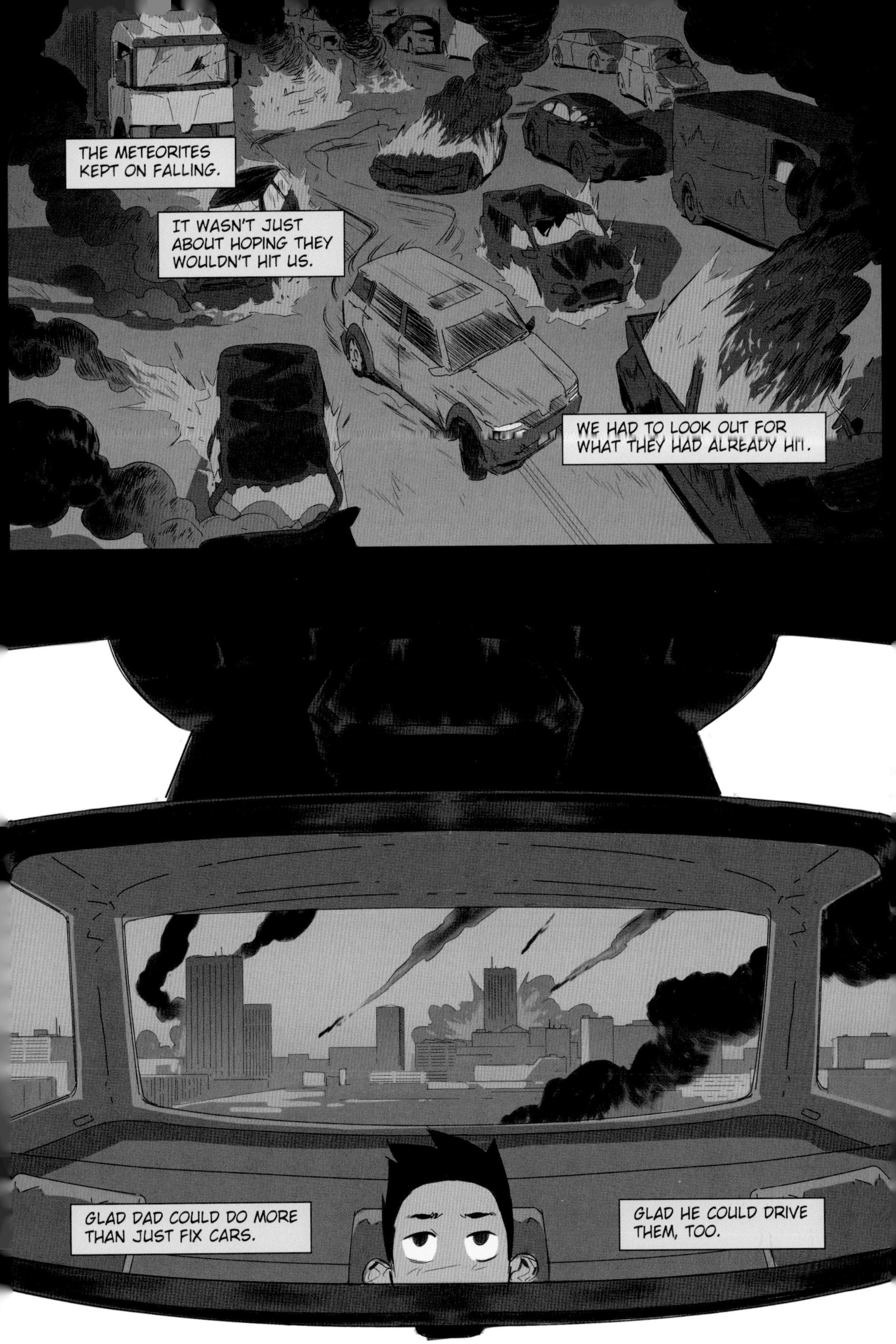
THE METEORITES KEPT ON FALLING.
IT WASN'T JUST ABOUT HOPING THEY WOULDN'T HIT US.
WE HAD TO LOOK OUT FOR WHAT THEY HAD ALREADY HIT.
GLAD DAD COULD DO MORE THAN JUST FIX CARS.
GLAD HE COULD DRIVE THEM, TOO.

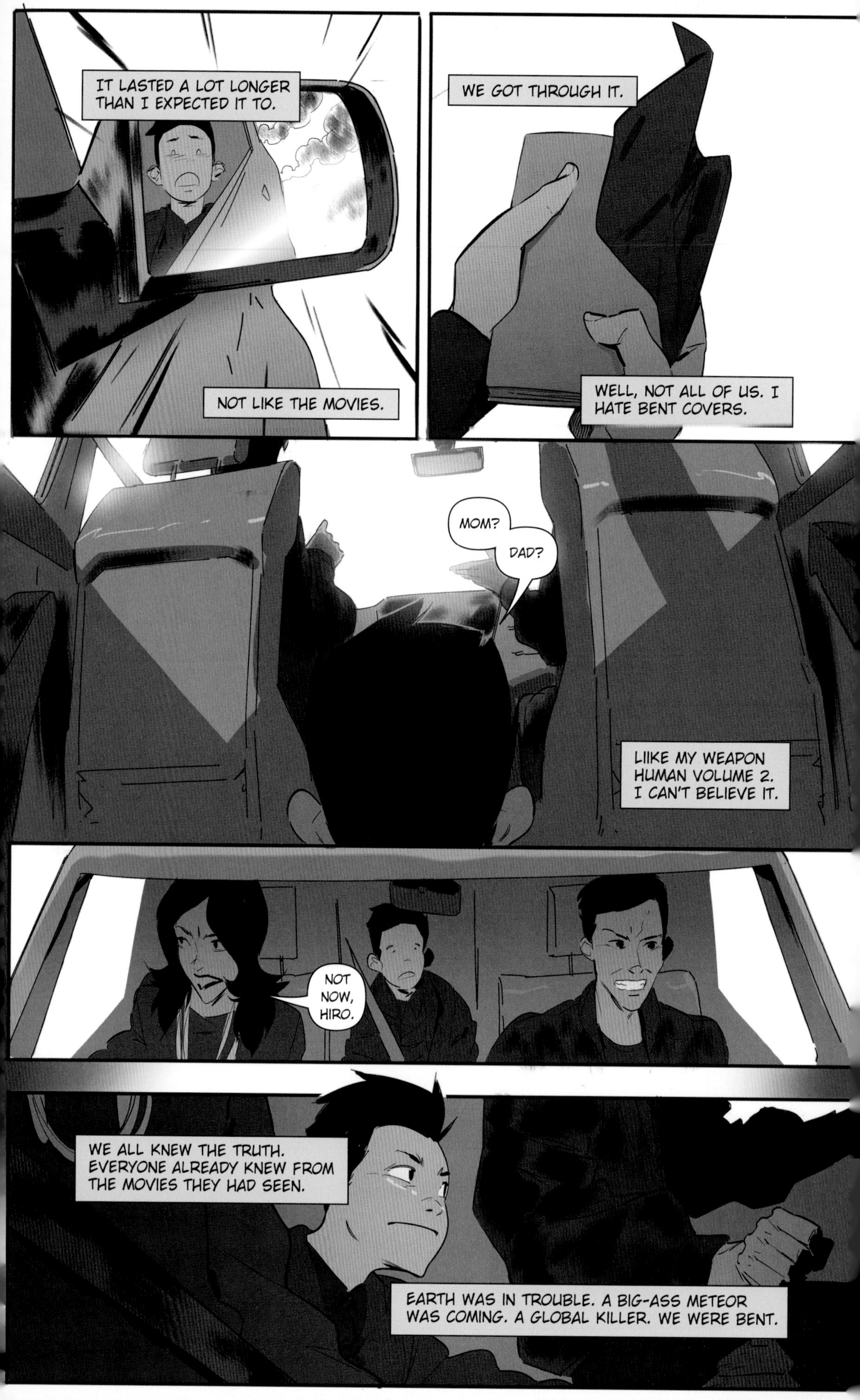
IT LASTED A LOT LONGER THAN I EXPECTED IT TO.
NOT LIKE THE MOVIES.
WE GOT THROUGH IT.
WELL, NOT ALL OF US. I HATE BENT COVERS.
MOM?
DAD?
LIIKE MY WEAPON HUMAN VOLUME 2. I CAN'T BELIEVE IT.
NOT NOW, HIRO.
WE ALL KNEW THE TRUTH. EVERYONE ALREADY KNEW FROM THE MOVIES THEY HAD SEEN.
EARTH WAS IN TROUBLE. A BIG-ASS METEOR WAS COMING. A GLOBAL KILLER. WE WERE BENT.

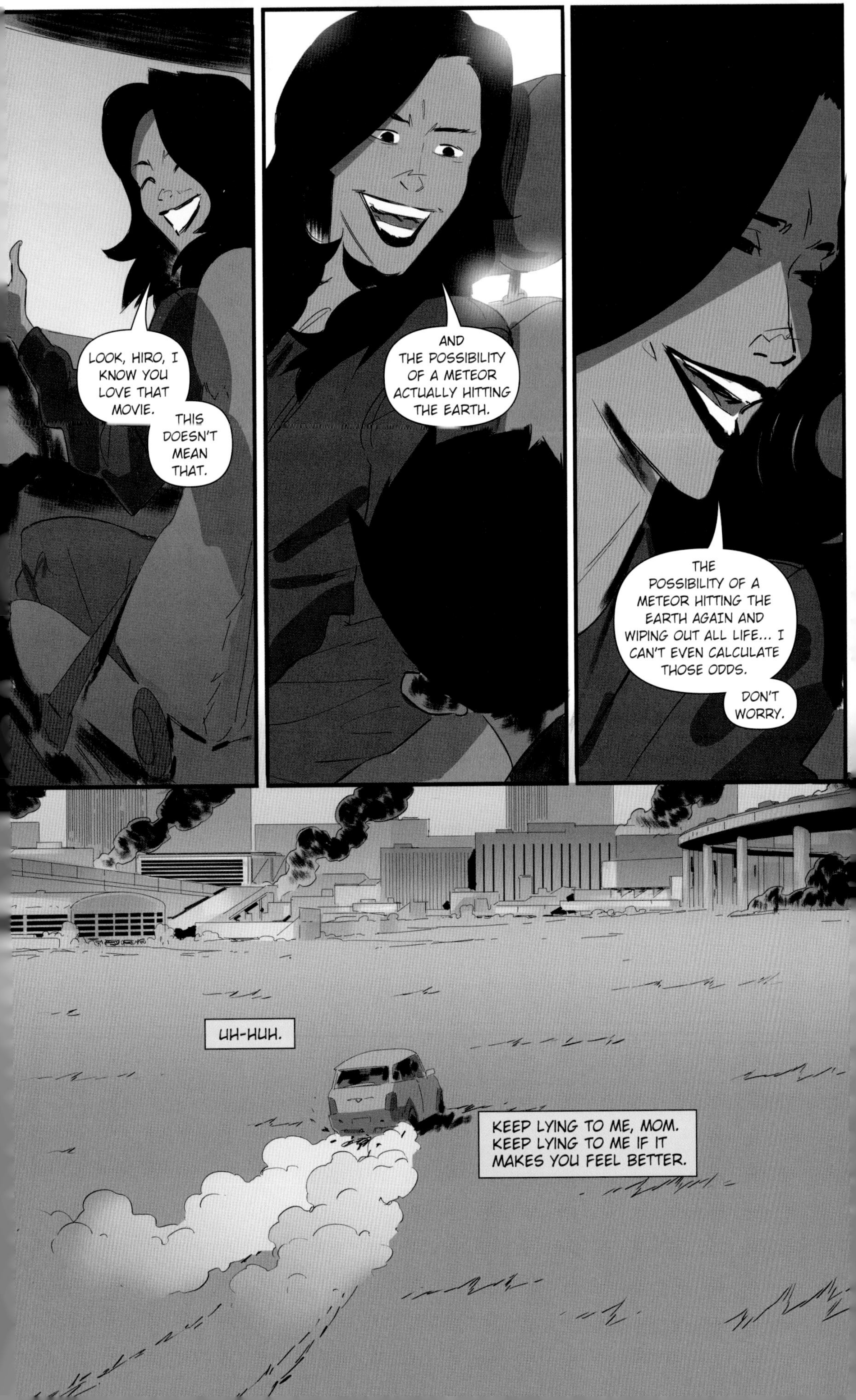
LOOK, HIRO, I KNOW YOU LOVE THAT MOVIE.
THIS DOESN'T MEAN THAT.
AND THE POSSIBILITY OF A METEOR ACTUALLY HITTING THE EARTH.
THE POSSIBILITY OF A METEOR HITTING THE EARTH AGAIN AND WIPING OUT ALL LIFE... I CAN'T EVEN CALCULATE THOSE ODDS.
DON'T WORRY.
UH-HUH.
KEEP LYING TO ME, MOM. KEEP LYING TO ME IF IT MAKES YOU FEEL BETTER.

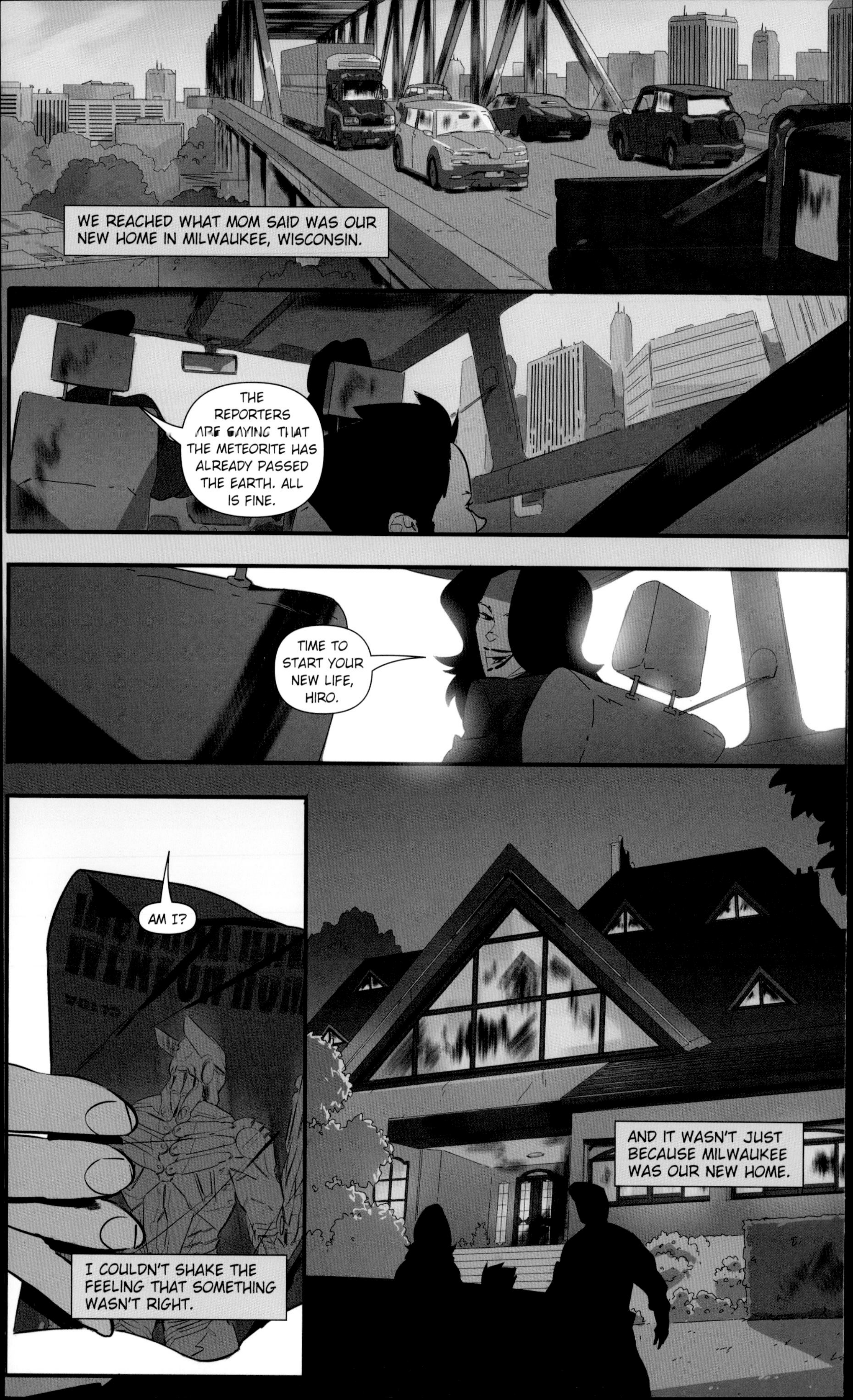
WE REACHED WHAT MOM SAID WAS OUR NEW HOME IN MILWAUKEE, WISCONSIN.
THE REPORTERS ARE SAYING THAT THE METEORITE HAS ALREADY PASSED THE EARTH. ALL IS FINE.
TIME TO START YOUR NEW LIFE, HIRO.
AM I?
I COULDN'T SHAKE THE FEELING THAT SOMETHING WASN'T RIGHT.
AND IT WASN'T JUST BECAUSE MILWAUKEE WAS OUR NEW HOME.

HiroQuest

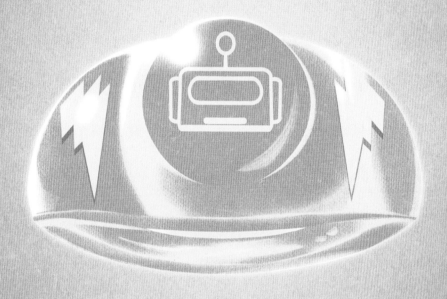

RING FIVE
ROBOT RING

PART FIVE

THE FACTION OF
THE TAUROBONS

CHAPTER SIXTEEN
NOBODY

"But my heart feels so lost in the dark."
Steve Aoki and PollyAnna

When I woke up again, when I could see again, I was on another world. Was it hours later? Days later? Weeks later? I don't know. I had no idea what happened to the zombie world of the Extants, or to Tom the pin-cushion boy, or to the healer, Goth Holly. Did I teleport away without even thinking about it? Or was I brought here? And what was that voice? The one that told me I was only the hero of one world? To leave the Extants to their own? Was Goth Holly right? Is there something wrong with me?

Something that needed her to bring healing to me?

I wondered, Doctor Snow, if I have been somehow compromised by visiting these other worlds. I guess they all have diseases and problems that my body may not have the ability or the immunity to take on.

Is it possible I could bring the rings back to save Earth only to spread a disease there, like what happened with the Sasquatches? I don't know, maybe one of the rings that I find will be a healing ring. Or Holly will have to come back with me, assuming, of course, that I can find her again. Though I guess I lost her once already and found her. My third eye wasn't telling me anything either.

I don't know. No matter how much smarter I feel like I'm becoming, I just don't know. I may have to figure out a way to get the rings to you even if I will be denied breathing the air of Earth again. Like I said, I do not know.

I think the truth was that I was realizing that I didn't need nobody. As in anybody. If I saved Earth only to not be allowed to return, that's fine. I can be the somebody that nobody knows about. Forget the parade. I needed to do the right thing and that was that.

When I opened my eyes, I at first thought I was once more on the OIO world. This was a mechanical city and there were Taurobon all around me. Like before, they moved through the streets and ignored me.

Everything was ordered and in its proper place. Like a well-oiled machine. Which I suppose it was. A machine made of machines.

But it didn't have to stay that way. I have the ring from the OIO world. I could do something here. I spoke the source code.

"OIO IOI." It sounded like "Oh Eye Oh Eye Oh Eye." It triggered something in the ring from the Artificial Intelligence world and it caused three of the Taurobons to rebuild themselves and advance their ability to become the next evolutionary step, in mechanical terms, at least. They evolved mechanically before my very eyes, taking the form of three new robots. Three new Taurobon. I didn't encourage them to turn to each other and perhaps get lost as a Heart Brain, like on that other world.

No, I wanted them to focus on me. To focus on what I wanted.

Two of them were mechanically winged. The third was not.

The first told me its name was R-1134. It was one of the new Taurobon with wings.

The other Taurobon with wings told me its name was Nexus.

The third Taurobon, this one without wings, told me its name was Otis.

I asked about the ring. There was no argument on this planet. There was no sense of dual and multi-perspectives. There was only one, linear, telescoping value system. How to serve. How to give. How to fulfill one's purpose.

I couldn't help, in light of everything, being grateful for this place, its simplicity.

We started talking. Me and the advanced Taurobons.

I learned that the robots from this world were waiting for a star that looked like a giant eye to take them to another world. They were lining up and waiting; the star promising to give them identity and purpose and to make them into beings that can make up their own minds and make their own decisions. The star basically promised that they wouldn't be slaves on this other world.

They wanted to leave or to aspire to become something else (Two options? A binary proposition? Like computer language?) did seem like something a robot would say. Especially the desire not to be a slave.

But I'm afraid, Doctor Snow, that they will become slaves. I was afraid that whatever that eye-star was, which they called the Pixel Pupil, it was serving the OIO. And it was merely moving the Taurobons from this world to that world so that they could become slaves there for more Heart Brains.

I asked the newly advanced three Taurobon if they had ever seen the Pixel Pupil? They had. And more than this, it had interacted on a global level with the Taurobon. That was my answer. This thing from space had changed their programming. The Taurobons don't have desire, they're just programmed to believe they do. And to leave this place would be contradictory to their initial programming.

I was never good at history, Doctor Snow. I mean, I probably would be now, but then, before you made me into what I now am, I didn't care. That said, though, I know how on our world, one nation played other nations. One race played other races. Even one class would play another class.

Was I now on another world that was playing another world? Is this the way of the worlds?

THE THREE ROBOTS

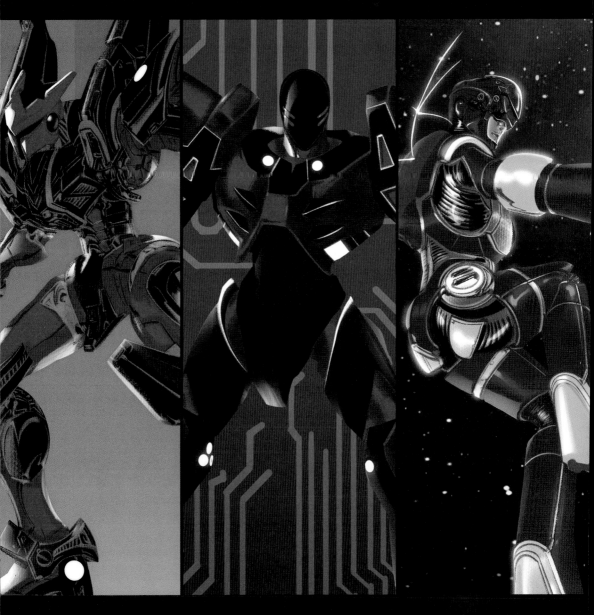

R-1134   NEXUS   OTIS

There were three Taurobons that I used the OIO ring to rebuild themselves into Artificial Intelligences. Three that I thought would explain and help me understand the relationship between this world and that of the OIO. What I did not realize was that by advancing them, I was endangering my mission.

THE PIXEL PUPIL

The Pixel Pupil does two things. It's from the OIO world. It has reprogrammed the Taurobons to ignore their previous programming and repurposed them to become slaves of the OIOs. The EYE is also a transport vehicle for them. And is the way they are taken and put to work on that other world. In some ways, it is like a god to the Taurobon. And maybe that makes sense to a degree. After all, a robot knows that it was created for a purpose. Most of the people I know, do not.

CHAPTER SEVENTEEN
DEMONS

"The deeper I'm diggin' the further I have to fall."
Steve Aoki and Georgia Ku

So here I am on this planet. And I see that not all the Taurobon programming is legitimate. The question is should I use my OIO ring to transform them all? All the robots? All the Taurobon? Should I do this programming? The Pixel Pupil thing will return and it could change them all again. But I could give them independent thought. I could make them all OIOs.

The question was this: Do I do on this planet what I was not allowed to do on the last one? Making them AI would be like "saving the Extants." I listened for the voice again. But it said nothing.

On that prior world, I would have brought the dead back to life. On this one, I'm giving life to the never-have-lived.

But wouldn't that still be great? Or at least good?

And what do I want for those worlds I visit? Am I taking or giving? If I take a ring, is there something I can give in return?

How do I affect the future and not just the past?

I want to advance the robots. No more slaves. A new life.

I asked the advanced Taurobons about the ring for this world. I told them about my quest and then realized my mistake. Advanced as they now were, they did not want me to take it.

It was not only that, they wanted the other rings as well. They reached out to me and I then thought that I teleported out of their immediate reach. But I was too slow. One of them teleported with me, having grabbed hold of my arm. Its mechanical, iron grip took hold of my wrist. Doctor Snow, as strong as you made me, I could not break it off.

I tried to fly off the ground. But two of them had wings as it was.

Another grabbed hold of that Taurobon. And then a third. They climbed each other, ultimately taking hold of my other arm and one of my legs, no matter how I tried to fly up and escape. They were trying to pull me apart. My body would have been pulled to pieces if you hadn't augmented it. But that still seemed like what was going to happen.

I was about to black out when I heard the voice again. The one that told me I was a hero to only one world.

The voice told me that there was an army there, ready to help me. Ready to come to my aid.

But all I could see were more Taurobon going about their mechanical tasks.

The three advanced robots kept pulling, trying to even rip my hands from my arms. And then I saw it, my ring. It wouldn't let me turn them back to what they were. The ring doesn't work in reverse, but I realized that I could advance the other Taurobon around me. I could advance them taking a page out the Pixel Pupil's handbook.

"OIO IOI!" I screamed, willing every Taurobon on the planet with new programming. I used the ring to repurpose them. If the ultimate program of a robot is to serve, I commanded them to kill all those robots that insist upon being served. I made the OIO the enemy of every Taurobon.

There were so many of them. And now they had a new purpose. To kill AI.

As robots attacked the three advanced Taurobon that were trying to kill me and steal the rings, I was released. Perhaps self-preservation was now part of their intelligence.

The three tried to escape, but no matter where they went, there were Taurobons that turned on them and pulled at them. Until finally there was nothing left of them but pieces.

Pieces, ha ha. I hurt all over, but at least I was still only in one.

The voice, whatever it came from, helped me. There was someone there. But not anyone I could see.

It was back. That same black cloud, even more fully formed now. There was someone in the darkness.

No.

They weren't in the darkness.

They were the darkness.

It's the same thing I saw on the Extant world. I was starting to see a bigger picture.

"It's Death," the voice whispered to me. "It's Death. Death is following you."

THE
TAUROBON ARMY

They were robots. I had to remember that. And they had already been reprogrammed. I didn't do anything but actually give them another purpose. And so I commanded them to destroy the Taurobon A.I. They rescued me. And therefore, I am still alive to finish my mission and save Earth by seeking out the rest of the rings. I may need this army one day.

DO I OWE THE OIO BETTER THAN WHAT I HAVE DONE?

I may have condemned the OIO on that other world. These robots are planning on riding the eye to that world and destroying the OIO there. Maybe even freeing the other Taurobon while they are there. That may be wishful thinking on my part. I find that as time goes on, I am lying to myself more and more. The Ends justify the Means is fast becoming the only way I can keep doing this.

CHAPTER EIGHTEEN
STARS

"I'm waiting for my final day."
Steve Aoki and Lil Xan

"Why are you following me?" I spoke to the shadow. It like a black sheet blowing in the wind, but it had form, too.

There was no answer at all, Doctor Snow. But the other voice, the one that's been helping me, it told me to use the ring to make the robots find and bring me the ring

I did as the voice suggested and I watched as the robots scoured everywhere. I ran for my life from Death, but Death did not seem to follow me. It hovered above the spot where the Advanced OIO I'd created (and that had later then turned on me) had been when they were ripped apart.

If Death was following me, why was it not following me now?

A worse thought: Was it only following me because more and more people were dying because of this quest of mine?

Is Death like a dog eating the scraps I leave behind? Or is it more?

And what's with the voice? Perhaps Death was not the only one following me.

I turned to find the Taurobons all standing in formation behind me, like I'm some sort of General and they are awaiting further instructions.

One of them was holding out its robotic hand. On the hand was a ring. The ring. The ring of this world. My third eye struggled to understand its source code. I guessed that that was because it is telepathic and empathic in nature and this is reading a digital code.

I asked the Taurbon what the source code was, and they spoke in unison.

"GNUTTER-SPIN."

It seems this ring has a sort of hypnosis or "technosis" ability to impart. It makes anyone I command with it a robot. A slave. I have no idea how this could be used to save Earth; unless, of course, I could tell the meteor that would kill everyone to go the other way!

I was wrong when I said the Taurobon were waiting for me to command them. They were not waiting for me … they had a new service to perform. To kill the OIO. They were waiting for the Pixel Pupil to come and take them to the planet I found my second ring on.

I thought about the Half-Heart that I met on that world, how it killed its partner. I assumed it killed, deconstructed, its partner. And I thought that maybe it would not be such a bad thing if the AI on that world no longer existed. I didn't know. At least it would keep Death busy, I guessed. But there was something else that distracted me in that moment.

In the Taurobons' shiny metallic bodies' reflection, I saw someone that looked like me. But different, darker. Scars on his cheeks. Even scarier; it whispered in my ear to take the ring. I asked the voice what its name was, and when it answered, I was filled with a terrible sense of dread, Doctor Snow.

I took the ring, of course.

But when I turned around, to see him, there was no one there.

I was right. Death was not the only one who was following me.

Its name, Doctor Snow, it said its name was "Hyro".

THE TAUROBON RING

This was a slave ring. Whoever wears it can command others to do whatever the wearer says. It's therefore the power of a god, I suppose. I'm imagining that as the meteor gets closer to Earth, that it will make my planet a pretty scary place to live. There will be rioting, I'm sure. And other problems including arguments and debates about what to do and how to respond. This ring should help counter that.

SOURCE CODE TO
ACCESS POWER: GNUTTER-SPIN

HYRO. HE SAID HIS NAME IS HYRO

He just wanted me to know that I was not alone. I seem to remember one of the scientists accidentally calling me Hyro. A lot of people did. It was always pronounced "hero" though. What's happening? And now Hyro was sent here to help me? That's what he told me. That you sent him, Doctor Snow. And that there was a way to save all ten worlds, not just Earth.

Hyro told me that I should kill Death. That's what Hyro said I should do. Kill Death. Will it take our combined efforts to actually do this?

And if we do, won't it be like I'm saving every other world as well? It's how we will find and make better days. For Earth and every other world.

Yeah, that's it. I'm going to Kill Death and save everyone.

I'll just need the other five rings to do so.

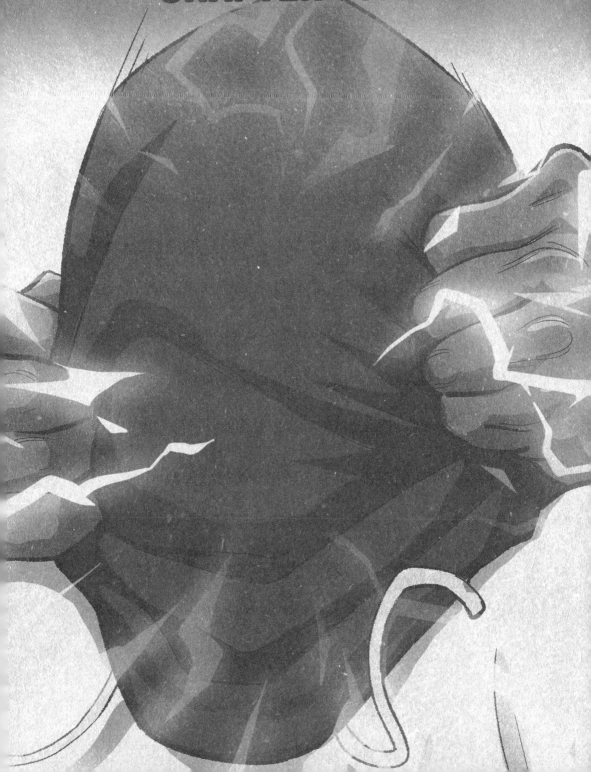

HIRO's JOURNEY
CHAPTER FIVE

WHAT CAN I SAY, THE NEW SCHOOL FELT A LOT LIKE MY OLD SCHOOL.

THE NEW LIFE, A LOT LIKE THE OLD LIFE.

INSTEAD OF HURRICANES, WE GOT BLIZZARDS.

BLIZZARDS AND...

MEN IN BLACK?

HIRO? COULD YOU COME HERE PLEASE?

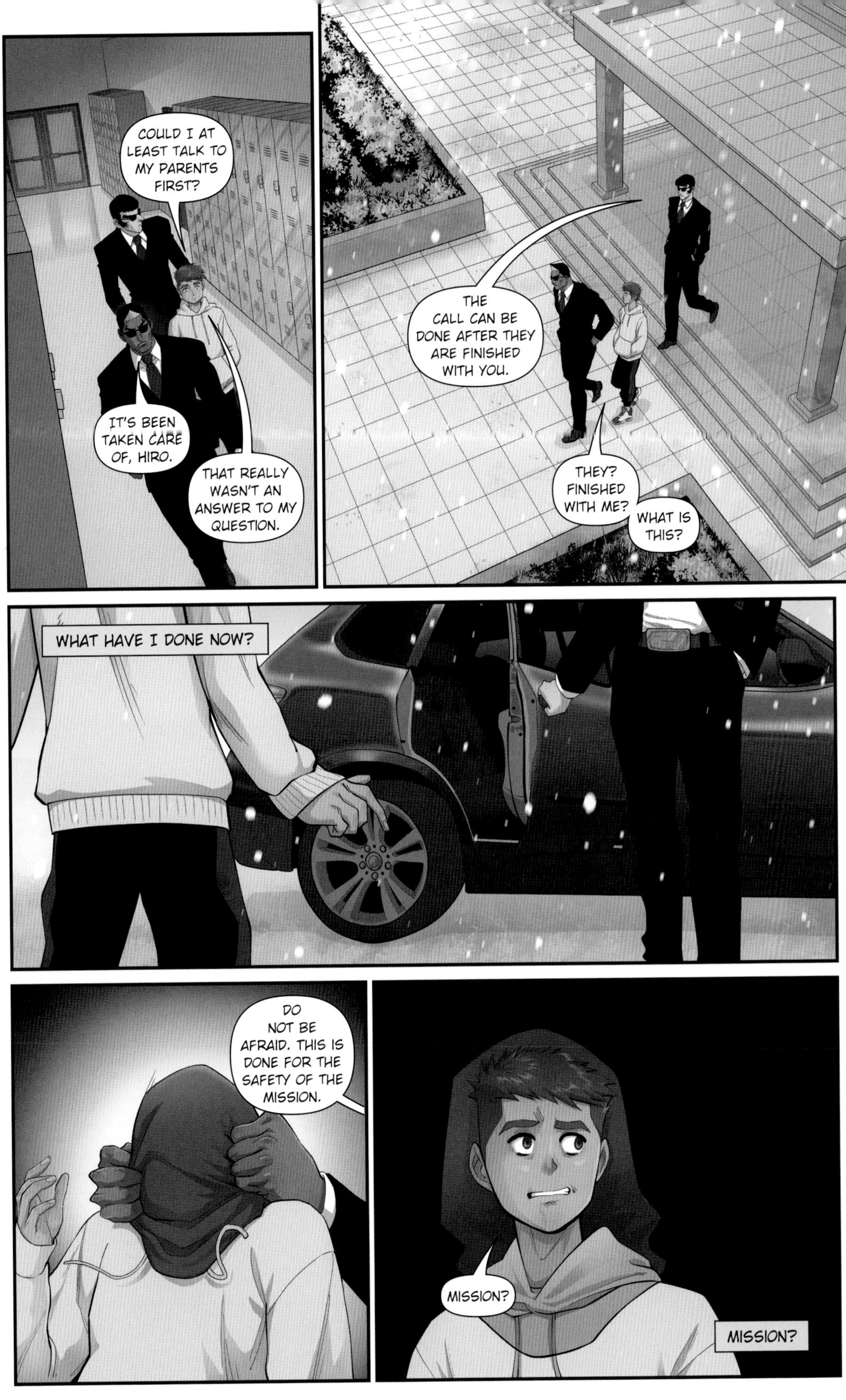
COULD I AT LEAST TALK TO MY PARENTS FIRST?
IT'S BEEN TAKEN CARE OF, HIRO.
THAT REALLY WASN'T AN ANSWER TO MY QUESTION.
THE CALL CAN BE DONE AFTER THEY ARE FINISHED WITH YOU.
THEY? FINISHED WITH ME?
WHAT IS THIS?
WHAT HAVE I DONE NOW?
DO NOT BE AFRAID. THIS IS DONE FOR THE SAFETY OF THE MISSION.
MISSION?
MISSION?

WE DROVE FOR OVER AN HOUR BEFORE WE FINALLY STOPPED AND GOT OUT AGAIN.

THEY DIDN'T TALK MUCH.

I DON'T KNOW EXACTLY WHERE THEY TAKE ME. BUT I CAN TELL IT'S FANCY.

THEY DIDN'T LIKE MY JOKES EITHER.

SHOULD I TAKE MY SHOES OFF?

I DON'T WANT TO BE RUDE TO MY ABDUCTOR.

I COULDN'T SEE A THING THROUGH THE HOOD THEY HAD ON ME.

BUT I COULD TELL SOMEONE ELSE HAD COME INTO THE ROOM.

'YOU HAVEN'T BEEN ABDUCTED, MISTER HIRO.

BUT SECRECY HAD TO BE MAINTAINED.

YOU SEE, HIRO, WE NEED YOUR HELP.

THERE'S NOT A PERSON ON THE PLANET WHO DOESN'T, ACTUALLY.

END OF
PART ONE

HIROQUEST

CREATED BY
STEVE AOKI

WRITTEN BY
STEVE AOKI AND JIM KRUEGER

GRAPHIC NOVEL CREATIVE DIRECTION BY
MATTHEW MEDNEY

HIROQUEST PART TWO:
DOUBLE HELIX

PRELUDE

Hi, Doctor Snow, as you know I am no longer just able to be a hero of our world, I want to be a hero of all the worlds I am getting rings from. Maybe even beyond that.

I know you sent Hyro to help me, to keep me on my mission, and for that I am exceedingly grateful. His messages to me reminded me to remember Earth, no matter what. He told me I could only be a hero to Earth. But, I disagree with the message, because there is something now that you could not have known.

Death.

As in, I don't know, the Angel of Death, is following me. I'm somehow defying it, or it's collecting up all the dead from the worlds I've been visiting. I don't know. The point is that Death is following me and I think, maybe with Hyro's help, I can kill it. I mean, I already have the Resurrection ring from the Zombie World of the Extants. And other rings. Maybe Death is pissed because I can defy IT now? Truly. Like no one else ever has. So, if I can kill Death, then everyone on every single world I visit from this point onward could live.

Please don't misunderstand me. My mission to collect all ten rings and to save Earth has never been more personally important to me than now; and so I have never been more committed to it than even before. I am grateful to my parents. I love them. And I love my world.

I now have a ring that had the power of resurrection, a ring with the power to advance technology, a ring with the power to teleport, a ring with the power to see the future of a person, and a ring with the power to control others. That's a lot. And I assume it's not enough to save Earth, or you would have just put me on a quest for these five rings and not ten.

But I also don't want to just leave these worlds the way I found them. I think I want to help these worlds as well, even though I do not know how.

I was losing my way. I think I really was, but I'm back.

So, my plan is that I'm going to save Earth. And I'm going to save everyone else; I'm going to save these other worlds. All my new friends. I think about all the possible ways these worlds could have been better if maybe I had been here sooner? If the rings had been available earlier. So many ways; I don't always know at each moment what is best, but I know I could help do something about what is obviously not right.

It's what my parents named me to be.

I'm Hiro.

This is what I was made for.

HiroQuest

RING SIX
GOBLIN RING

PART SIX

THE FACTION OF
THE GREMBOLDS

CHAPTER ONE
HUNGRY HEART

"Every time you leave, I always fall apart."
Steve Aoki, Galantis, and Hayley Kiyoko

I haven't heard from Hyro since I got here to the world of the Grembolds. I'm assuming that because he warned me and showed himself to me in the past, that he is still with me. I assume that your attempts to send him to help me have met with some problems, Doctor Snow, and that's why he is not here fully yet, but I want you to know that I have heard him. And I am grateful. He's helped me get more than one ring.

I had now collected five of the ten rings and was dedicated to continuing my quest. I was very grateful that I was not alone, but 'not alone' was a strange thing on this world.

You see, this new world of the Grembolds is a world of creatures and beings that seemed to be in perpetual 'Goblin Mode'. I mean, don't get me wrong. The inhabitants had claws and were green and looked like monsters, sure, like Goblins, yes, but it was also that, in the way they behaved as beings, they were in full-on Goblin Mode, because, in other words, they lived completely for themselves. They indulged themselves in whatever they wanted to do. The moment they had an appetite to do something, they acted on it; that totally ruled them.

Goblin Mode.

When I first arrived here, I realized that this world had certain similarities to the OIO and the Taurobon world. For instance, no one, not a single Grembold, at least initially, noticed I was here. They were all too busy pleasing themselves. Some of them were just hungry. But others, they had blood and the taking of it on their mind, and even the drinking of it in some cases. Others were destroying their neighbor's homes. And some were destroying their own. If there was something to do on a whim, it was being done here. If there was some dark desire to embrace, it was being done here, on this world.

I couldn't help but remember why the three of you scientists perpetuated the myth that Earth had been saved from the meteor while you were preparing and augmenting me for this quest to save a world that was going to be destroyed by a meteor. You talked about the fear and the doubt and the rioting that would happen if my fellow man knew about the impending doom that was coming.

And now I saw what it is like to live upon such a planet. If looting were to happen on Earth, if people gave in to their last wishes, it would have destroyed everything, probably even resulting in a population that might not deserve to even be saved. I appreciate now how your lie to Earth's people was a way of keeping their collective souls from being corrupted. I wasn't certain if I agreed with you then, but I do now. I see the wisdom of it all. Firsthand, you might say.

There was something unfinished about this place, too. Its cities were half-formed. Everything was in a perpetual state of being incomplete. Many things seemed to have been begun, but were ultimately neglected, including the streets themselves. And maybe that spoke to the world of the Grembolds, as well. It is a place where goals are abandoned and given up for the sake of any new distraction. If this was something in the air, like a curse, or some airborne problem, I wondered, would it affect me, eventually; would it keep me from finding this world's ring? Or any of the rings on any other worlds? Is this kind of laziness something I could catch, or had already caught?

I wondered if I would hear from Hyro again. And then I wondered about Goth Holly. How would she, as a true hero, heal this world?

How do you heal an out of control appetite?

If I was going to save each of these worlds, I felt like I needed to think about what it would take to save each particular world. Because they were not the same, although they had similarities. Like people, I suppose.

But I didn't have to think, because of her.

Alora.

She was green, and hot as hell. And she was right in front of me.

She wasn't like Goth Holly at all. Goth Holly loved me with big, deep healing eyes. But I loved Alora with all my heart. The moment I saw her. Sure, I was human and she was a Goblin. A Grembold.

But I needed to assume that no one would judge me for that, especially four hundred years in the future. Especially after I was mutated and augmented and saved all of Earth and everything.

I saw her and I wanted her. Wanted to be close to her. Not in a Goblin Mode way, please. There was just something in me, something that said that I already knew her, already had something with her that was deeper than I even understood.

She had Goblin hands and Goblin feet, but the rest of her was beautiful. Perfect.

She pretended like she didn't see me. And I let her know that that was okay.

This world was like a piece of trash neighborhood that had been gentrified. There were stores that sold clothing. Stores that sold food. Stores that sold tech. Some windows were broken because looting was the desire of the moment. Others had new windows because restoration was the new whim. And other stores were in between; they had wood in place of glass as if awaiting some sort of reparation.

The street I now walked on looked in a perpetual state of being torn down, and built back up according to a moment's temptation.

So, I decided to just sit and be unnoticed. I placed myself on a public bench. Unlike on other worlds, I chose to be quiet. To be still. All in the hopes that the ring might eventually come to me.

Alora. With her perfect lips and her only-hinted-at smile she came and sat with me on the bench.

"Hi," I said to her, with an eagerness that pretended to not be eager but clearly showed what a bad liar I was.

She looked at me and said nothing.

She was so amazingly 'hot', Doctor Snow. Did I mention that?

You and Doctor Scottski and Doctor Horse prepared me for zombies and monsters and robots, but in all fairness, you didn't prepare me for 'hot.'

"Hi," I said again, and hoped that she had just not heard me the first time.

"I heard you the first time," she said.

"Shit," I thought. If that had been a word balloon, like in a comic strip, there would be a thunderbolt that would then shoot down at me from that bubble like a cloud and fry me on the spot.

"What do you want?" she asked. And she then slid herself a little closer on the bench. Her lips even pouted a bit.

My name was Hiro. And I wasn't about to forget that. But I also knew what I wanted, and it was her.

ON THE ONE HAND, FIVE RINGS

Doctor Snow, I hope you are getting these audio files. I send them off to you every time I succeed in getting a ring from one of the ten worlds. I have five so far. I've visited worlds filled with robots and mutants and zombies and more. I'm not happy with everything I've had to do to get these rings. But I know this will save Earth.

ON THE OTHER HAND, NO RINGS.

As you know, Doctor Snow, there are five more rings to go. Five more rings to collect from five more worlds. I wish I could send each ring home to Earth as I get them. But sometimes I think that the only way I could keep doing this is because each ring gives me enough power to get the next ring.

CHAPTER TWO
WILD

"We burnt it down so that everyone comes around."
Steve Aoki and Vini Vici

"What I want is actually less important than what I am needed to be." I told Alora once we stopped kissing.

"What?" she said and looked deeper. "Not on this world. This is a world of perpetual want. Not responsibility. You are born for one purpose here. To be wild."

"Esse Quam Vidiri," I said in response.

"What again?"

"It's Latin. An ancient language from my world. It means 'To Be, Rather Than To Seem To Be.' I want to be real." That's what I said. Can you believe it? I responded to a girl, even a goblin girl, in Latin. I didn't even know that I knew Latin, Doctor Snow. Whatever you did to me, don't ever undo that part. I have real game now. You all kind of made me a player.

"I wish I knew someone who was real. More than in the moment." Those were the words she said to me. "I wish I was with someone who was real."

I looked at her and said, "Well, I wish I was with someone who wanted to be with someone who was real."

She smiled at that.

I smiled back and said "Your turn."

She smiled with those perfect Grembold lips of hers, and flashed those perfect Grembold teeth. I couldn't tell for certain, but I think she even had a goblin dimple.

Shit.

No one had ever told me that goblins could have dimples.

So I told her about the rings, Doctor Snow. I told her about my world. I told her about my quest. And I told her about how it wasn't enough to just save my world, I also wanted to save all the others.

She told me there was someone she thought I should talk to. But before we could talk to him, we kissed. And kept on kissing. Not saying anything at all.

Eventually ...

Alora took me to meet with a Grembold. He spoke to me like he knew me. He wore a hat and seemed like a show promoter. Well, like the goblin version of a show promoter. He said his name was Turbo Tanker.

I asked him how he spelled that. He said to spell it exactly like it sounds. That was a lot of help. But he said he knew me. That he had seen me before. That he was there, on the Astrals world, when I stole the secret of space travel from the Tribunal.

Before I could ask him anything about that, he turned back to Alora. "What does he want?" he asked her.

"The ring. This world's ring. He needs them all to save his world."

"No matter what it does to all the others?"

"We should help him," Alora told him and smiled at me. She winked a little. And I could still remember her goblin lips on mine. "Who knows, it'll be a new sensation for all of us if we give him the ring."

Turbo seemed to think about that. He nodded. "So it's the road, then, is it?"

She smiled at him and asked him if he was sure if it was okay.

"Does he love you?" he asked.

"Yes."

"Do you love him?" he asked.

"What I know of him," she said.

"Then, yes, it's okay with me. Let's go. The three of us. And Hiro, don't eat the first order of barbeque. Only eat the second helping."

I looked at Alora, and she already knew what I was going to ask before I asked it.

"It's because, Hiro, the first helping is not as clean a roadkill. It's more accidental, less planned."

I gulped, Doctor Snow. And grimaced. But I was getting closer to the sixth ring on a really weird-ass planet. I don't know why the ring would not teleport me right to it. Maybe some sort of goblin magic; I was not sure.

And maybe, the love I already felt for Alora, was getting in the way.

ALORA

When I first saw her, I was overwhelmed by how beautiful she was. I didn't expect to find anyone like her on that world. She was the first to try to help me and I love her. And she says she loves me as well, at least the part of me she knows so far. I wonder what that means?

TURBO TANKER

He hates me, this particular Grembold. But Doctor Snow, he was there, on a world before. There on the Astrals world. It was Turbo that was fueling the Kultists to worship the Astrals and helping the Astrals believe they were meant to be worshipped. He pitted the two groups against each other and now I fear for that world and the resentment that both races will have towards each other purely because of how Turbo Tanker manipulated them.

CHAPTER THREE
MOTOR

"Mash it up on di place."
Steve Aoki and Quintino

There we were, Doctor Snow. It was me; me and two Grembolds – in some sort of goblin–mobile – making our way along what I would probably call a highway, and there were strange 'goopy' purple and orange mountains on both sides of our 'truck'. The mountains were more like the inside of caves than mountains, too; as if these mighty sites had been made by being dripped down upon from space for millions of years in their formation.

But, Doctor Snow, before you think of this as something like an alien Route 66, it was more like Route 666. Because there were fires, lots of them, on both sides of the road after we cleared the mountains. And where there weren't fires then there was the clear signs of where there had been fires before: smoke still coming from those places where flames had gone out.

And skeletons. There were plenty of bones everywhere that suggested accidents of the past, or not so-accidental violence of the past, if you get what I mean.

But it wasn't all skeletons. There were also Grembolds on the side of the road either eating the rotten meat from some of the animals that still had some meat on their bones, or fighting with each other and maybe they'd become food again for other Grembolds.

This was a bad place, the road I found myself on.

I would call what we were driving a monster truck, but only because of who was with me inside of it.

There was the goblin Alora, who I was really falling for, and Turbo Tanker, who I think wanted me to fail in my quest to save Earth.

But it was interesting because I had a feeling he was more angry that I had brought some equality to the Astrals and the Kultists. So really, I was starting to think of my first mission in a different light. Maybe I didn't do such a bad thing after all?

The air on the road smelled bad, the kind of bad that made me think that more goblins had died here than I could even guess by counting skeletons. Every once in a while, I would look in one of the side mirrors to see if Death was following me. It was not.

I still needed, I assumed, five more rings to kill Death and save the other ten worlds as well. This thought got me thinking about Earth.

It's not just about saving billions of my people some four hundred years ago, I realized. How many new humans would have been born since then? Wouldn't I be saving them as well? The potential lives? What might my people accomplish if they were given those four hundred years? Those multiple generations? This is probably ... hundreds of billions of people. And how many other worlds would they visit in that time, now that we know there are other worlds? And how many other worlds filled with beings could the future heroes of my people save? This was staggering.

A rest stop was coming up, I was told by my travelling companions. The one that served BBQ. The one I was warned not to eat the first helping of. That said, just what is the difference between clean and dirty roadkill? Or is it that the second helping of roadkill had actually been orchestrated and the first was merely, well, accidental?

The hope was that we would reach the rest stop before the sun – well, what they called a sun in this world – went down. This was because when the daylight went, the chance of the goblinmobile hitting goblin nightlife was that much greater. And the chance of that same nightlife hitting us, also went way up.

So, both Turbo and Alora made it clear to me they wanted to get me to the off–road diner where we could sit and talk before we met their contact, this meeting being the next day, because, as I said, it wasn't safe to drive at night. Their contact was the one that would help me find the ring of this world, or who had the ring. I wasn't certain; which worried me.

When we finally pulled over, it was like there were gas pumps there. But not like the gas pumps I remember. These looked like a combination of things both ancient and futuristic, though the idea of refueling was still there, somehow. But the devices looked abandoned at the same time, and as if they'd been so for a long while now.

Turbo Tanker, I keep wanting to put a "the" before his name, but never mind. Anyhow, Turbo looked at me as we entered the diner and sat down. He surprised me when he asked what I would do if I had to choose between the ring and Alora.

I looked at Alora and she looked at Turbo Tanker. And then she spoke. "It's not love, if he has to choose between us. Even if he does not choose me, I choose him. I will love him even after you have tried to get your revenge on him."

"Come what may?" Turbo Tanker the goblin asked.

"Yes. Come what may. Come what will," she said.

"Come what will," I seconded. But I couldn't help thinking about what she had said about Turbo Tanker still wanting to get his revenge on me.

"Very well," said the male Grembold. "Very well. But first, a warning."

"Of what?" I asked.

"Techno Gaze."

"Who or what is that?"

"After you left that other world, he ... it appeared in the sky."

"I'm sorry, I don't understand. The Techno Gaze; what is that?" I asked.

Turbo Tanker paused. He took a deep breath. "I thought everything was bad enough when you stole the ring that made teleportation from one world to another possible. You have no idea how many years I cultivated and built up the Astrals, and made them into the celebrity gods to all who lived on that world. I didn't just have to build them up, either, I had to tear the native inhabitants down, and make them believe they needed something to make their lives worthwhile again."

"But why would you do that?" I asked.

"Because, man, it turns me on to see an entity being worshipped that shouldn't be. And another race bow who should be standing up for themselves. I dig it."

I hated this guy. I really did.

He continued, looking right at me. "I made something beautiful and you threw it away just by stealing a ring to save your people. And now Techno Gaze has arrived. And every one of them, from Kult to Astral, sees something in the sky that now lets them know that either they are not God and never were, or tells them they were bowing to a false one before. So, it's all over, man. That world, any potential I ever saw in it, it's all over."

"So, you're not going to help me find the ring here, after all?" I asked.

"Oh, I will. I want you to have it. I want you to get it."

"And why is that?"

"Because I don't think you're going to be able to give those rings to your precious humanity. I think that that much power is going to be too much for you. And after all the destruction you have caused, letting Earth die for the god you will have become is going to be something you are more than willing to allow."

"You're wrong about me," I said.

"We'll see. But this is how I'm going to get my revenge. I'm going to help you get exactly what you want."

MONSTER TRUCK

With the help of Alora and Turbo Tanker, we headed out on the old road in what felt like the type of monster truck you'd find on a monster world. I think it's the only thing that can keep us safe from this goblin-filled world. Everywhere I look, I see the Grembolds in the process of eating or being eaten. I hate to say it, but this makes me think of our world, Doctor Snow, and how people treat each other. Maybe when Earth is saved, you and the other doctors can find a way to change it as well.

THE TECHNO GAZE

Doctor Snow, there may be something else to deal with. I learned from Turbo Tanker that after I left the world of the ASTRALS there was something that appeared in the sky. It was giant and seemed ready to judge and destroy that world, Astrals and Kultists alike. I hate that I'm almost relieved. That this thing in the sky was coming anyhow. I hate the sense of guilt I feel over how I've left some of these worlds.

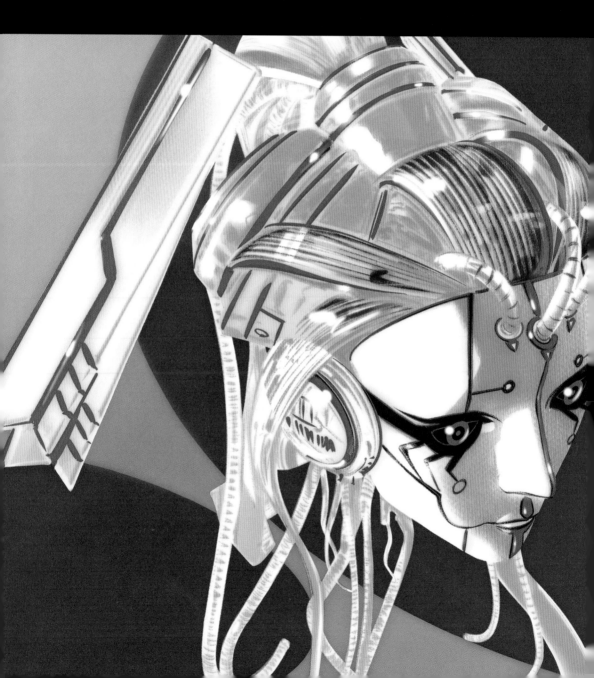

CHAPTER FOUR
BROTHERS

"We've got to slow it down."
Steve Aoki and Brohug

When I learned that Turbo Tanker had been there on the Astrals' planet, I started to actually feel better about my mission to collect the ten rings. His words of condemnation had the opposite effect on me compared to what he might have desired.

"It's just up this way," Alora said. We were back in the truck and it was the next morning. There were fires and more corpses along the road.

There was a way to get off this highway of sorts, off to the right. You almost wouldn't see it if you didn't know it was there. What you would see is a fire and a lot of smoke.

We drove through the smoke. There was a well-worn dirt road there waiting for us. It was rutted. Clearly this was not a road that trucks, even monster ones, normally drove on.

I could have flown, even teleported the three of us to where we were going. But their contact said that he wouldn't even meet with me if we didn't come by the road.

"Who?" I asked.

"He has many names. He'll want you to call him Harly."

"Harly?"

"Yeah, Harly. A lot of the skeletons you saw along the way, well, he's the reason they're skeletons. He eats what he wants and leaves the rest for the other Grembold scavengers to pick at."

"He killed them and … ?"

"Yeah, he ate them. He's the real reason it's only okay to see him during the day. Well, one of them. And even then, it's questionable. But he's hungrier at night."

The road up to Harly's home was littered with more skeletons. Some were put in certain positions. They pointed away from Harly's home. Poised as if they were warnings for anyone who would come too close to this place.

We parked the truck, exited and made our way to the door.

Harly answered it. I'd heard of something called road rash. It's what happens when you crash on your bike, slide along the pavement and have the scars to show for it. But this guy, he was the pavement. There were tyre-imprints and burns all over him. He'd been run over by bikes over and over again. It looked like there wasn't a smooth bit of skin on him. I once heard there was a version of the American flag that had the words "Don't tread on me" on it. This guy was treaded upon all over. And over again.

He looked at me, ignoring both Turbo Tanker and Alora.

"What do you want?"

"The ring," I told him.

He paused. I wondered if he was even going to tell me.

"Talk to the one with the patch," he said.

"The patch?"

"Maybe he'll give it to you, maybe he won't."

Harly shut the door in our face immediately.

I looked at the other two Grembolds. "That's it?" I asked them, disappointed with how short that meeting was with everything that had led to it. "All this, for that?" They nodded in response. And then they hurried me back to the car. "I don't get it. Why are we rushing?"

Alora looked at me and there was real concern on her face. "The sun's going down. And he'll be after us soon."

"Who? Harly?"

"Who else," she responded. "We're all in this together now. Different rules at night."

"Different rules?"

"Yeah," she said. "As in no rules. You're going to have to fight him."

HARLY

On the way to finding the ring of the Grembold world, we went in search of the cannibal goblin known as Harly. He had the information I needed to find the ring, I was told. He road a type of motor-cycle and was feared by all who live here. Especially when the goblin sun goes down and he gets hungry.

ROUTE 666

Harly is not the only cannibal on this world of the Grembolds. But he might be the most feared. The road to finding him was strewn with his prey. And if he doesn't finish a meal before moving onto preying on the Grembold, there were many ... others to finish his scraps.

CHAPTER FIVE
KIDS

"Days when we'd fight, we'd fight 'til I would give in."
Steve Aoki and Tony Junior

Harly was coming after us. It was night. Even Turbo Tanker seemed nervous. We all looked in the rearview mirrors. It didn't help that that just made Harly look all the closer.

We passed the diner we had camped out at the night before.

Harly's bike, the one he was chasing us on, was like something out of a Hell-Racer comic book, which, you know, was my other favorite manga other than Weapon Human. I couldn't tell if his bike was actually aflame like in Hell-Racer or if it was just on fire because of the flames he was going through to get to us.

Alora was scared. Turbo Tanker was scared as well. And Harly, well, I'm pretty sure Harly was just hungry.

I didn't have to worry about upsetting Harly anymore, though. He was almost upon us and I tried to time things perfectly.

Our truck was on fire. He was trying to get us to stop. Or, trying to barbeque us like he had so many others and bring us to a stop already cooked. I reached forward and touched both Turbo and Alora and I teleported us out of the truck. The now passenger-less truck spun out of control and crashed, flipping over and over again. While still spinning, it also burst into flame in its last couple flips, and took at least a light pole or two with it until it crashed into an abandoned road-side hotel.

I thought that that would be it. Expecting that we were over-barbequed, Harly would just go back home, or move onto something else or someone else to eat. I know that that was not the way to think about other intelligent beings, but I did not think I had much of a choice, especially on this world.

I have to say, that explosion would have been fantastic if it wasn't so bright. And, unfortunately, it revealed exactly where we hid in the shadows-that-didn't-stay-shadows.

Harly turned his bike around and came after us.

I remembered a year before, well, four hundred and one years before, I guess. I remembered how I stood up to this kid who had always put me down. I stood up to him in front of his friends and smashed him in the mouth. When I left the school that night, he found me in the parking lot and beat the shit out of me. All I had gotten in was a lucky punch. That was all. I had no real power then. But I did now.

I launched myself at Harly using both my ability to fly and my strength. I tried to knock him off his bike, but he spun it around, his tires spitting what felt like hot lava in my face.

I punched him like I did that kid, hoping to get lucky.

And just like before, I got unlucky; he spun towards Alora and I realized he was going to go after her. I threw myself with the speed of a bullet in front of Alora, and Turbo Tanker technically. And hoped that maybe I could save her.

We would have been dead, Doctor Snow, if an arrow didn't shoot through the air and hit Harly, knocking him off his bike, before he could reach us.

But it didn't kill him. Harly, bleeding, got to his feet and pulled the arrow out of his chest. At first he was snarling and enraged. And then he looked at the arrow. He looked up and saw who his attacker was. His look changed from anger and hunger to just plain fear. He simply got back on his bike and rode away.

"What was that about?" I asked.

"That was about me."

We turned. And there he was. Bow and another arrow in hand, just in case he needed to shoot another at Harly. This thing before me had an eye patch. And a robot arm.

"Are you the one with the patch? I mean, that's obvious. But are you the one who can help me get the ring of this world?"

He nodded. Alora literally ran away. What was it with this guy?

I didn't understand this at all. This was the guy that Harly told me to talk to, but he was also the Grembold that made Harly go home.

"It doesn't matter whether you understand this or not," he said. Turbo Tanker was still around, and he seemed frustrated as well, or maybe scared, too. He kept backing away from the guy with the patch. Was there some sort of history between them, or was it something else? I figured I didn't need to know what it was, regardless. If Patch here had the ring, that's all that mattered.

And, Turbo Tanker was suddenly nowhere to be seen; he'd clearly made a decision and disappeared like Alora. Alora; yes, who was gone, which broke my heart.

"You didn't need to seek me out, Hiro. I was coming for you the moment you came to this world. My name isn't Patch. It's Gilgamar."

"I did have a feeling that what I was here for was just going to come to me, eventually. Have you brought the ring to me?" I asked. Was it my third eye, Doctor Snow, that made me think or know this, or was it something else?

Gilgamar said nothing. There was clearly more to him than I knew. Or could know at this point, I was pretty certain. But I did have the sense that this Gilgamar was a friend.

"I have the ring. But first let me explain what it does. It has the ability to mask the wearer as a creature to be feared. That's why Harly backed away when he saw me. That's why Turbo Tanker did the same. Why Alora ran.

"Then why aren't I afraid?" I asked.

"Because I don't want you to be."

"I don't understand. How did you find me?"

"There are some things I won't explain. At least not until I see you the next time."

"Next time?"

"Never mind that. The way to access the power of the monster ring is by speaking the word 'Nilboggerize' and saying it slowly."

I looked at Gilgamar's hands. He wasn't wearing the ring on either. Not the normal one, well, normal for a Goblin. And not the robotic one.

"So where is the ring, I asked him?"

"I have it on me," he said. "Know, Hiro, that there is more at work here than merely your quest. You are part of something much larger. What will happen, will happen."

"I don't understand." I was saying that a lot. But I was being truthful.

"Sometimes a wound has to be made larger before it can be healed." Gilgamar said.

"I'm sorry, the doctors that augmented me and mutated me to save my world didn't give me much in the realms of philosophy." I muttered.

"I understand," Gilgamar said. "There isn't a lot of good discussion in this world. The Grembolds live to interrupt each other and change the subject. You want the ring and you should have it."

He reached up to his eye patch and flipped it up. Inside the socket of where an eye would be, there was something else. He pulled it out and unfolded a small bag. Inside the bag was the sixth ring. He took it out of the bag and handed it to me.

"Thank you," I said. And watched him flip down the patch again. "We will see if your gratitude will last the tests that are coming."

He nodded and warned me that Turbo Tanker was not so far from the truth. "Be careful, Hiro. Don't lose yourself."

GILGAMAR

Gilgamar is, in the world of the Grembold, the person who ultimately had the ring of this world for me. He carried it in his eye socket. Harly, Turbo Tracker and even Alora were all frightened of him, but I think that has more to do with the ring than him. I don't know. He also warned me, Doctor Snow, that I may see him again.

THE GREMBOLD RING

The Grembold Ring, I think, has some sort of telepathic effect on how its wearer is seen. To wear it is to be seen by others as the most fearsome presence they would imagine. I think it's different for everyone. What someone personally fears most. If Gilgamar had let me see him with the ring, I think I would have seen Earth destroyed by that meteor, Doctor Snow. That's the image that keeps me going. It's the one I'm most afraid of.

SOURCE CODE TO
ACCESS POWER: NILBOGGERIZE

HIRO's JOURNEY

CHAPTER SIX

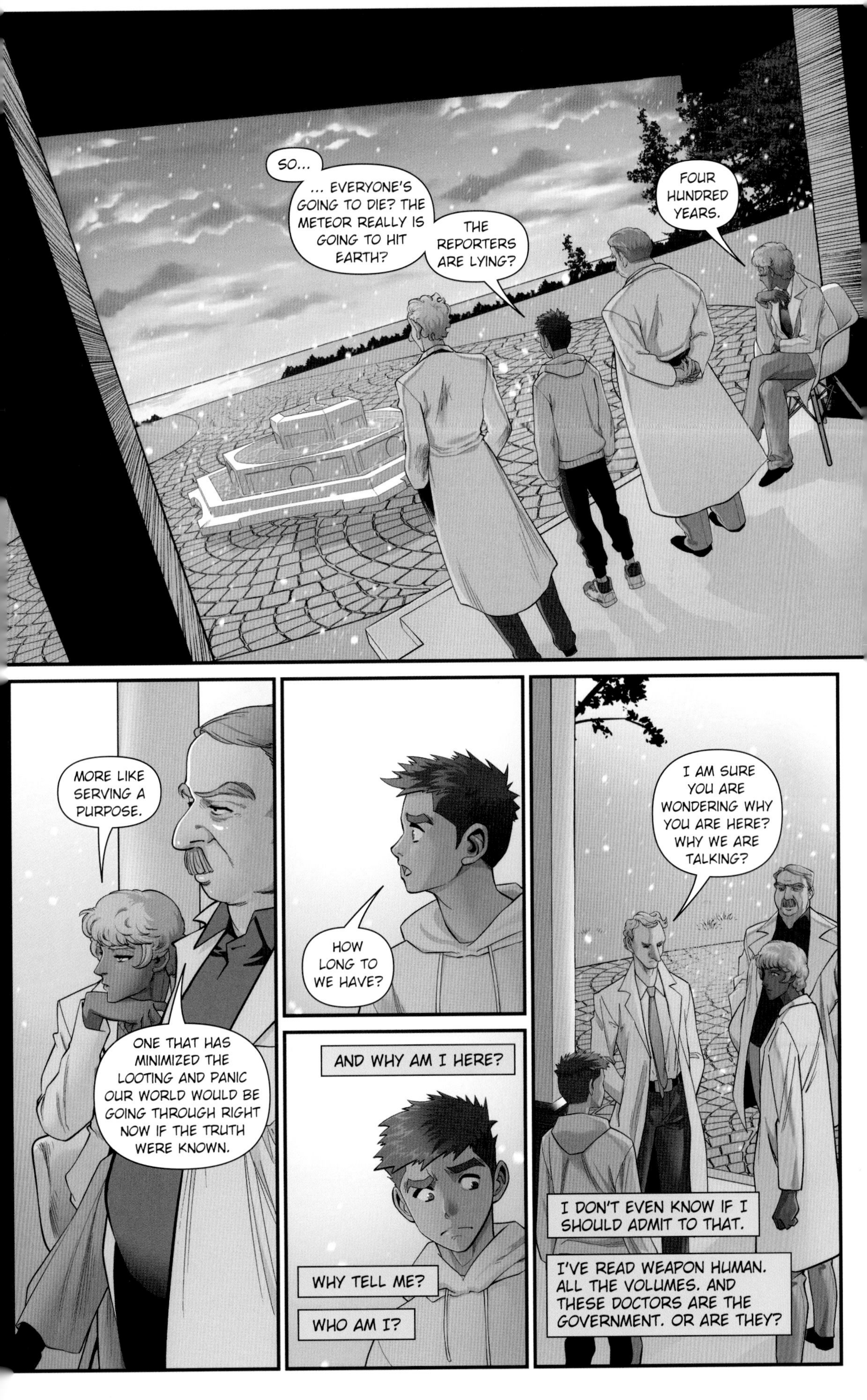
SO...
... EVERYONE'S GOING TO DIE? THE METEOR REALLY IS GOING TO HIT EARTH?
THE REPORTERS ARE LYING?
FOUR HUNDRED YEARS.
MORE LIKE SERVING A PURPOSE.
ONE THAT HAS MINIMIZED THE LOOTING AND PANIC OUR WORLD WOULD BE GOING THROUGH RIGHT NOW IF THE TRUTH WERE KNOWN.
HOW LONG TO WE HAVE?
AND WHY AM I HERE?
WHY TELL ME?
WHO AM I?
I AM SURE YOU ARE WONDERING WHY YOU ARE HERE? WHY WE ARE TALKING?
I DON'T EVEN KNOW IF I SHOULD ADMIT TO THAT.
I'VE READ WEAPON HUMAN. ALL THE VOLUMES. AND THESE DOCTORS ARE THE GOVERNMENT. OR ARE THEY?

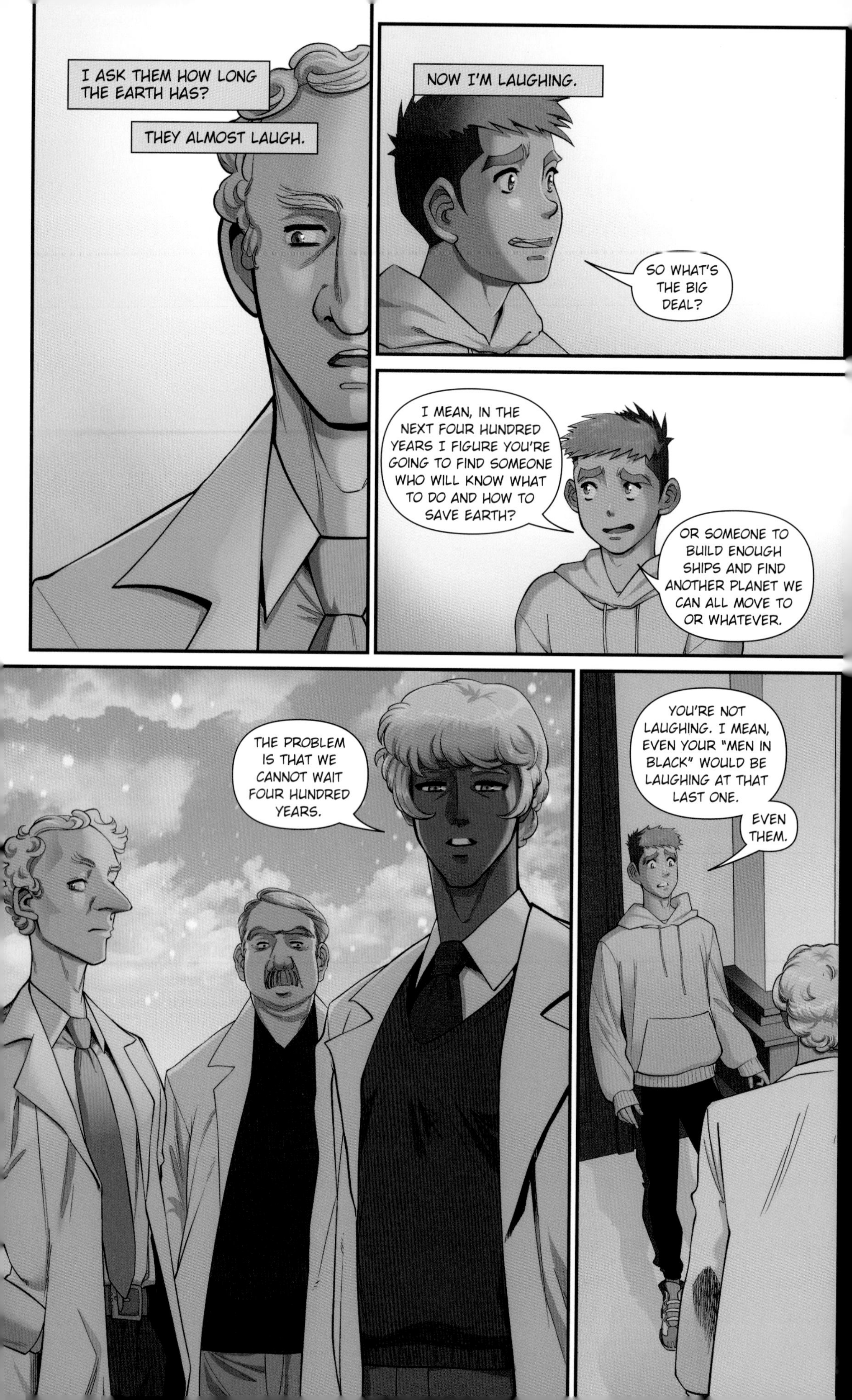
I ASK THEM HOW LONG THE EARTH HAS?
THEY ALMOST LAUGH.
NOW I'M LAUGHING.
SO WHAT'S THE BIG DEAL?
I MEAN, IN THE NEXT FOUR HUNDRED YEARS I FIGURE YOU'RE GOING TO FIND SOMEONE WHO WILL KNOW WHAT TO DO AND HOW TO SAVE EARTH?
OR SOMEONE TO BUILD ENOUGH SHIPS AND FIND ANOTHER PLANET WE CAN ALL MOVE TO OR WHATEVER.
THE PROBLEM IS THAT WE CANNOT WAIT FOUR HUNDRED YEARS.
YOU'RE NOT LAUGHING. I MEAN, EVEN YOUR "MEN IN BLACK" WOULD BE LAUGHING AT THAT LAST ONE.
EVEN THEM.

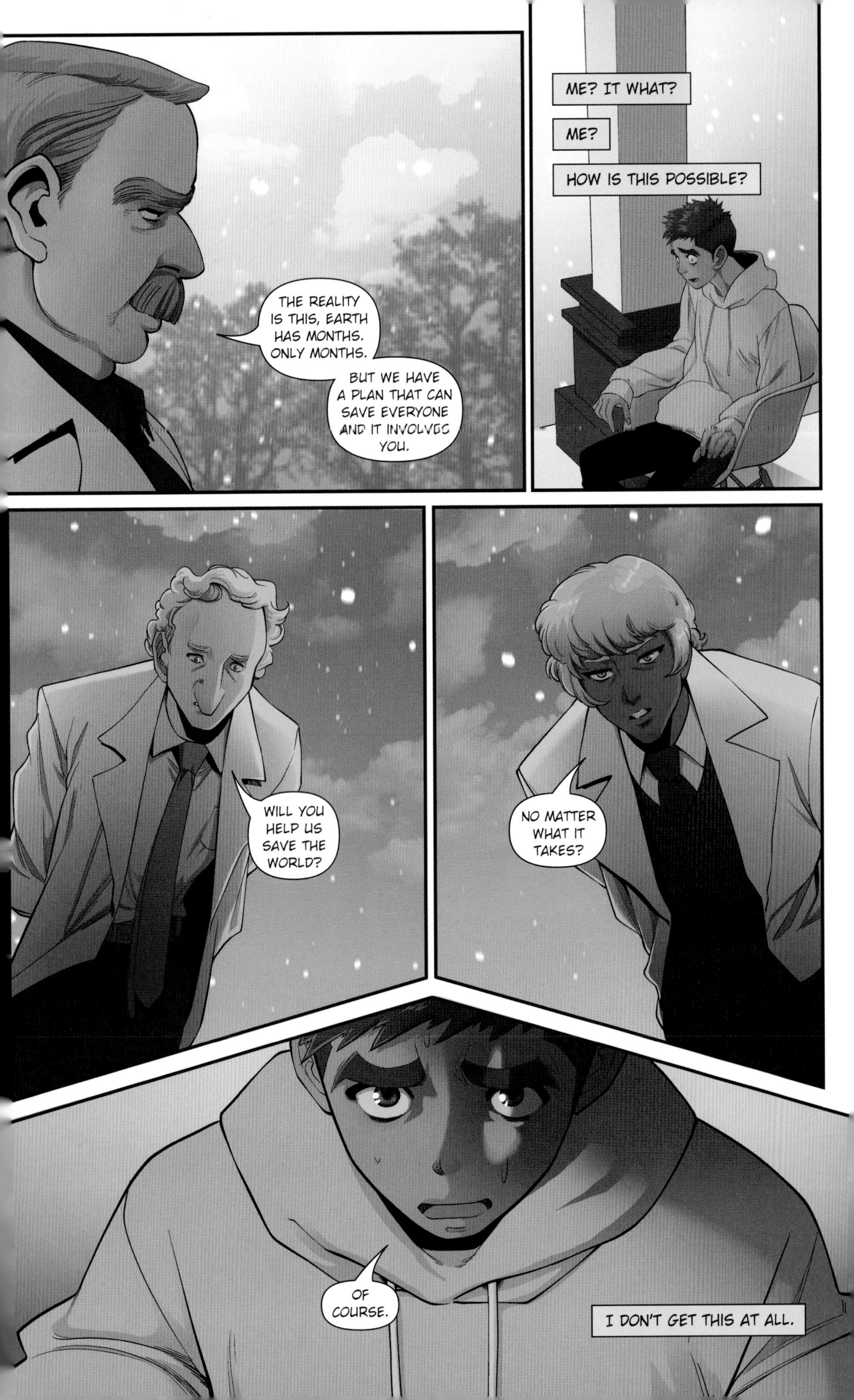
THE REALITY IS THIS, EARTH HAS MONTHS. ONLY MONTHS.
BUT WE HAVE A PLAN THAT CAN SAVE EVERYONE AND IT INVOLVES YOU.
ME? IT WHAT?
ME?
HOW IS THIS POSSIBLE?
WILL YOU HELP US SAVE THE WORLD?
NO MATTER WHAT IT TAKES?
OF COURSE.
I DON'T GET THIS AT ALL.

I'M SO PLEASED TO HEAR YOU SAY THIS HIRO.

OR SHOULD WE SAY "HYRO"... NO, HERO?

THE PROBLEM IS THIS. WHAT WE NEED TO SAVE THE WORLD DOESN'T EXIST YET.

I LIKE "HERO."

BUT IT WILL IN FOUR HUNDRED YEARS?

SO WHAT ARE YOU GOING TO DO, SEND ME TO THE FUTURE TO GET WHAT YOU NEED SO THAT EARTH CAN BE SAVED?

UH... THAT WAS A JOKE.

HiroQuest

RING SEVEN
GIANT RING

PART SEVEN

THE FACTION OF
THE GRAVITONS

CHAPTER SIX
NEW YORK

"Don't know what's real."
Steve Aoki, Regard and Mazie

I missed Alora not being with me anymore, but my third eye kept flashing pictures of her; memories that weren't mine, but were of her in my arms, and I felt like it meant I would see her again. I could tell that she didn't want to get to close. But I think it was too late for that. Maybe after I had gotten all ten rings, I thought. Maybe then we would be together. It was probably better that she wasn't with me now, anyway. I would have been too distracted. At least that's what I said to myself.

"Welcome to the world of the Gravitons," a voice said. But I knew the voice well.

"Hyro? Where have you been?" I couldn't see him. But I could hear him. And had a sense that he was near. Almost like one radio station crackling in on another.

"I'm almost there, Hiro. Almost there," said Hyro through what was like a static and at the same time felt like it was coming from inside me.

"What is this place?"

"It's a world of giants. Everything is huge there. The ring you're looking for can make the wearer either really small or really large. 'Mammothus' is your source-code."

"Thank you. Do you have any idea of where to begin?"

"Not yet, but I will find out."

I flew into the horizon, seeing vast forests and even a city off in the distance. Anxious to talk to someone, anyone, I headed to that city.

When I finally reached the city I found buildings that were only a few stories high, and that was only because every floor was hundreds of feet tall. This was truly a world of giants. Of the Gravitons.

The first of these giants I met, I met because he wouldn't get out of my way. He was known as Levi, and he would not shut up. His opinion was the only opinion that mattered to him, unless of course, I could shout louder than him; which I couldn't because I was so small in comparison. To disagree with him was to just have his opinion repeated, but still louder and louder. He seemed like he came from New York.

When I asked him about the ring, he told me about a lot of them. Lots of rings. Lots of things. About greater giants than he that were much smaller beings. He told me about the cities that dwarfed this one, where the greatest minds lived and hoped for a smaller world, because the air they breathed was thinner because of their height.

He spoke of the regrets he had for mountains he had stomped into deserts, and of his lack of appreciation for nature (which seemed a contradiction, but, as I said before, he had opinions).

He spoke of broken promises and sadness, all because I was willing to listen. This was no giant. This was a small being; at least emotionally. He was a giant like so many of his kind that lived in the regrets of maybe becoming too large. At least, too large too soon.

He knew about the ring I spoke to him of, though, but would not say any more than that. Levi asked what was in it for him? Not for his world. For him. And, so I left. And when I did, he called out as I was going, and said he wanted to renegotiate. He wanted to talk some more.

"Aren't you supposed to be one of the greatest of the giants? Isn't that what you said?" I asked.

"I am the greatest," he said, more gruff than honest.

"I don't believe you. If you indeed were the greatest, you would tell me where the ring of this world was, because there's nothing it could do that would limit you. You're bigger than that. Or any little ring."

He thought about this for a while. And then he buckled, and told me that I should seek the prisoner, the Tormenter, a four-armed Graviton that had been made small when he was incarcerated.

Levi also told me to be wary of the trees. The trees were killing giants now. Maybe even people my size. But they were especially killing giants.

LEVI

Levi was the first of the giants I met on the world of the Gravitons. He was overwhelmingly self-absorbed and even though he was a giant, as my mom would say, he had a big head. What was sad was that, as a giant, he seemed to miss the days when he hadn't been one. Maybe the days when he'd he still had to prove himself for real, and not just talk.

HYRO IS COMING

I'm so happy, Doctor Snow, that you sent Hyro to help me. He's not here yet, but he has been sending me messages that have helped in collecting the rings so far. I can't wait for him to get here. To tell you the honest truth, these rings are a little heavy. Like I can't look at them on my fingers without thinking of all I've had to do to retrieve them from these worlds.

CHAPTER SEVEN
LOCKED UP

"They won't let me out, they won't let me out."
Steve Aoki, Trinix and Akon

The former prisoner known as the Tormenter didn't need me to release him or help him escape. When I met him on my journey, he was already free, already wanting to make all those who had unfairly incarcerated him pay for what they had done.

I also think he was quite mad. But he said that he was in his last moments, and that in that short time, he wanted to help me understand this world.

"How did you escape?" These were my first words to him.

"Who says I did?" He asked. He had four arms, hence his name.

"I do," I said and used the ring from the Grembold world. I knew it would make me look like a monster to him. Like someone he would be afraid of.

"You're scary, kid, but not scary enough. After all, you're only five and a half feet tall."

"I'm sorry."

"You don't understand the prison system in these parts, do you?"

"Care to explain?"

"No."

"Will you anyhow, please?"

The Tormenter paused. He started to speak a couple times, always stopping himself. He walked back and forth in front of me, like he was imprisoned again, this time, not by bars, but by his own indecision. Finally, he turned back to me.

"There are a lot of criminals on this planet. A lot. And on the world of the Gravitons, this presented the rest of society with some real trouble. After all, the prisons themselves were giant, and the inmates themselves were giant. Do the math."

Doctor Snow, 'Math' was never my thing, as you know, but now I know Latin, and more. But this wasn't math. This was about things adding up in a real way. I'd seen enough of this place to know that it wasn't a prison world. There was a lot of nature here. And cities. But not prisons. So, something he was saying was out.

I turned back to the Tormenter. "So, what does it mean to be a prisoner on this world?"

"On some worlds, prisoners pray that their sentences would shrink. On this world, being shrunk is the sentence."

"What?"

"The prisons are small here and they house many; and that is because they shrink you once you are imprisoned, and you're given a number. My head used to be in the clouds, and now I am forced to try to look over the blades of grass. That's what they do to you. They make you small. They make you nothing. They give you a number, but to be honest, there are so many numbers that a number isn't even really even a number anymore. And once in, they won't let you out, they won't let you out."

"I'm sorry. It's interesting. I met another giant who regretted being a giant. Is there something that suggests a 'grass is greener' idea?"

"Do not mention the grass or the trees. They are killing the giants now."

"Okay, but the giants want to be small again, and it seems like those who have been shrunk want to be giants."

At this, the Tormenter thought for a moment. "Perhaps it has something to do with the freedom to choose. I am not certain."

I wanted to call him "Four-Arm" as in fore-warned is fore-armed. And, of course, because he had four arms.

"You mentioned before that you were given a number. I feel like if I don't find the ring that will help me save my world, my world's number will be up. No matter what that number is."

That's one of those things, Doctor, another part of your augmentation to me. I felt like I knew how to respond to people, whether a situation required humor or cleverness or pride or humility. And I innately knew what it would take to talk with Four-Arm. Well, I mean, the Tormenter.

He looked at me. "Ha, yeah, a number is still a number. So, you're trying to save your world, is it?"

I nodded.

"Would you accept my help while I was guilty, or not guilty? Whether I was seen as a good Graviton, or not?"

"Yes."

"And why is that?"

"Because there are things that I think I am actually guilty of." I told him. "Some bad. And there are things I would be blamed for that are probably unfair as well."

"Okay."

"But more than any way I might look at it, there are billions of lives on the line and I'm not certain it's okay for me to worry about my own mortality, not with the futures of so many others at stake."

To this the Tormenter seemed to respond.

"Look kid, I want you to find your ring. I really do. And I think it'll help make things right. I'm more than happy to tell you everything that I know. And even take you to where you want to go. But there will be a cost. I have a price."

"And what is that?"

"I want to tell you my story and I want you to promise to believe me even if you don't."

"Wait. What?"

"Even if you don't believe what I'm about to tell you I want you to believe me anyhow. I want you to ignore any hunches or conclusions you might have and believe me no matter what."

"That's a tall order," I told him.

"That's all they are on this world. Unless you become a prisoner."

I laughed. Well, I chuckled. And continued. "I'm not sure I understand."

"Let me put it this way, then. You want me to believe, without any proof, that I should help you find a ring that might be of real use to this world. But giving it away to you, that's better: and by doing so I will help save billions and billions. You want me to believe this no matter what?"

"Yeah."

"Well, I want the same from you. No matter what."

I couldn't help but think of what Alora had said to me. "Come what may."

I looked back at the four-armed Tormenter. "Okay, yeah, no matter what."

THE TORMENTER

I met a hero here, who became a criminal here, who I think will become a hero again. This Graviton was imprisoned for something he didn't do. At least that's what he says. But it was in the process of being a prisoner that I think he became a bad guy. His name is The Tormenter. He just wants to be a giant again.

THE PRISONERS OF GRAVITON

In the midst of my search for the ring of this world I came upon the fact that to be in prison on this world is to be denied even free air. They all wear a helmet of sorts. Maybe they inhale a gas or something through it that keeps them small. The Tormenter still remembers what being small before being giant before being a prisoner was like. I think that now that he is free, he hopes to one day become a giant again.

CHAPTER EIGHT
WON'T FORGET THIS TIME

"Take my hand in the prayer into the sky."
Steve Aoki, KAAZE and John Martin

"First of all," the Tormenter said, "I was completely innocent before they shrunk me and imprisoned me. But I'm not innocent anymore. I'm what they called me before I was guilty. I'm the Tormenter."

"I'm sorry, I don't know if I understand what that means."

"It means that I didn't become a criminal, I didn't become a thief, I didn't become a murderer, until after I was incarcerated for crimes I never committed. You see, I was blamed for a murder. I was with this girl. And I came home one night to find her in the arms of another guy."

"I'm sorry."

"You know, the worst part is, he only had two arms. There's the irony for you. Look at me. I'm twice the hugger, twice the holder, this guy ever was. I might have even been a little taller. It's hard to tell with us giants. But that's love, I guess, right? Anyhow, horrified, I confronted her, in anger. She filmed me on her smart phone being angry, and I stormed off."

"The next day, Two-Arms there, he winds up dead. Strangled. I did not do it. If I had, it would have been with something more than my bare hands. Still, he's dead and they pin it all on me under some lame legal umbrella the no-good lawyers called 'reasonable cause.'"

"I'm sorry," I told him.

"Not nearly as sorry as she was. Well, would have been if she had lived long enough to be sorry. But she didn't. Live long enough, I mean. Because no one ever pays any attention to the little guy. And after being incarcerated, after being shrunk down to be a part of the penal system, I was indeed the little guy. All these words are so insulting. Anyhow, the point is that I made sure from the inside, from the ant's point of view, that she didn't live to be sorry."

I told the Tormenter that I understood what he meant.

He asked if I had ever been betrayed.

I told him about a girl in junior high. He didn't know what junior high was, and misunderstood what "high" meant altogether. So, I explained and told him about some other friends that I thought were friends but it turned out they weren't. But that was well before I was augmented, of course.

He told me my story was nothing compared to his experience. His was like having your heart ripped out, without anesthesia. And without the proper surgical tools. He said it was like his life was ripped out with something I can only guess is this world's equivalent of a weed-whacker.

Anyhow, there was blood on his hands. All four of them. That said, because he was now shrunk so small, in other words, the size of me, he said there wasn't much blood on his hands.

I really didn't understand that logic. I mean, if he was small and she was giant, wouldn't there have been more blood? (As I mentioned earlier, math is not my thing.)

"So how did you escape from prison?" I asked.

"Some Graviton died on the spot and collapsed onto the prison. No one cleaned it up because everything is a giant disaster in this world. "Bigger fires to put out, you know."

I nodded.

"Anyhow, the flies and maggots that affected the giant, well they were bigger than even the walls of our shrunk down prisons. And so, the walls weren't that strong and the maggots and the moths and whatever else, they were really hungry."

"Is there anything else you want to say to me? Or have me hear? Because I believe you. I really do. And I'm not even trying to convince myself of anything. There was a girl on another world that I thought was going to betray me and she didn't, but I still thought it was going to happen. I still felt all those moments."

"No, I think I'm finished. Thank you for believing me. But be warned, one day you will be betrayed."

"Why do you say that?"

"Because you are a hero and it is the very structure of the hero's journey and story that you be betrayed."

"I'm not sure I like that," I said. "But I also can't worry about that now. I need to find the ring to this world."

"We need to talk to the trees," he said.

"The trees?"

"Yeah, there are too many giants on this Earth. They aren't happy about that. But because we are small, they will speak to us."

"Thank you."

So, I teleported myself and the Tormenter into the woods outside the city.

We walked through the moss and the grass and the mud at the base of trees higher than any I had ever seen.

The Tormenter asked me if I had the patience to climb. I said we wouldn't have to and I teleported us up onto a branch at the back of a certain tree that seemed to be the largest, most dominant of the clump of trees here.

We walked along that giant branch and spoke to the tree.

"I have heard you are angry at the giants." I said
to the tree.
The old tree spoke back in a voice that didn't make me feel any better or safer.

"They use too much of the air we produce. We hate them. We hate all air-breathers for stealing and taking so much from us."

"But me and the Tormenter here, we use very little air."

"Well, maybe we do not hate you, then. As long as you don't get any bigger."

That was a relief. I had hoped that we might be able to find some sort of way to negotiate. I had even wondered if there would be a way to use whatever thing it was that shrunk the prisoners down to shrink everyone down. Then they'd all be using less air.

"I'm looking for a ring that could save billions of people's lives. Do you know where it is?" I said.

"No."

The answer came so quickly, that I'm not even certain the entire question was heard. It was the kind of answer you got when you knew that no one wanted to talk about a particular subject matter.

I looked at my four-armed friend. He looked back. This time, he spoke.

"The ring might make a giant difference to others. They might be so grateful to the trees afterwards that they would seek out ways to take care of all vegetation on their worlds, and others' worlds."

There was a cacophony of leaves rustling and branches creaking in response as if it wasn't just this old tree responding but the entire forest.

And then, after a crescendo of more creaks and the meekest of twigs - there to crunches— from the mightiest trunk to the meekest of twigs—there was silence.

"No," responded the tree.

The Tormenter was not happy about this. He paced back and forth on the branch and finally turned to face the trunk of the tree and the majority of the trees in general. "I have axes," he said.

And they seemed to laugh at his response. As if he was no threat at all. As if he was an insect. I told him they were grumps. He said Forest Grumps. I thought about the movie and laughed.

"Forest Grumps is the funniest thing I've ever heard, I told him. But he didn't pay any attention to me. He was directing his words at the trees.

"I have four arms. That's twice the swing of the axe."

They laughed at him again. But he had a plan. I didn't realize it yet. And finding the ring was part of his revenge. Whether these trees deserved it or not.

ESCAPE FROM THE GRAVITON PRISON

So, the Tormenter, from within the prison, was able to get his revenge on the girl who betrayed him and pinned a murder charge on him. He became guilty even though he was innocent. Is this my story, Doctor Snow? Am I becoming more and more guilty of crimes as I walk the path of being a hero and saving Earth? The Tormenter was able to escape his prison. What escape will there be for me and my own conscience once this is over?

THE ELDERWOOD

Okay, they're not called Forest Grumps, but the Elderwood are giant angry trees. From what I understand they feel overworked because of how much air they produce that the giants of this world inhale practically all of. As a result, they are fighting back and now attacking the giants themselves.

CHAPTER NINE
OLDER

"We still got time, we still got time, we still got time."
Steve Aoki, Jimmie Allen and Dixie

So, the Tormenter and I made our way through the woods, undetected for the most part because we were so small. Every once in a while, the branches would seem to turn towards us, almost hostile, like they were sensing us. We would calm our breathing and try to inhale as little as possible until the branches returned to their normal positions.

We needed to use the same caution when it came to certain root systems that were not altogether underground. They snaked towards us many times.

Eventually we reached a clearing and trudged across a massive field, at least it was massive to us. We reached the other side where there was a giant stone. The Tormenter grabbed another rock and started striking the stone. Over and over he hit it. He used four rocks in all four of his hands smashing the old stone over and over again. We must have been in a place that had some sort of perfect echo because the bashing of the rock seemed to reverberate everywhere around us.

He looked back at me. "I used to be a giant, you know. A gargoyle. But that was before."

"Thank you for your help," I said.

"I'm not helping you, I'm helping me."

"Well, as long as I get the ring." I said.

"No matter what?" he asked.

"Sure. For the most part." I didn't like the way he said that, Doctor Snow. It'll be good once Hyro gets here. He'll be able to help me deal with things like this.

I felt it coming before I saw it or heard it. Him. Not Hyro. The one the Tormenter was signaling. I felt him coming before I heard him or saw him.

"Maximus, first of the giants, is coming. You won't have to bow because we are so far beneath him. But you may hurt your neck looking up at him." That's what the Tormenter said.

Maximus didn't rise out of the valley. He only lifted his head, which we now faced, which we stared up into. His head was as big as a house. A big house. Each of his teeth were probably as big as a door. None of which I wanted to go through.

"Why are you here?" it ... he, asked.

"The trees are getting angrier all the time."

"Grumpier. Forest Grumpier," I added in, glad to use the phrase in a sentence. I don't think in retrospect that the Tormenter had a sense of humor. Just as I'm not sure he would have laughed even if he had ever seen Forest Gump.

The Tormenter ignored me. "The giants in this world are using too much of the air. It's over-working the trees and they are beginning to strike back. They resent our use of what they call their fruit."

At this Maximus sighed, and actually seemed saddened. "It was me, you know. I was the one who started this. And it is not all the trees, just the one."

"The one?" I asked.

"Yes. Its roots have intermingled with all the others, over the eons. Once that one tree is brought down, it will stop producing the type of air that makes the small things become the large things, as well as all those it has interwoven its roots with.. The air they make is an engine for building giants. Like myself. To a very real degree, they have created their very own destruction and anger. Just as I did those many years ago, when size and a being's stature and greatness was determined by what they did and the quality of their thoughts."

I was shocked with what I next heard.

The giant admitted that it was his fault the world was the way it was. "This world's air was terrible, polluted, and was making the other inhabitants sick. There were mutations amongst my people and something needed to be done to undo the destruction we had caused to ourselves through industrialization and greed."

So he'd planted a very special seed that would make a certain tree grow. He'd done this in the hopes that the tree would clean the air and produce an atmosphere that would nurture and bring health to the people of this world.

It had made them giants as well. But there eventually were so many giants that even the suburbs of certain areas became overcrowded.

And then those giants began to use too much of the oxygen in the air, forcing the trees to be overworked. Forcing them to strike back. It was a new vicious cycle. A new way in which the Gravitons, by trying to solve one problem, created another.

"Then ... " continued the Tormenter, "when they incarcerate us and make us small, what they are really doing is denying us the actual air."

"Yes," responded Maximus.

"Good," said the Tormenter.

"No. Not good," said the giant. "This is destroying the fabric of our world."

"I want to be big again," the four-armed gargoyle said.

"Are you big enough to bring this world crashing down?"

"Big enough?"

At this, the giant produced a flower and told the Tormenter to breathe, and breathe deep. With each breath that the Tormenter took, he started to grow larger and larger until he was a giant again. I stared at him.

"I'm big."

"Are you big enough?" Maximus asked.

"Big enough for what?"

"To take down the tree. I've wanted to do so many times, but alas, I am not, as I say, big enough. Will you be this world's hero?"

I heard the words. He wanted to be a giant, but to do what he wanted to do, it would mean he would never get what he truly wanted. Could I make that kind of choice? Would I make that kind of a choice when it came to my world?

Maximus had axes that he gave the Tormenter. The Tormenter put me on his shoulder and we went to the tree, the tree that seemed to infect all of the others. The tree looked at us, with its senses, but not senses like I have–it didn't have eyes, for example, it was a giant vegetable after all.

It shot out branches at him, causing those branches to grow thorns as it did. They stabbed and skewered him. They whipped at him, drawing blood. Again and again and again. But he fought back like a hero would. Maybe it was the years of incarceration for no reason. Maybe it was because he was part of a system that tried to make him small, less than he actually was. Or maybe something even deeper than that.

Something had been planted in him a long time ago and it had grown to a size that could not be cut down. Could not be pruned back. Could not be transplanted into a different life. Maybe the roots of his anger just went too deep. He was mad as Hell and he was not going to take it anymore.

The Tormenter just kept chopping at the tree, chopping and hacking and hacking and chopping. It was hard to tell his hands from the axes they held. He just continued no matter how much blood he lost, or how much sap splashed up on him.

And finally, the old tree began to fall. And completely crashed into to topple it did. It crashed into other trees, uprooting them, ripping them from the soil, almost like in the way that dominos fall, or bowling pins crash into each other, but much more violently. The collapse shot dirt and giant worms and gargantuan insects and weeds into the air that then fell like the worst storm you could imagine in the winter.

Bleeding, the Tormenter looked down at his fallen enemy.

I stepped through the area where the tree had been chopped down. And looked at all the rings of the tree that revealed how old it was.

What was amazing was that in the center of the rings of the tree was a different ring entirely. It was the ring. The Graviton ring. This was the so-called seed that Maximus planted those many years before. This was what caused the trees to grow to produce the air that made everyone in this world into giants. It was the ring in the center of the rings.

I picked up the ring and put it on, ready to leave this world behind.

The air already smelled better.

The Tormenter knew he would not remain a giant for too much longer. But I could see that he wasn't angered about it anymore.

If anything, he had found a part of himself that had been cut down years ago.

Doctor Snow? I wasn't the hero of this world, but I also didn't have to be. The Tormenter was. And while he was innocent and then guilty in this life, I think he felt somewhat redeemed for bringing an end to the days when the so-called giants would look down on the little people.

MAXIMUS THE GIANT

Maximus is the oldest of the Gravitons I think. He, like the Giant called Levi, and maybe all the giants, missed being small. He misses, I think, seeing great and giant things and was tired, from his vantage point of only seeing small things. I wonder, Doctor Snow, if I am becoming too accustomed to the fantastic. I hope, when I am myself again, that I will be able to feel wonder again.

THE GRAVITON RING

The Graviton Ring has the power and ability to make the wearer either really large or really small. On this world, it is in the center of a tree that produced air that turned everyone into giants. I wonder, Doctor Snow, if you could use the ring to make the meteorite that's going to destroy Earth really small? That would make sense to me. But why then, would you need nine other rings?

SOURCE CODE TO
ACCESS POWER: MAMMOTHUS

HIRO's JOURNEY

CHAPTER SEVEN

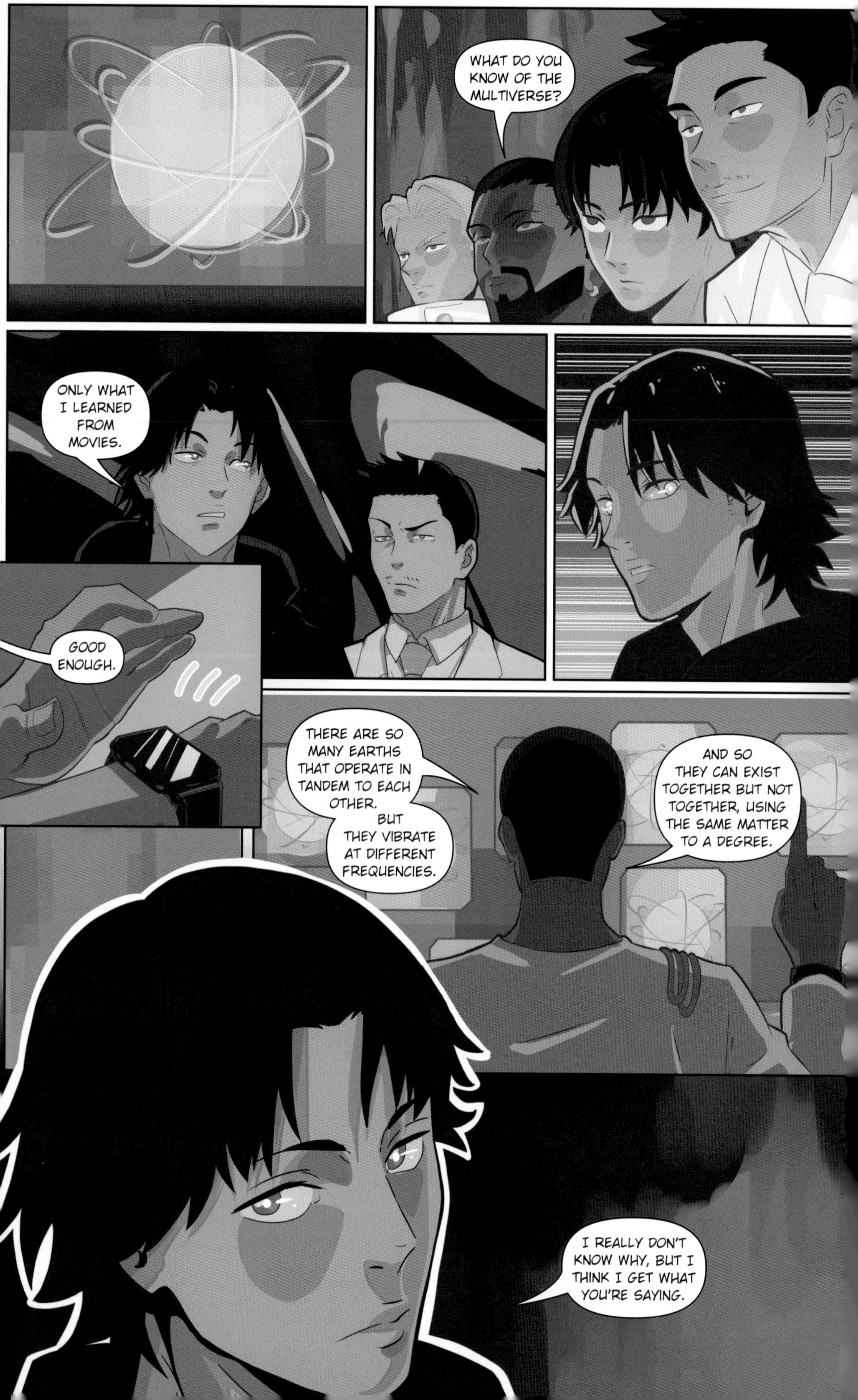
WHAT DO YOU KNOW OF THE MULTIVERSE?
ONLY WHAT I LEARNED FROM MOVIES.
GOOD ENOUGH.
THERE ARE SO MANY EARTHS THAT OPERATE IN TANDEM TO EACH OTHER.
BUT THEY VIBRATE AT DIFFERENT FREQUENCIES.
AND SO THEY CAN EXIST TOGETHER BUT NOT TOGETHER, USING THE SAME MATTER TO A DEGREE.
I REALLY DON'T KNOW WHY, BUT I THINK I GET WHAT YOU'RE SAYING.

UH-HUH.

I'M SURE THIS IS CONFUSING. IT WOULD HAVE BEEN FOR ME.

BUT WE'VE FOUND WORLDS WITHIN THE SPREAD, WHEREBY, TAKING FROM THEM WON'T AFFECT THE OTHERS TO A DEGREE THAT WOULDN'T BE... I DON'T KNOW...

THE EQUIVALENT OF KILLING A BUTTERFLY IN A PREHISTORIC ERA, LET'S SAY.

SURE... AND WHO HASN'T DONE THAT?

EXACTLY.

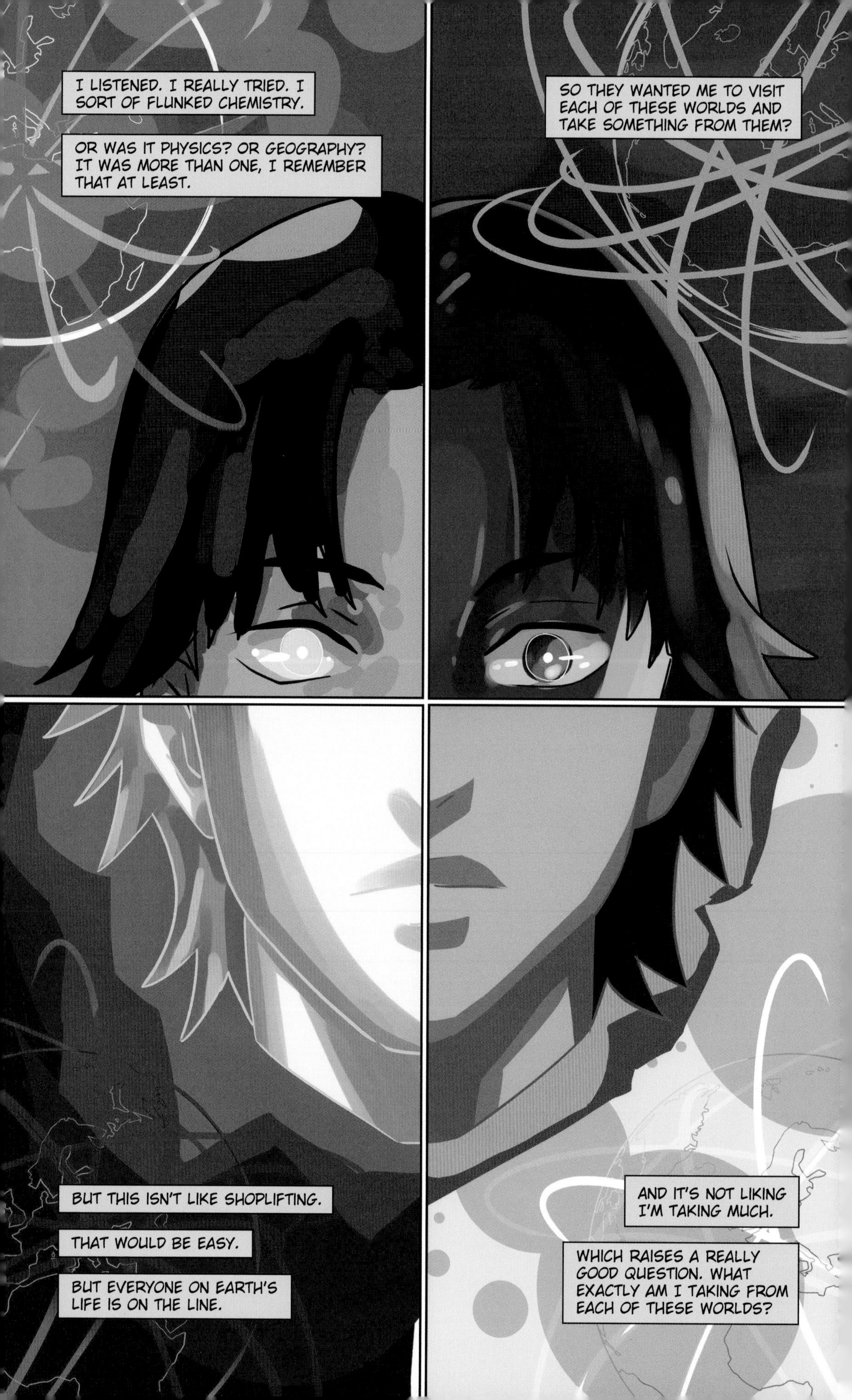
I LISTENED. I REALLY TRIED. I SORT OF FLUNKED CHEMISTRY.
OR WAS IT PHYSICS? OR GEOGRAPHY? IT WAS MORE THAN ONE, I REMEMBER THAT AT LEAST.
SO THEY WANTED ME TO VISIT EACH OF THESE WORLDS AND TAKE SOMETHING FROM THEM?
BUT THIS ISN'T LIKE SHOPLIFTING.
THAT WOULD BE EASY.
BUT EVERYONE ON EARTH'S LIFE IS ON THE LINE.
AND IT'S NOT LIKING I'M TAKING MUCH.
WHICH RAISES A REALLY GOOD QUESTION. WHAT EXACTLY AM I TAKING FROM EACH OF THESE WORLDS?

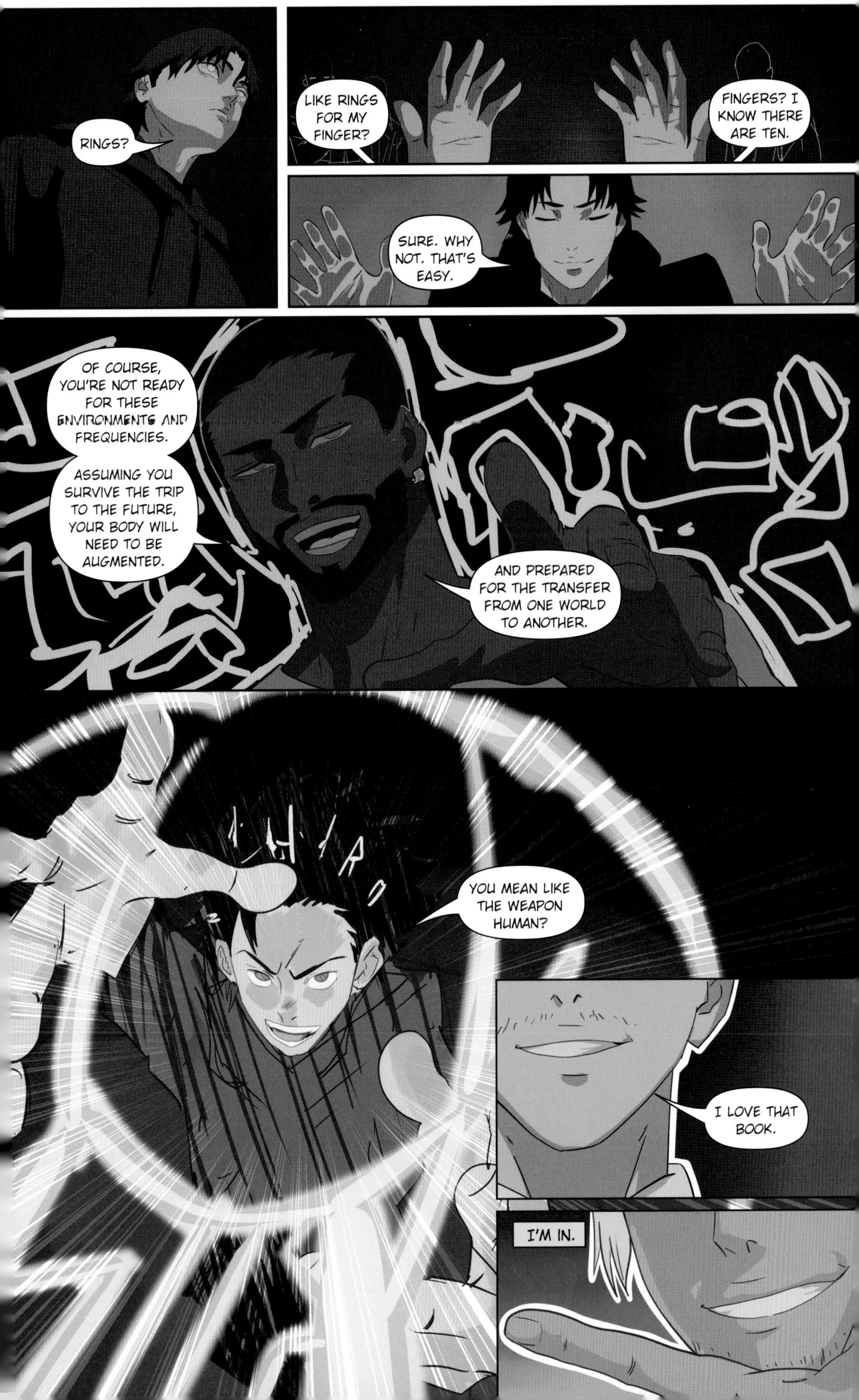
RINGS?
LIKE RINGS FOR MY FINGER?
FINGERS? I KNOW THERE ARE TEN.
SURE. WHY NOT. THAT'S EASY.
OF COURSE, YOU'RE NOT READY FOR THESE ENVIRONMENTS AND FREQUENCIES.
ASSUMING YOU SURVIVE THE TRIP TO THE FUTURE, YOUR BODY WILL NEED TO BE AUGMENTED.
AND PREPARED FOR THE TRANSFER FROM ONE WORLD TO ANOTHER.
YOU MEAN LIKE THE WEAPON HUMAN?
I LOVE THAT BOOK.
I'M IN.

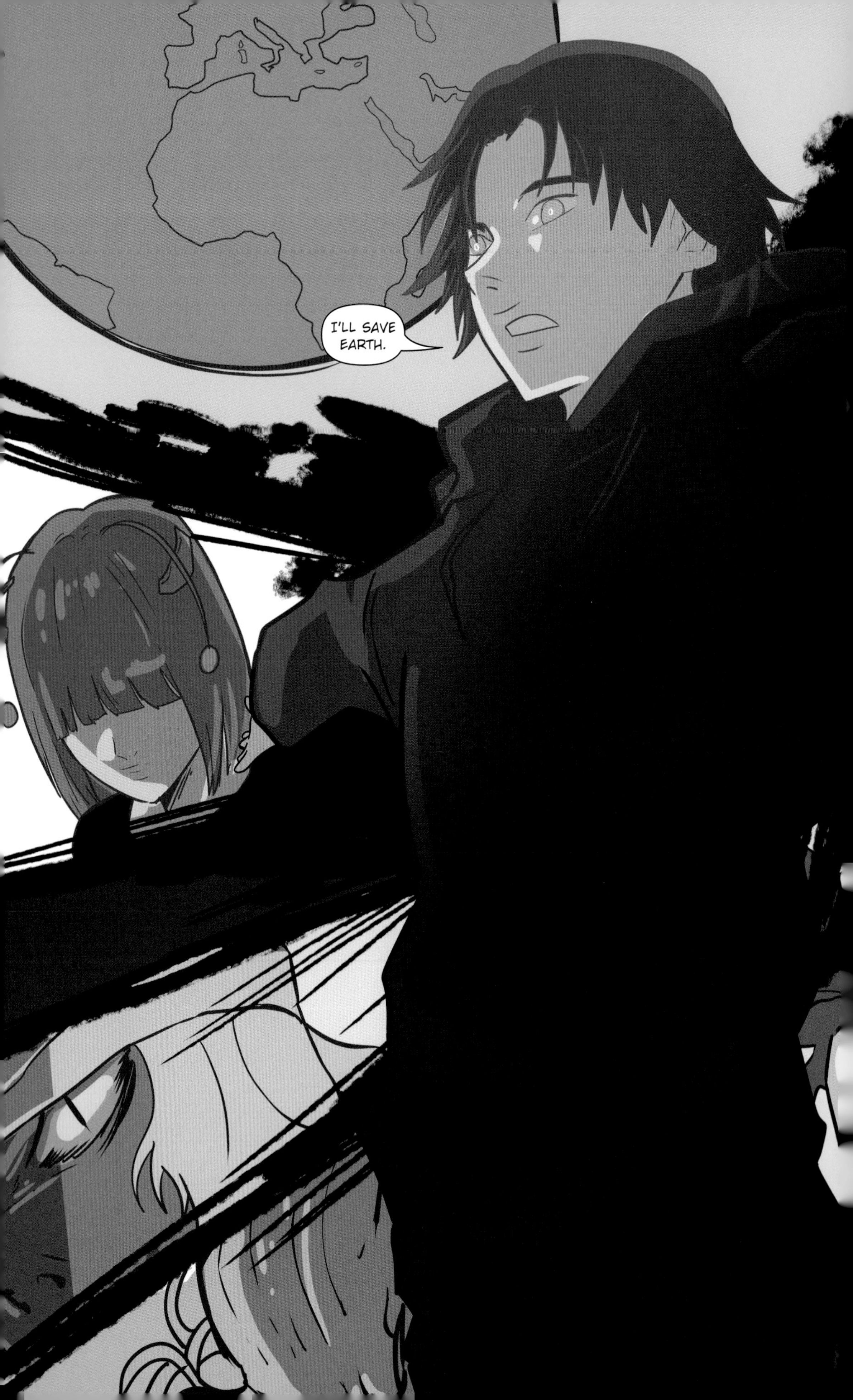
I'LL SAVE EARTH.

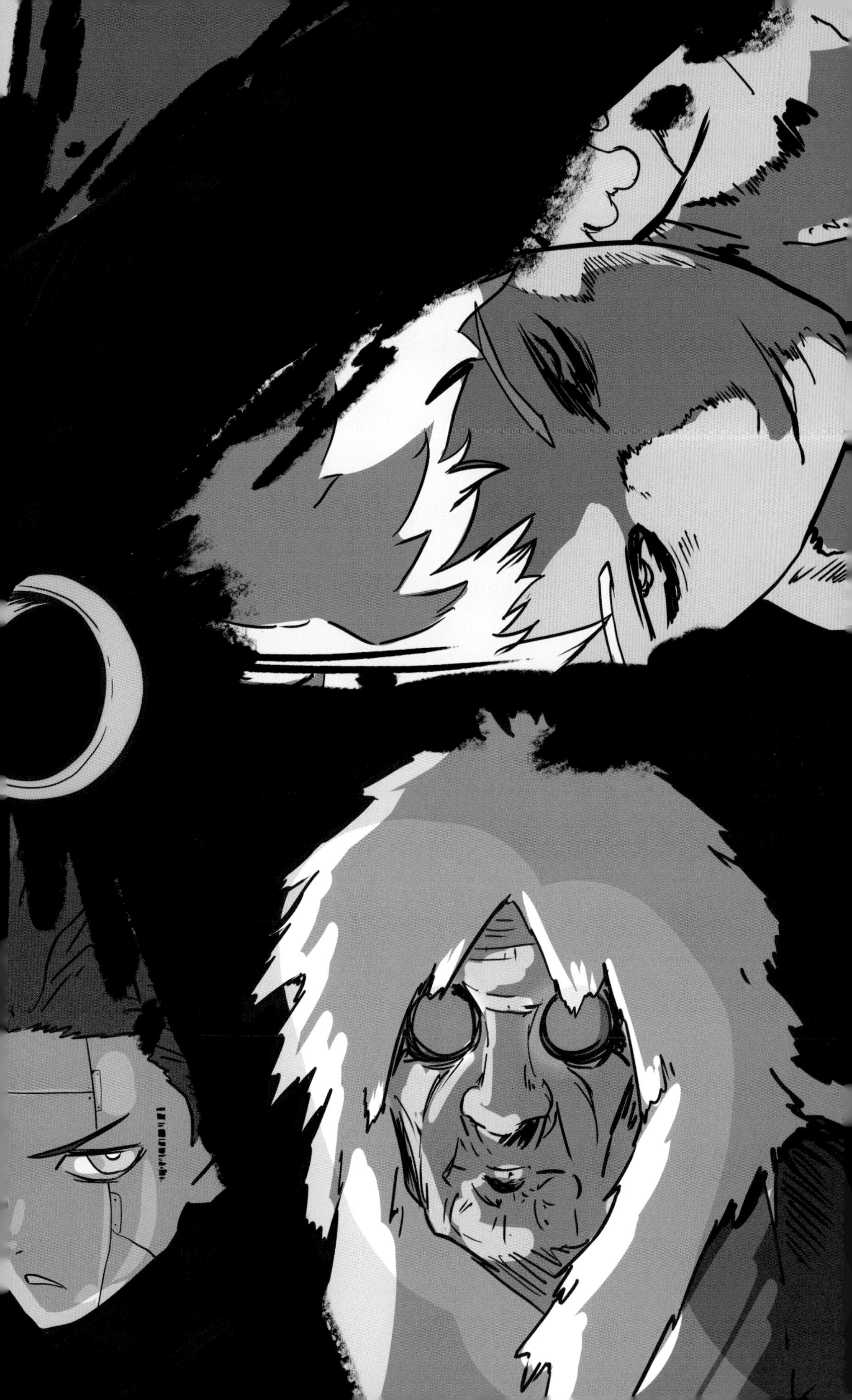

HiroQuest

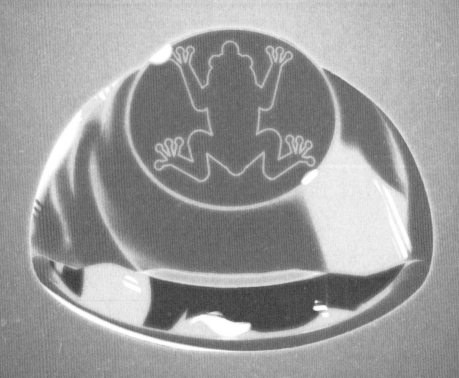

RING EIGHT
AMPHIBIAN RING

PART EIGHT

THE FACTION OF
THE PROTEA

CHAPTER TEN
THE SHOW

"I don't wanna be like them."
Steve Aoki and JJ Lin

I was now on an Amphibian world, of sorts. There was water and there was land and there was an area in between, a swamp-like half submerged world that was like nature dipping its toes in the deep end of the pool. The beings of this world were either swimmers, walkers, or in the process of growing legs.

It made me think about the Tormenter on the giant world and the stand he took at the end. It made me wonder what it must be to have to wait to have the legs to stand on. What it must be like to have to wait to take a stand. To have to wait to be a hero even.

I don't like being alone. I wondered how long it was going to take for Hyro to get here.

It made me wonder for a moment if I had gone through the proper way things have to be to become a hero. Have I earned this yet? I do have seven of the rings. I'm close to being finished. I'm closer to Earth being saved. But have I earned this?

"You're earning it along the way," said Hyro in my mind. I was grateful to hear him again. "I'm bringing you Alora. You'll see. Dude, how did you score her? I cannot believe it. Anyhow, I'll see you soon. I'm almost there."

"Who the Hell are you?" said a voice and it wasn't Hyro's.

I turned, and there before me was the closest to a Jack Kirby drawn character I had ever seen. He was amazing. Like DC's Etrigan meets Triton of the Inhumans. A Marvel/DC Amalgamation that never happened and wasn't ever going to happen. He already had legs and knew how to stand on them.

"My name is Hiro and I am looking for a ring that will help me save my world." I said to him.

"And my name is Masa. I'm a bounty hunter. In other words, you want me to find something, I will. And can. Above the water and below. But for a price, of course."

Alright, he was Etrigan, The Demon, Triton, and a little Funky Flashman (a weird character that Kirby modelled on Stan Lee) at the same time. Wow, I'm realizing Jack Kirby has really helped me understand the world.

I explained the plight of Earth and what I was searching for. So Masa went in search of the ring for me. And I continued to search this area both above the water and below. I think I had forgotten, Doctor Snow, that you also gave me gills.

My third eye was especially helpful while I searched below the waterline for the ring just in case Masa couldn't find it.

What I found, however, was a whole other world. One that had existed but had become lost. One that had died. Whose inhabitants, the survivors, crawled up on the lands above the sea. It was not just adaption. Not just evolution. Maybe something of destiny or fate. And this made me think of the Earth when there were dinosaurs on it and that first meteor struck it.

Humanity came from that. Would we have even been born at all if the dinosaurs hadn't been wiped out? I wondered, if perhaps, were I not to bring the rings back, if there wouldn't be something that would live on and adapt and evolve if that meteor did hit Earth? Was I somehow getting in the way of humanity becoming something even greater, even more important?

No. I'm sorry. That meteor would wipe us all out. There wouldn't be anything to adapt or evolve or transform from. These diary entries, these messages to you, there's a certain aspect of free-thinking and free thought to them. Please forgive me. I want to save our people. I really do.

Masa eventually came back to me but he did not have access to the ring yet. He had been investigating its origins and had discovered important information, though. This ring has adapting powers. It allows the wearer to adapt to whatever environment they find themselves in. And the source code was "Phibiana."

He then told me about the battle he fought against a frog-like creature called Jinsu. And of what it took to even find the information he did. I expect he would have liked to have me pay him something at this point, but he knew better to wait until the end. That said, I had no idea what I would pay him, or how.

This was a world that seemed to constantly be evolving, constantly adapting. I just kind of wanted to go back to me. The old me. In my simplest form. My true self. I missed reading Weapon Human comics. And Hell-Racer. I'm sure there will be some new volumes when I get back to just being me. I just wanted to sit and read and stop carrying not just one world on my shoulders, but ten more to beat. I'm like the Atlas of the multiverse.

There was a time when I really wanted to be a hero, Doctor Snow.

What's funny is that I no longer want to be one anymore. And I fear for that phrase I've heard about heroes. They either die ... or live long enough to become the villain.

MASA

Masa's a sort of bounty hunter, I guess. I didn't even have to look for the ring on this world because he offered to find it for me. He's pretty courageous and is able to go anywhere as part of what I guess is like an amphibian nature. He is another of the heroes that I have met on my way.

THE LOST WORLD

In my search for the ring of this world, Doctor Snow, I found a sunken city that was clearly a lost realm. It was a warning to me of what would happen to Earth if I fail in my quest. And a reminder that not every world can be saved.

CHAPTER ELEVEN
LOVE ME

"But I like flying towards the sun."
Steve Aoki and PHEM

She said her name was Treela and she had an amazing ability to go anywhere and everywhere. Her fingers had, like, organic suction cups on the end of them, and so did her toes. She could do anything, walk on any ceiling or wall. I had similar, but not the same feelings, for her that I kind of had for Alora. Not cool, Doctor Snow. You should have done something about my teenage hormones. You really should have.

I spoke with her about the ring of this world and she seemed confused. That said, she was still on my side no matter what. She was like that girl I would never ask out but who I was still attracted to and knew would be the very best girl for me. The girl I would probably regret and think about for the rest of my life.

But instead of her, I thought about Alora. Was Hyro really bringing her to me? He said he was.

Anyhow, Treela joined Masa in the search for the ring of this world and while they looked, I became aware, once again, of the cloud that was Death, that was following me.

But it was different this time.

Death hovered in front of me. "You want to kill me?" it asked.

"I do. It's how I can save not only my world, but all the others."

"What are you saving?"

"I'm not allowing them to die. I'm not allowing you to take them, you bastard."

"Bastard?"

"Yeah, bastard, you bastard."

"Death is transformation too. Have you considered even for a moment, Hiro, that by denying these worlds the gift that is me, you deny them change? You deny them happiness? You set up the roadblocks to their personal Heavens?"

"What?"

"By saying 'no' to me, or trying to kill me, you deny all of nature the autumn and the winter and therefore the spring and the summer. You deny growth and change."

What was Death saying to me?

"Imagine a person shot, but not killed. My touch could end their suffering and allow them to become what their next form is. For energy does not die, it only changes. And what of the sick? If I do not bring my kind embrace, they just remain sick. Is that what you desire? An end to healing? Hope will therefore be gone for those who need it most."

I was confused, Doctor Snow. This was not the Death I expected. Something inside of me ignored the words Death spoke. I needed to think about Earth. I needed to think about saving lives, not allowing for a 'necessary evil' argument to creep into the subtext of my mission.

I used the Monster ring. I became more terrible than Death itself.

Do you know the form I took, Doctor Snow? The Monster form I took to send the Death cloud into its own form of self-banishment?

I became a different kind of cloud. A different kind of formless thing. One that suggested that Death was a curse and a waste and there was no good to it. I became Death's greatest fear. That it served no purpose at all. And Death pulled away from me. As it left, it told me that I had to be stopped.

Death was gone. And maybe because I didn't just scare it with an illusion, but because I suggested that I could so change the world that Death would mean nothing anymore.

Have I really become that powerful?

I was grateful when I saw Treela and Masa coming towards me. They had the ring to this world.

Oh my God, that was number eight. Earth was almost as good as saved. I only had two more rings to find. I was getting more powerful all the time. And felt better and better about every world that I had taken a ring from.

Masa and Treela held the ring before them. They told me of someone called Ruby Rana that they had stolen it from.

And then I couldn't see anything. It's not that everything went black. It's that I couldn't see what it was that was attacking me. It was like invisible. Was this Death again? Or something else? What was this?

And not just me. It attacked Masa and Treela as well.

A few moments later, Masa and Treela were barely able to stand.

Treela was bleeding. Masa even more. Why or how was this happening? They were both being struck but I could not fathom who or what was striking them. I did not see anybody. What was happening? Was this the Ruby Rana that they stole the ring from or something else?

They fell at my feet.

And then I was struck. Again and again and again. I tried to rise. I tried to use all the ways I was augmented and given power. My strength. My insight. My abilities. And then I tried to use the power of the rings.

I used the ring from ASTRALS. But my attacker was there, ever present with me, wherever I went.

I used the ring from OIO. It didn't work. My invisible foe was clearly not mechanical.

I used the ring from the DIASOS World. But I didn't see anything. No future. Nothing.

I used the ring from the TAUROBON World.

And the one from the GRAVITONS. I thought that maybe if I shrunk down to nothing, I would lose this invisible enemy.

Even the GREMBOLD ring brought no defense.

Nothing helped me. Not even the rings. Nothing saved me. I had failed and I now thought that Earth was certainly going to be struck by that meteorite and everyone I ever loved was going to die.

And then, when all seemed lost, I heard him. He was here. Actually here. It was Hyro.

"Don't worry, Hiro, I have this. I'm here at last. This thing is no match for me."

It wasn't just a voice anymore. Wasn't just static. Hyro was here. He looked a lot like me. Except he wasn't spitting blood like I was. He was here. To fight for Earth. To fight for me.

I think that was about the time I passed out.

TREELA

Like Mesa, Treela joined in the search for the ring. And like Mesa, she is an acrobat and a hero. She's exactly the kind of girl that I would fall for if it wasn't for Alora from the Grembold world. I can't help wondering, Doctor Snow, why a guy falls for the wrong girl, and a girl falls for the wrong guy. It's what it means to be human, I suppose. And I can't help seeing basic humanity in certain ways on all these worlds.

DEATH, THE COWARD

You should have seen it, Doctor Snow. Because of the ring from the Grembold World, I was able to scare the shit out of Death. It pulled away from me as soon as I took the form of the thing it was most afraid of. That it had no purpose other than to collect souls or lives. That it was nothing more than a messenger boy. Maybe I should not be so quick to judge, though. If it weren't for the fact that this mission of mine is the way we save Earth, I would just be collecting rings, wouldn't I?

WEAPON HUMAN AND THE HELL-RACER

I cannot wait, Doctor Snow, to just have five fingers on each hand again so I can sit and read the latest issues of Weapon Human and Hell-Racer. I'm not sure why I love conspiracy heroes so much. Like the Hell-Racer made a deal with the devil to save his family, but he didn't know it was a deal with the devil. Just like Weapon Human was about a rogue government turning a normal guy into a weapon.

THE PROTEA RING

The Protea Ring is about adaption; pure and simple. And I assume, Doctor Snow, that this is a ring to be used should the meteorite somehow affect the environment on Earth. Somehow this ring will help change humans maybe into what we will need to become in the future. There's a part of me that also hopes it will help us become more kind.

SOURCE CODE TO
ACCESS POWER: PHIBIANA

HIRO's JOURNEY
CHAPTER EIGHT

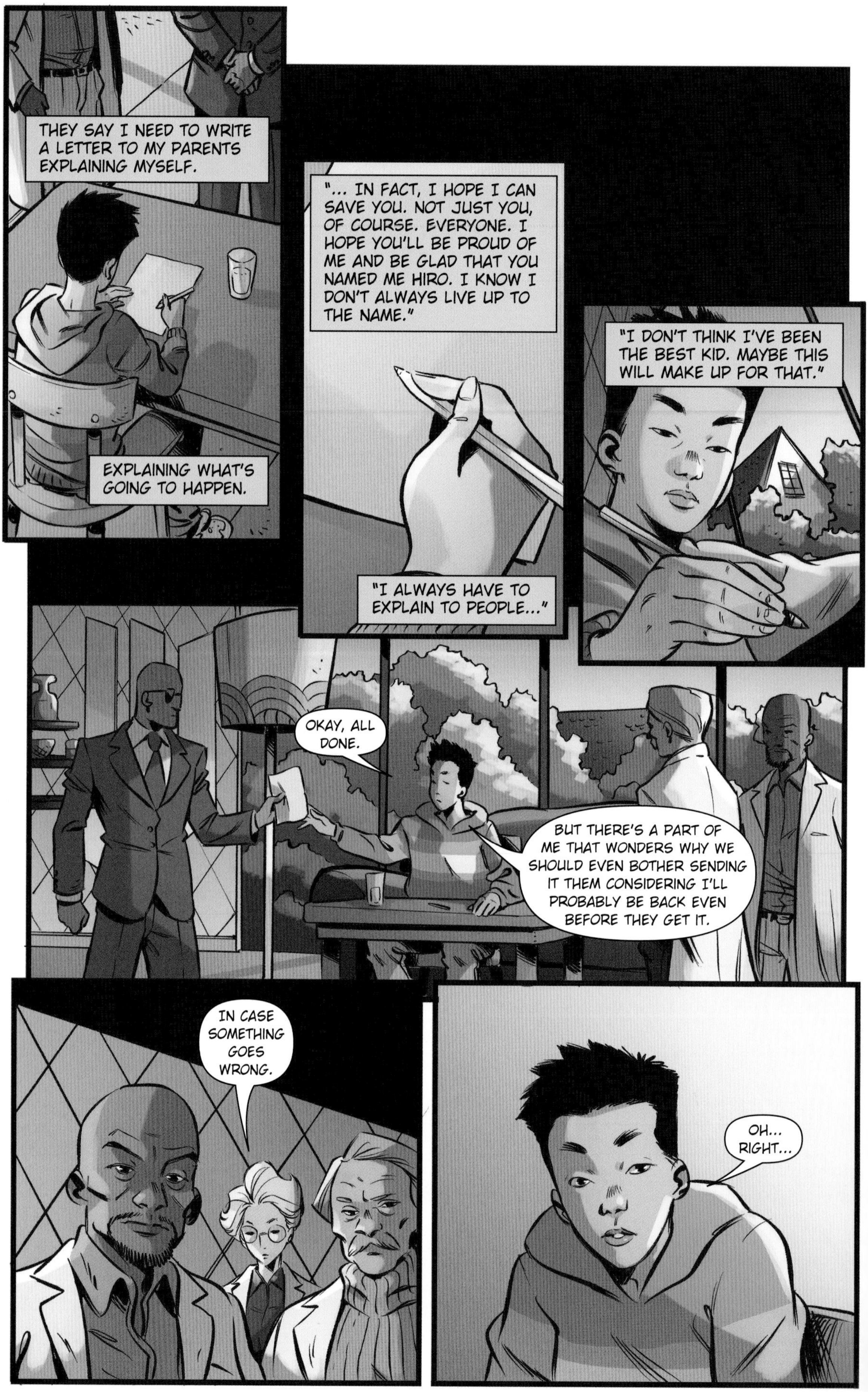
THEY SAY I NEED TO WRITE A LETTER TO MY PARENTS EXPLAINING MYSELF.
EXPLAINING WHAT'S GOING TO HAPPEN.
"... IN FACT, I HOPE I CAN SAVE YOU. NOT JUST YOU, OF COURSE. EVERYONE. I HOPE YOU'LL BE PROUD OF ME AND BE GLAD THAT YOU NAMED ME HIRO. I KNOW I DON'T ALWAYS LIVE UP TO THE NAME."
"I ALWAYS HAVE TO EXPLAIN TO PEOPLE..."
"I DON'T THINK I'VE BEEN THE BEST KID. MAYBE THIS WILL MAKE UP FOR THAT."
OKAY, ALL DONE.
BUT THERE'S A PART OF ME THAT WONDERS WHY WE SHOULD EVEN BOTHER SENDING IT THEM CONSIDERING I'LL PROBABLY BE BACK EVEN BEFORE THEY GET IT.
IN CASE SOMETHING GOES WRONG.
OH... RIGHT...

THIS ISN'T A COMIC BOOK. I NEED TO REMIND MYSELF OF THAT.

BUT IT FEELS LIKE A COMIC BOOK.

THEY SAY THAT THE PROTECTIVE GEAR THEY ARE PUTTING ON ME WILL NOT ONLY PROTECT MY VITAL ORGANS...

... BUT HELP WITH THE TRANSFORMATION.

THIS BETTER NOT BE INDIANA JONES AND THE ADVENTURE OF THE BOUNCING REFRIGERATOR THOUGH.

I REALLY DIDN'T BELIEVE THAT HE'D LIVE THROUGH THAT. THE BOUNCE. NOT THE RADIATION OR THE BOMB PART. THE BOUNCE.

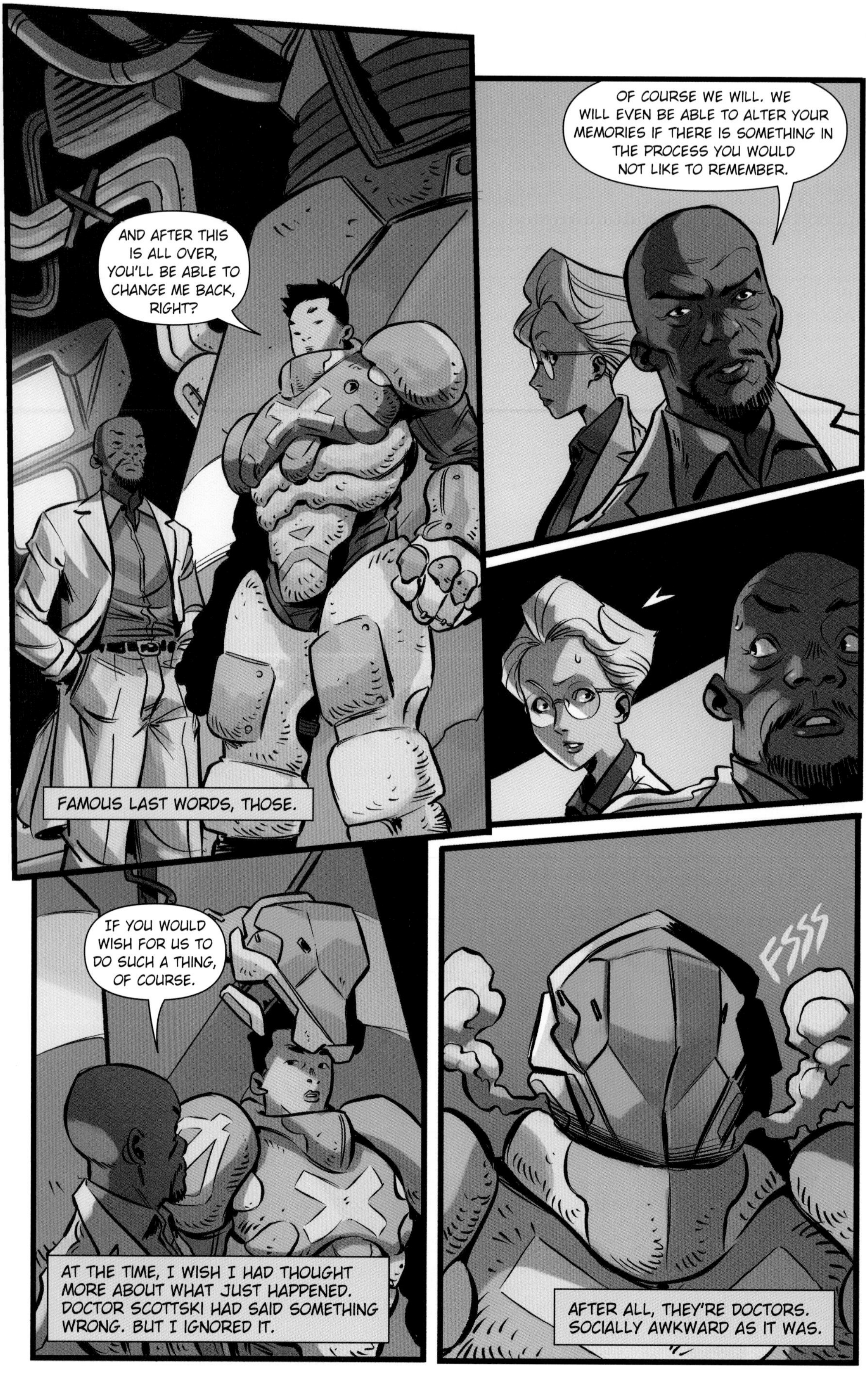
AND AFTER THIS IS ALL OVER, YOU'LL BE ABLE TO CHANGE ME BACK, RIGHT?
FAMOUS LAST WORDS, THOSE.
OF COURSE WE WILL. WE WILL EVEN BE ABLE TO ALTER YOUR MEMORIES IF THERE IS SOMETHING IN THE PROCESS YOU WOULD NOT LIKE TO REMEMBER.
IF YOU WOULD WISH FOR US TO DO SUCH A THING, OF COURSE.
AT THE TIME, I WISH I HAD THOUGHT MORE ABOUT WHAT JUST HAPPENED. DOCTOR SCOTTSKI HAD SAID SOMETHING WRONG. BUT I IGNORED IT.
FSSS
AFTER ALL, THEY'RE DOCTORS. SOCIALLY AWKWARD AS IT WAS.

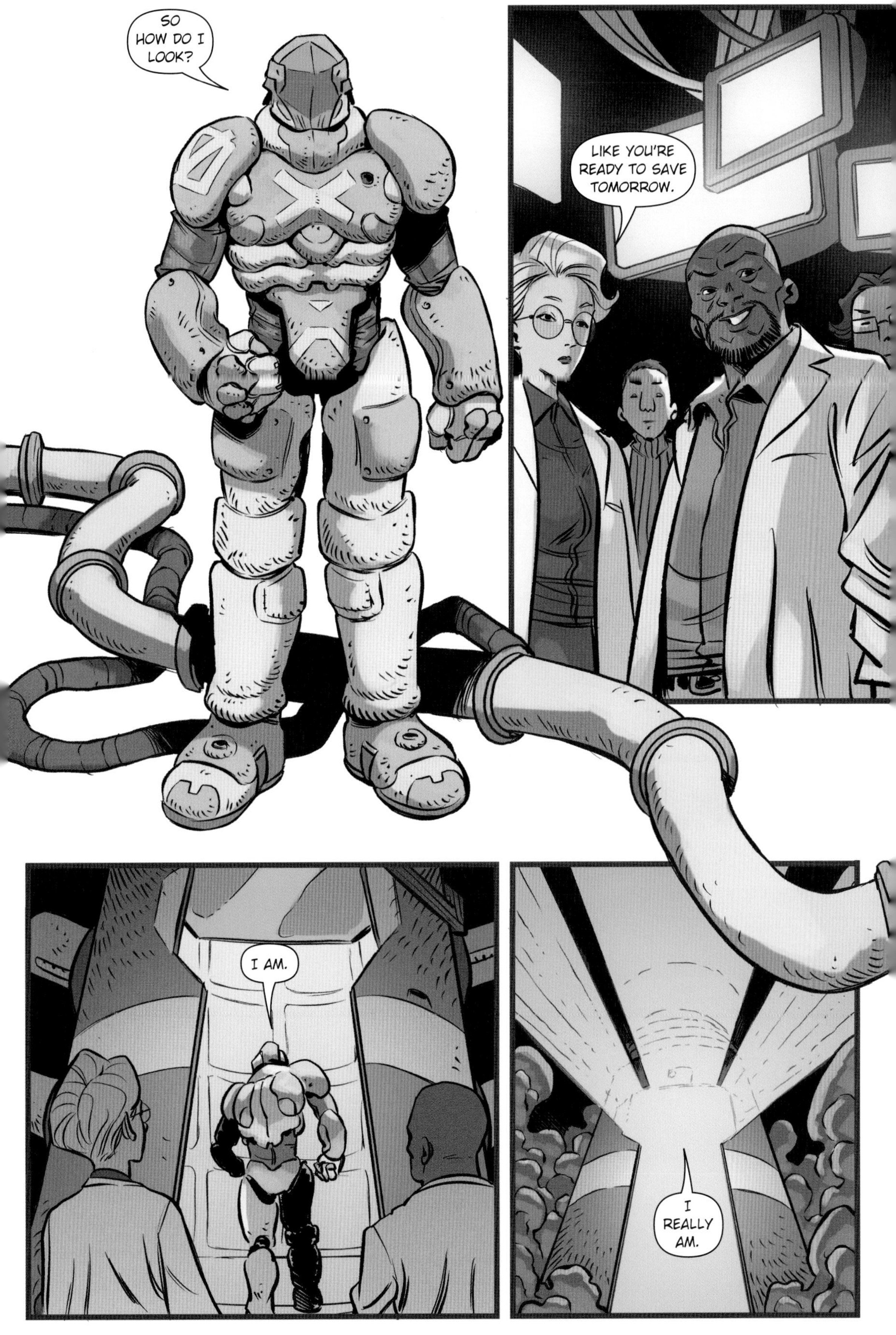
SO HOW DO I LOOK?
LIKE YOU'RE READY TO SAVE TOMORROW.
I AM.
I REALLY AM.

HiroQuest

RING NINE
WIZARDS & WITCHES
RING

PART NINE

THE FACTION OF THE SHAMASAYA

CHAPTER TWELVE
LIGHTER

"Lighter ‥ without you."
Steve Aoki and Paris Hilton

When I came around, the ring of that other world, of the Protea world, was on one of my fingers like all the others.

I had eight rings now and felt a sense of accomplishment. I had made this happen. I would see my parents again. I would experience my world, and even as a human once again.

But I was on a new world now.

And there was no sign of Treela or Masa. But I knew that Earth would be saved. I knew it. Because there before me was Hyro. He had been trying to get to me for so long and he was finally here. Right in front of me.

"Hey Hiro."

"Hey Hyro."

"I'll bet you're wondering about what happened on that other world?"

"I am. I really am. What was that thing? And what about Treela and Masa? Are they alright?"

"I really don't know what happened to them, Hiro. Once I got the ring from them and rescued you, we left for this world."

"Okay, okay, okay. But what was that thing? I couldn't see it at all."

Hyro smiled, but it was a dark smile. A knowing smile. "That was an Amphibian world. The beings of that world are defined both from the sea and from the air. It's the things in-between that you have to be most guarded against.

"The creature that attacked you was not invisible at all. It was the Ruby Rana. Its nature was more like an emo- or meta-chameleon. I'd imagine. But it was also even so much more than that. It was able to not only copy your abilities with the rings, but also copy your abilities as you apply them to the environment around you. It was able to mimic and replicate your powers. So, it could also blend in with the environment to an uncanny degree."

"It was worse than facing Death."

"Of course it was, Hiro, because it was a sort of mirror-being. And like all mirrors, it made you face yourself. And that can be hard, especially in light of how much you've been changed. And how much is resting on your shoulders."

"Who and what are you, exactly? I mean, you're like me to a degree. Your costume is cooler though."

"I'm a clone of you, Hiro."

"Really?" I remembered the comic books I read, well, four hundred years ago. Clones never want to be clones."

"You're wrong, I want to be a clone."

I laughed.

"Well, I'm glad you're here. It's going to make getting these last couple rings that much easier."

"Not really," Hyro said. "This is the world of the Shamasaya. It's a Witch world."

"Which world? I thought it was the ninth."

"No. A witch – W. I. T. C. H. - world. As in witches and warlocks and wizards. As in magic spells and curses. This may be one of the most difficult worlds of them all, Hiro. Because this is a world where even words are magic. Even words bring curses. And a sentence here can be a sentence for eternity."

"Shit," I said.

"Oh yes, shit." That was Hyro's response.

We were twice the target now. And it's always easiest to hit a bigger target. But there were two of us now. And we were stronger for it as well. Me and my shadow, you could say.

We cautiously moved down a street that felt more like Doctor Doom's Latveria than anything else. Like this was a town that was urban-planned by the gypsy mom whose son was the wolfman. Like in the old school black and white monster-vision movie. Gargoyles on buildings. Cobblestone roads. And everybody in this place walked with a cane. I was pretty sure that every handle of every cane was in the shape of a silver wolf's head. Or of the Devil's hoofprint. Or of a pentagram. Or of a six-six-six monogram. This was a world of darkness and both Hyro and I were a target.

We needed to find some lederhosen soon. The sooner we looked like a "festmeister" or an "Octoberfestrian" the better, because we looked too different to everyone else and for once that made me feel really uncomfortable. I hoped that this was something like Fall-fest or a Halloween or a Krampusnacht even. Anything to maybe give us an opportunity to get clothes that would be good as a disguise to walk around in. I also hoped no one would ask either one of us to play the accordion.

There were things in the air as well. Like ink squiggles that would move from house to house or person to person. They were curses. They looked like moth wings without the caterpillar center. Sometimes they landed on people, and were breathed in like smoke. Other times, there would be a barrier of sorts on the person that would keep them from being inhaled.

We made our way along the streets and the back alleys and found some things to disguise ourselves on a clotheslines to make us fit in better with the locals. Of course, if anyone caught us stealing their clothing, that would have been a cursed for certain.

People lived in fear here. They lived in fear of a neighbor putting a curse on them. As a result, everyone was very polite.

But it was not graciousness. It was not kindness. It was, like I said; fear. Like behind and beneath the perfect manners was a sense of self-preservation that felt like a fool's folly. Like they knew it was never going to work.

There was music in the cobblestoned streets. It suggested some whimsey but there was a darkness to it as well. A sadness that suggested a depression that hinted at a greater universal curse upon the people of this world.

It was then that she appeared to us. She was beautiful. Gorgeous. But she would not give us her name. She said that to give her name was to allow others to have power over her.

So she gave us a made-up name and referred to herself as Morgana Grimfeather.

She told me that behind every person who is cursed, was the knowledge of the person's name.

But she was breath-taking, and wanted to know how she could help us. When I told her that we were looking for a ring, she laughed. But then she told me that the fate of Earth would be with the final demon.

I did not know who that was.

The name she said was 'Diablo Finales' That was Spanish but she said it with a German accent which made it sound even more evil. It meant 'the last devil'.

I told her that I didn't know there was more than one devil. She told me that in my case there were three. Maybe four.

Hyro asked her a question, but she seemed to ignore it until I repeated the question. "So how do we get to the so-called last devil? How do we get to the four of them? The devils, I mean."

I was not happy with her answer at all, because she encouraged me to leave my crusade and quest behind. She said that it would be better if Earth died than the alternative. At this Hyro screamed in my ears that this was witchcraft, and she was trying to trick me. That some magic words are subtle. Some come in the form of lies. He reminded me that we needed to find the ring. He told me that my mission was sacred and that I needed to remember my Mom and Dad and all the people of Earth.

I asked her name once more. But she said nothing. Morgana Grimfeather was all she said. To offer a name, she said again, was to give someone the power to call on you. The power to curse you and use your name against you. She asked my name.

I told her. "Hiro."

"Is it?" She asked.

What kind of question was that?

She encouraged me to seek out the "Udor the Monsters Man."

"Udor the Monsters Man?" I asked. And she told me about a poor wretch who had been cursed so many times, there was nothing left of his humanity to curse.

This was the Monsters Man.

MORGANA GRIMFEATHER, THE WITCH

She wouldn't even tell me her real name. But she still told me more than I expected. She was a witch, Doctor Snow, and told me more than just where I could find the ring of this world. She told me that I should also give up my quest and it would be better to let Earth die than to continue on. She suggested something bad was going to happen. That something bad was coming. Of course, I ignored her. She's a witch. What does she know?

THE STREETS OF SHAMASAYA

This is a world, Doctor Snow, where the air above the streets is filled with curses. Everyone looks at each other with a sense of courtesy and good manners, but above them, in their thoughts, they curse each other. It is a world of witches and wizards. It is a world, not unlike Wisconsin, where how people speak to each other can be very different than what they think of each other.

CHAPTER THIRTEEN
LAS MUNECAS

"They don't know anything about us."
Steve Aoki, TINI and La Joaqui

This is a world where so many have been cursed that all seem to be looking for not a cure, per se, but a counter-curse. This is a place where everyone was afraid that they might both help and betray a person at the same time.

The witch whose true name she would not say also said that we needed to meet with the monster that was all monsters.

It sounded like a Frankenstein of sorts. But instead of being made of the parts of men, it would be made from parts of different monsters.

This sounded like another giant quest, especially in this world, but it was not. There was just a street address and that was it. It was really normal. And the address didn't have "six, six, six," in it or anything. It was almost disappointing.

The monster of all monsters was there. She said his name was Udor. And so we left the witch (who looked better than any witch ever deserved to look) and headed to where this so-called creature of creatures was.

Hyro noticed me as I glanced over my shoulder.

"What are you looking for?" he asked.

"I keep on thinking that I'm going to turn around and I will see that Death will be following me again."

"You said at one point, though, Hiro, that you were going to kill Death, and that was how you were going to save not just our world, but all ten of the other worlds, as well."

"I remember," I told Hyro.

"What if it's not just an ambition? What if, with the rings you have been collecting, and the power you were given, you could actually kill Death. And Death knows it. Seems to me the last thing I would do if I were Death would be to follow you around. Maybe he got the message and is actually afraid of you."

"That made sense," I told Hyro. What an amazing thought. Everyone everywhere fears Death at one point or another. What if I'm the one that Death actually does fear?

I wondered if there would be a point where everyone feared me. But that did not seem like a good thought. No, I'm the one who can take away their fear, especially when I save Earth. There will never be a point where people fear me.

"It's just up here," Hyro said.

We went to the door. On it was a giant knocker in the shape of a gargoyle. It made me think of the four-armed Tormenter from the world of the Gravitons. He said he was a gargoyle. A giant one. While each of these worlds are so different, there are some amazing similarities between them as well.

Wouldn't that make sense though? They were all using the same matter, but each world, each faction, was vibrating at different frequencies. Did that also mean that I was meeting the same people, the same souls? But just in different forms vibrating at different frequencies? Do souls vibrate just like matter does?

My questions would have to wait because the monster or monsters came to the door.

It turned out that this poor being had been cursed so many times that he was more like a monster soup, or a stew. Actually, in this case, he was a goulash. Well, he was a Ghoulash, actually.

"So you are the Monsters Man," I asked when I finally met him.

"I suppose I am," he or it responded.

"The Ghoulash." I said, wanting to make my joke again. And this got me thinking about what the hot witch said. If you name something, do you therefore have power over it, magic wise?

The creature that was so many creatures nodded, if such a thing was possible. "I am Udor." If this was once a man, I'm not certain there was even a neck here. I guess that if there were vampires in this world, at least he'd be safe from them. Or maybe, I don't know, maybe he was part vampire as well.

"I heard you can help me find a ring." I said.

"What else did she say?" Udor the Monsters Man asked.

"I asked her if I should continue on my quest to collect the ten rings to save my world. She told me that I should indeed. Not just because of my quest but because a greater good would come from it." I continued, but was still frustrated with the words that she'd told me. "I asked if I would be considered a hero.

"She said no," I continued. "But maybe, eventually, I might be. She said I needed to fail if I was ever going to be the hero I wanted to be."

The Monsters Man nodded. "I hate to say this, young man, but the want to be a hero often leads one to walk the path that leads to becoming a villain."

There was that idea again. I hated being told this. Wasn't it the right thing to want to be brave? Wasn't it right to want to be appreciated and have one's actions cheered on by others?

DON'T KNOCK IT

I know this isn't about one of the beings I have come across on these worlds, but it did seem worth mentioning, Doctor Snow. There was a gargoyle door knocker on Udor the Monster Man's house that looked a lot like The Tormenter from the Graviton World. It got me thinking about the similarities between these worlds. And if they all vibrate at a different frequency, while using the same matter, is this the Earth of the future? And doesn't me being able to visit these worlds suggest that Earth will survive anyhow? To some degree or another?

UDOR THE MONSTERS MAN

I called him Ghoulash, though I know it's spelled goulash, because he is like what you would get if Harly made soup of every monster he ever wanted to eat. This guy has been cursed over and over again, he's become like every single creature at once. And while everyone is really frightened of him, he's actually really nice. And there was a moment, where I saw him, I think. And he didn't; look like a monsters. Or like monsters. He looked like a Wizard. I wonder if I will be cursed, Doctor Snow. By the worlds that I have taken these rings from. Is there to be a penance for me to face for saving Earth?

CHAPTER FOURTEEN
2 MUCH 2 HANDLE

"Nah nah nah"
Steve Aoki and Alok

I asked the Monsters Man about the last devil. The "Diablo Finales" that the hot witch had told me about. I assumed or figured that if this thing was every monster put together somehow, he would know all about devils. You know, because he should know all about all the various monsters that there were to experience.

Well, he didn't know what she might have been talking about, but he did have something to say about devils, Doctor Snow.

"It's not just that a devil wants to convince you that it does not exist. It wants to convince you that even if it does exist, that it does not matter. It's insignificant to your life. And therefore, something to be overlooked even if you notice its presence."

"Notice its presence?"

"Yes, in most cases we don't recognize the devil in our life."

"How many are there? The hot witch, Morgana, whose name was not Morgana really, she told me I had four devils."

"Perhaps I have had more than that. Perhaps every curse I've experienced came from a different devil, I don't know. But in the same way that knowing a creature's name gives you a sense of power of it, recognizing one of your devils, well, it takes some of that devil's power over you away from it. After all, those that cursed me can't control me anymore. I see them for who they are."

I wasn't sure how to respond to this. Or why I was being told these things. Did the hot witch want me to have this conversation with this creature. Was that why?

I asked him about the ring of this world again.

"Oh, yes," he said. "I have it here somewhere. Just give me a moment."

The creature went into the other room while I whispered to Hyro.

"What do you think that was all about?"

"I have no idea. But I think that we need to get out of here. It's all happening way too easy and that usually suggests something bad. Like really bad."

I couldn't argue with Hyro on this. And I didn't have to.

"It was in a drawer. I think I wore it at one point in my life, but the various curses made my fingers too hairy and scaly and fat."

"Can I have it?" I asked the Monsters Man.

"Of course. I wish I had never had it at all."

"Why do you say that?" I asked.

"Because the ring has power. Real power. The fact that I had the ring is probably why I was cursed so many times."

"I don't understand."

"My neighbors were afraid of me. And so they put curses on me because they were afraid. And they are so much more so afraid of me now. Look at me."

We did.

"There's irony for you. They made me a fearsome creature because of their fear. And that fear they had of me is now coupled with their own guilt, which they carry out into the streets and is doubled every time they look in my direction. Whether they can actually see me or not."

He put the ring in my hand. The Shamasaya Ring. And for a moment, when he passed it to me, he didn't look like a creature or a monster at all. He looked like an old man in a cloak.

He explained that the ring would allow me to make magic spells that lasted till dawn.

"Kolarraw," I learned was the source code to access the ring's power.

I thanked him for just giving me the ring. But it didn't seem like he thought he was doing me a favor. Not at all.

"Be careful, for monsters often create monsters. My neighbors are only one example of this," he said. "And if you ever come back to this world, beware of the Vumas. She is different than all who live here. For she has cursed herself."

"What does that mean?" I asked.

He didn't answer. He just said he was sorry. So very sorry. And then, as we were leaving, he began to weep.

INSIDE THE MONSTERS' DRAWER

Udor gave me the ring, just like that. The Monsters Man had it in a drawer, Doctor Snow. Can you believe it? Makes me wonder what else was in that drawer. It also made me realize that this guy was probably a wizard of sorts because he had all this stuff. Also makes me wonder if giving the ring to me might not also be some sort of trick. I hope you will be careful with these rings, Doctor Snow. Everyone I get a ring from seems to be warning me about who I am becoming.

THE SHAMASAYA RING

The Shamasaya Ring has the power to cast magic spells, Doctor Snow. I think it's kind of like Green Lantern's ring, then, because it's almost the imagination and the creativity and maybe even the will power of the person who wears it that makes it work. But here is the catch. The spell the ring casts only works until the next morning's dawn. Does this mean we have to hope that the meteorite comes at night? I'm sorry, that's a dumb idea. I mean it's always night in space, right?

SOURCE CODE TO
ACCESS POWER: KOLLARAW

HIRO's JOURNEY

CHAPTER NINE

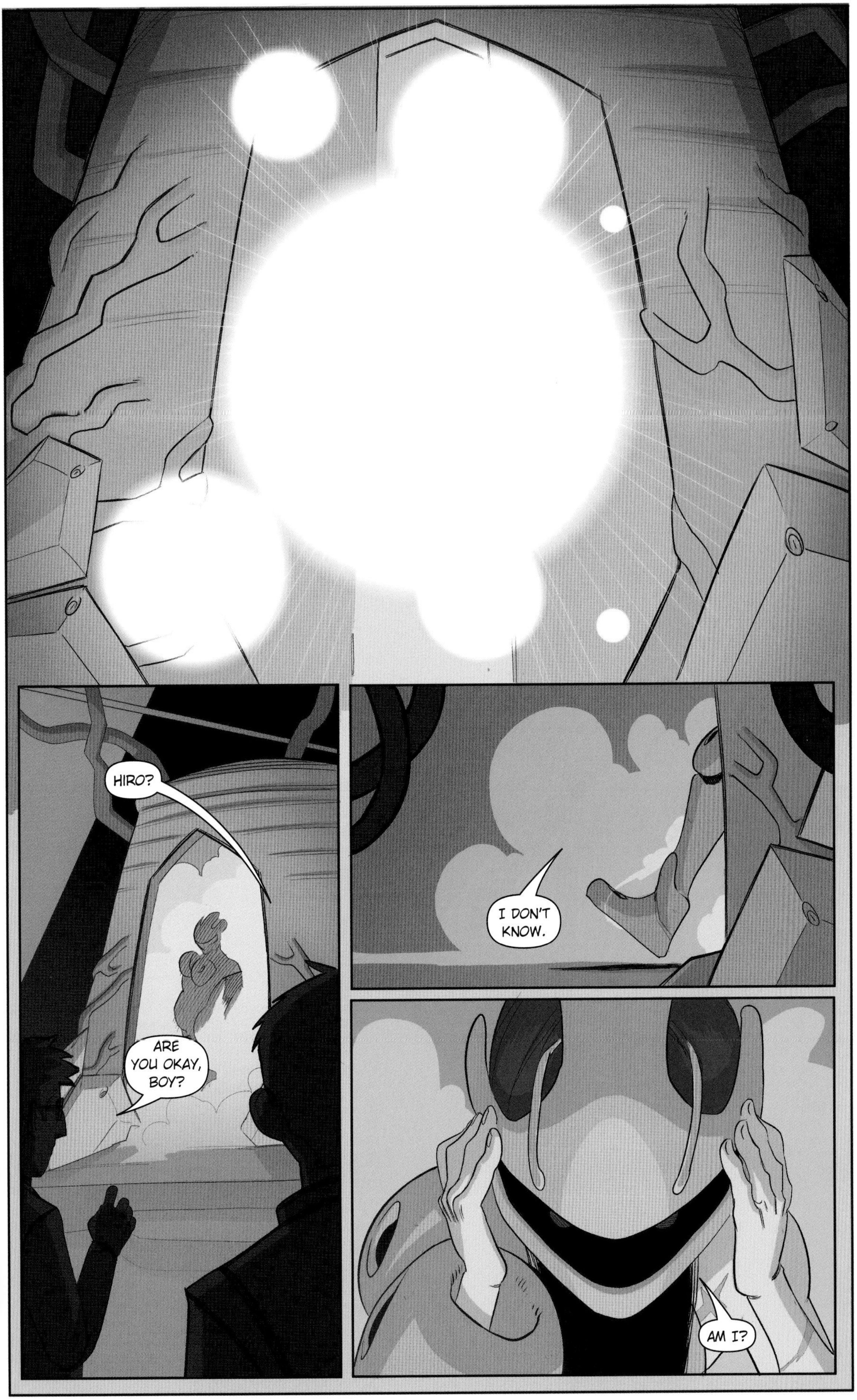
HIRO?
ARE YOU OKAY, BOY?
I DON'T KNOW.
AM I?

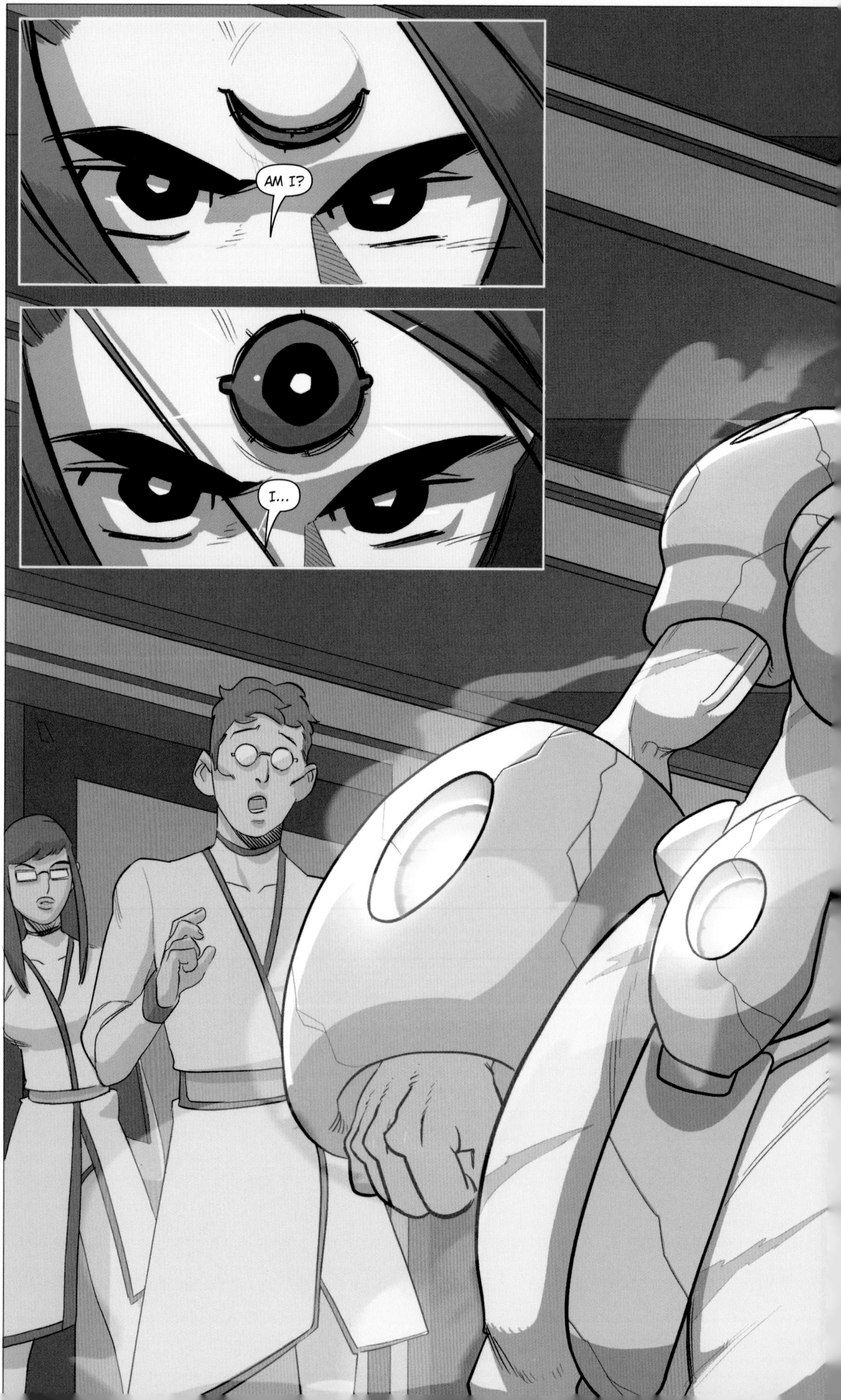
AM I?
I...

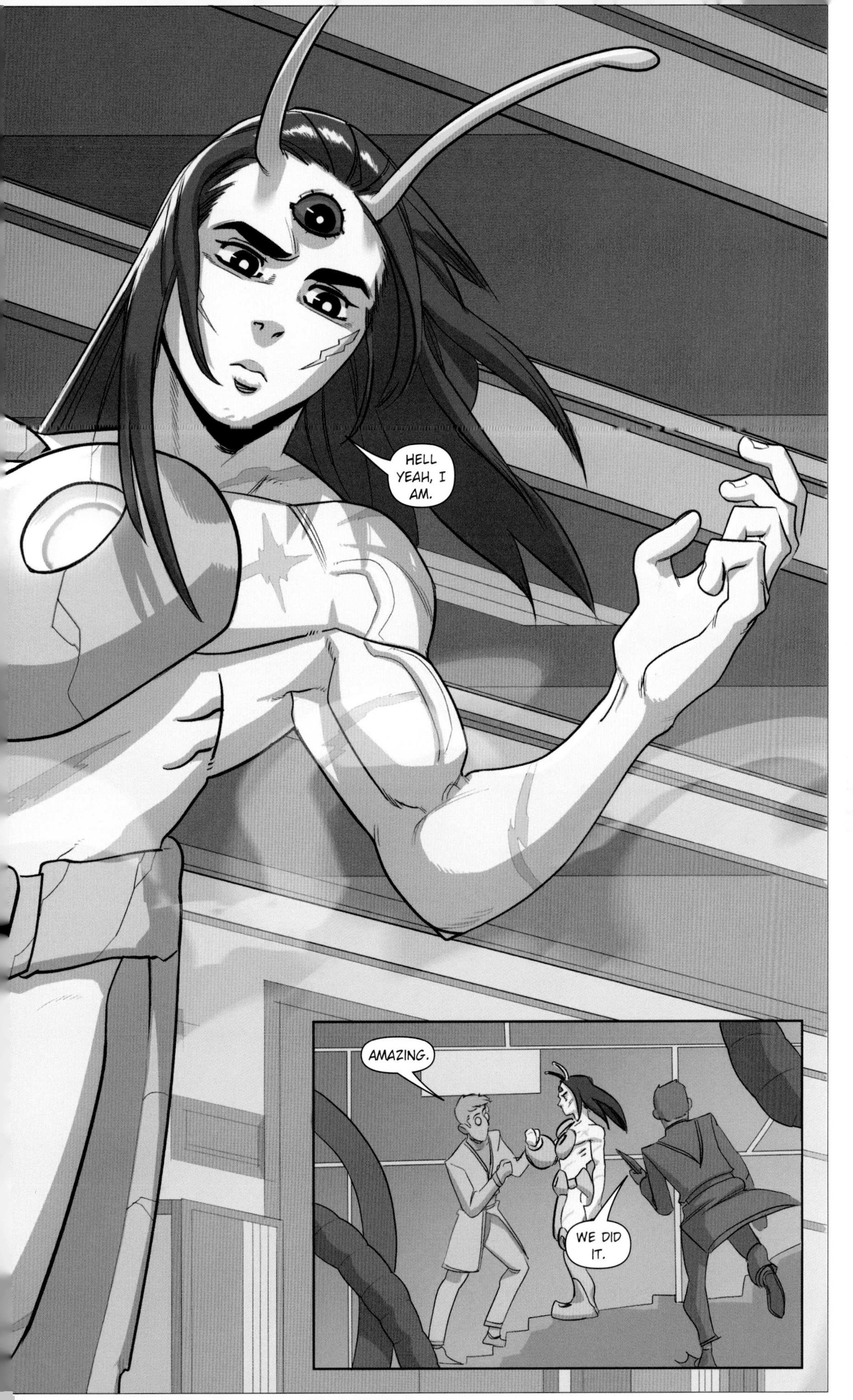
HELL YEAH, I AM.
AMAZING.
WE DID IT.

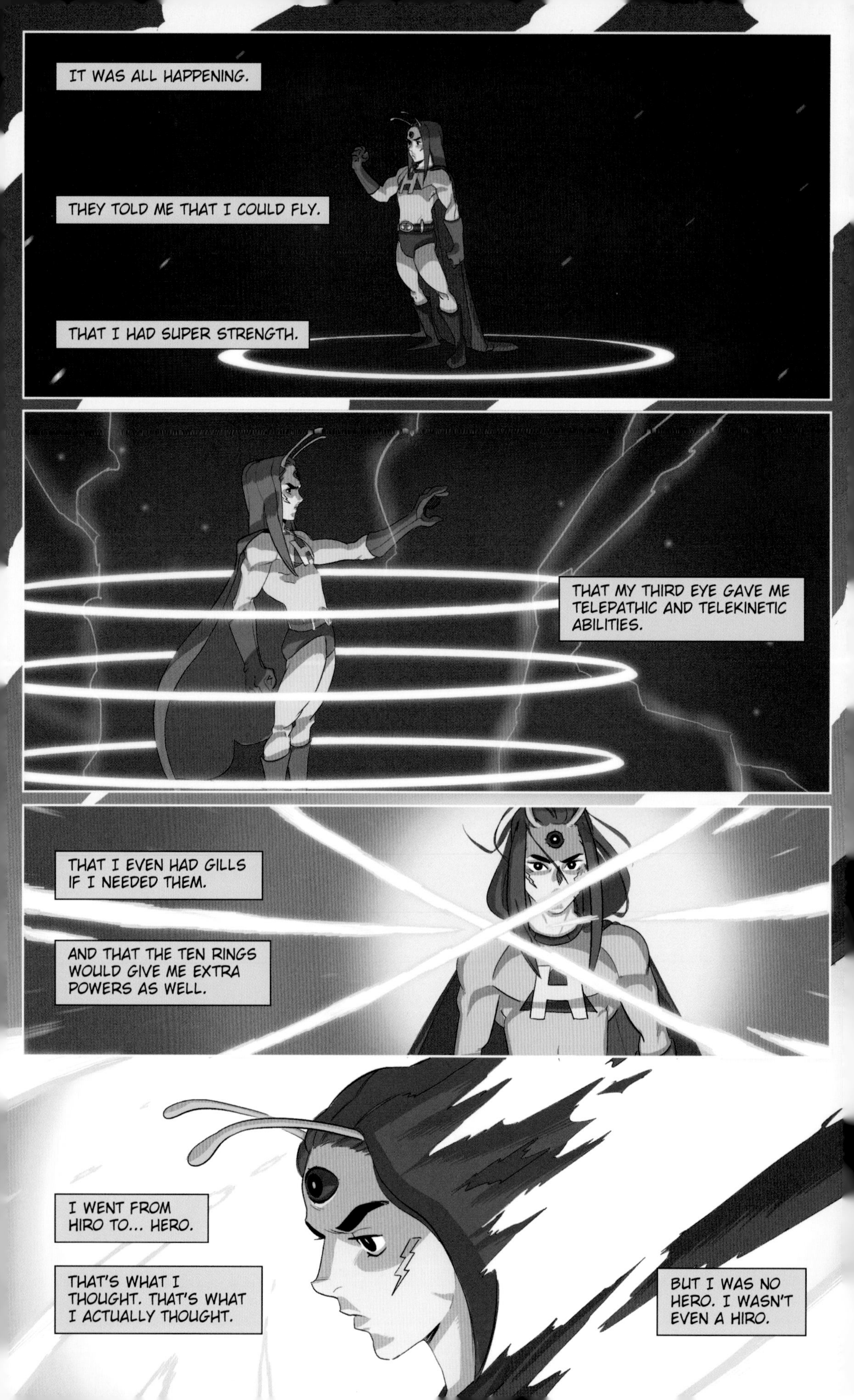
IT WAS ALL HAPPENING.
THEY TOLD ME THAT I COULD FLY.
THAT I HAD SUPER STRENGTH.
THAT MY THIRD EYE GAVE ME TELEPATHIC AND TELEKINETIC ABILITIES.
THAT I EVEN HAD GILLS IF I NEEDED THEM.
AND THAT THE TEN RINGS WOULD GIVE ME EXTRA POWERS AS WELL.
I WENT FROM HIRO TO... HERO.
THAT'S WHAT I THOUGHT. THAT'S WHAT I ACTUALLY THOUGHT.
BUT I WAS NO HERO. I WASN'T EVEN A HIRO.

HiroQuest

RING TEN
FAIRIES RING

PART TEN

THE FACTION OF
THE BLOODLINS

CHAPTER FIFTEEN
DIFFERENTE

"What we were before is no longer."
Steve Aoki and CNCO

We had come to a world that had fairies flying everywhere. They were called Bloodlins. Fairies fly like humming birds. They seem to hover and whip around through the air. Kind of spastically, actually. This was a world that was always in motion, always in movement. Whether it was the Bloodlins themselves or the dust and weeds in the air, glistening like snow caught in the sunlight, or something else, I could not tell. This was a world that seemed to defy gravity in every way imaginable.

Both Hyro and I, of course, could fly. So, we could follow them, but it was not as easy as it might sound, Doctor Snow. The Bloodlins fly in a way where they are always changing their minds as to where they want to go. It's like trying to walk fast anywhere in an amusement park. Where people in front of you just stop, or spin to take a picture, or back up into you.

This was a difficult world to navigate.

We landed, finally, getting tired of trying to follow the Bloodlins. There was a creature there, an amazing creature who said its name was simply "Fun Guy."

It kind of looked like the fairy version of a soldier, you could say. But I couldn't tell if it was animal or vegetable. His head was kind of helmeted, but the helmet part was kind of like a mushroom. The rest of him seemed like the other fairies of this world.

He looked at us. "Let me get a better look at you," he said. And then his eyes went grey ... and then white and his face began to dry, as well as the rest of him.

"Very interesting." I heard his voice now behind us. I turned to find that he was growing a new body behind me while he allowed the first to dry up and be scattered by the wind.

"You're not from around here, are you?" He asked. "I mean, you can fly, but you don't even have wings. That's amazing. But how?"

"I don't know." I hunched my shoulders and looked at Hyro. "There were these three doctors and they had a way to change me into this, I guess you could say I'm a super hero."

"What's a super hero?"

"On my world, a super hero is a made-up character that is able to do things that no one else can. Like fly. Or turn invisible. Or be really strong. They usually exist to save the world. That kind of thing. That's why I'm here. Why we're here."

"We?" Fun Guy asked. "Oh, right. Anyhow, is that why you're here? Have you come to save our world?"

"Well, no. I mean, I will, I guess. Death is afraid of me."

"What's Death? Or is it a who?"

"Well, I guess it's a who. It's also kind of a what, I suppose. Death is the end. It's a being who visits you when you take your last breath. He kind of claims it."

"There are no last breaths here. We have different seasons but the process is never the end of anything."

"There are some people on my world that think that Death is not the end."

"How could it be?" asked Fun Guy. "Do you have seasons on your world?"

"Especially in Wisconsin. When I lived in Florida, not that much, but in the Cheese State, the seasons are really different from each other."

"All your words are so silly," said Fun Guy. He grew two more bodies without letting this one dry out. The three of them surrounded Hyro and I.

They spoke in unison, though, which was kind of creepy.

"If you are not here to save my world, why are you here?"

I looked at the Fun Guy that I thought was the original one, well, the first one he regrew, I mean. "I'm here to save my world?" I said.

"Wisconsin or Florida?" they asked.

"Well, both, all of them. There are a lot more places on my world than just those two."

"So how does coming here save your world?"

I feel like I have had to tell of my quest for the ten rings so many times. But this was it. One ring left. I was so close. I explained the power I had found on other worlds and of my many adventures, and even of some of the friends I had made along the way.

"Interesting," said the Bloodlin. "And you did this all by yourself?"

I looked at Hyro. Then back.

"Well, in the beginning, yes, but then Hyro here came and helped me. I really don't feel alone at all."

"Who's Hyro?" Fun Guy asked.

"You know, Hyro. Him." I pointed at Hyro. One of the other Fun Guys was standing behind him.

What was strange was that that Fun Guy pointed at himself.

"Me?"

"No, Hyro." I said and pointed again.

And again, that same Bloodlin pointed at himself but explained to the others that we just met today. The explanation was still spoken in unison with the others which made the exchange even more confusing.

It was like they couldn't even see Hyro.

It was like to their eyes he wasn't even there.

Wasn't even …

"Hyro?"

FUN GUY

The first Bloodlin that I met on this world, Doctor Snow, was like half fairy but also half vegetable. He did help me on my way. He could grow new bodies of himself and this was how he travelled from place to place. It was like, I guess, teleportation to a degree. He could also grow multiple copies of his body. Speaking of which, my clone Hyro is finally here. The fact that you could clone another me makes me wish you just clone all of earth and send them to the future. That would be another way to make certain we all survive even if the meteorite hits.

THE HUSK OF FUN GUY

When Fun Guy leaves one of his bodies behind, it dries out very quickly and can be pulled apart by the faintest of breezes. What will be left of me after this is all over, Doctor Snow? I'm beginning to fear that there won't be anything to come back to. That even though you'll make me human again, maybe even wipe out some of the memories of what happened here, that I will never be the same again. Never be me again. Is this the cost of saving Earth? If it is, I understand. But I don't think I realized what this would all mean before.

CHAPTER SIXTEEN
INVÍTAME A UN CAFÉ

"You leave, and I stay here."
Steve Aoki and Angela Aguilar

More and more Fun Guys were growing around us. It was quite a crowd as I looked at Hyro. A Hyro that they could not see.

"This is becoming quite interesting," they said in unison to each other, growing more and more of their mushroom-headed Bloodlins.

"Why can't they see you, Hyro?"

"I don't know, Hiro. I really don't. I mean, they see you."

"They do." I admitted. Between robots and witches and goblins and giants, I had gotten pretty willing to pretty much accept everything at face value.

One thing that I was pretty certain of, Doctor Snow, was that Fun Guy was not going to be a help. There had to be others here on this world that could assist us.

So, we flew up into the weed-speckled air, past the other Bloodlins that skittled around and littered the sky.

I don't know what you would call it, Doctor Snow. Maybe it was I don't know, a vampire test. You know how you look to see if someone is a vampire by trying to see if they cast a reflection in the mirror? Well, I did something like this with Hyro.

In this case, as we were flying over the tall grass and I looked down at the shadow of me flying. And then I looked, and was careful not to make it look like I was looking, but I looked at Hyro's shadow. Accept there wasn't one there. He cast no shadow. Not at all.

Doctor Snow, I'm worried that it may be possible that he isn't here to help me save the Earth. I started thinking about these rings. And I started thinking about the kind of weapons they might be in the wrong hands. Well, on the wrong fingers at least.

"There," said Hyro. "Down there."

There was another Bloodlin down there. It had so many colors it was almost confusing to look at. But it wasn't flying around like the other Bloodlins. It just sort of hovered there.

We flew down and floated near her.

She looked at us, and acted as if she was grateful. Gratuitously grateful.

"Have you come to help me?" she asked.

"Who are you?" Hyro asked.

She said nothing.

"Who are you?" I asked.

"I'm Aurora Glitterwing."

"Glitterwing?"

"Glitterwing," she smiled.

Hyro turned to me. "Not only does she not seem to see me, she can't hear me either. Maybe I'm not here completely yet, even though I thought I was."

That actually made sense. And if you didn't send him to me, Doctor Snow, then who did? And his look is so similar to mine, it made me think that I was just not trusting.

"Glitterwing?"

"Yes?"

"You can't see him yet, but we're here to find a ring that will help us save the world. Our world. This is a beautiful world. It doesn't need saving but our world does. Do you know of this ring?"

"I know who has it and I will be happy to help you."

"Thank you."

"Saving a world is like healing a world. And I live to heal."

"That's nice," I told her.

"That's why I chose the name Aurora Glitterwing. It's not enough that it's just me, you know? I needed a name other fairies could believe in. My name has power."

I nodded but I'm not sure I really understood. She seemed to be saying that exact opposite of what Morgana whose name was not Morgana said to me on the past world.

"Not everyone wants to be healed, you know? Sometimes the Bloodlins that need the most healing don't even know they are sick. So it becomes my job to have to make certain they know they are sick before I can heal them."

Hyro, I assumed, now knowing he could say anything in front of her and it wouldn't affect our mission, let me know how bananas he thought Glitterwing was.

"The power of the ring of this world might not be of much use to you two then," she said.

"Why?" I asked.

"Because it gives the wearer the ability to fly and you two obviously have that ability."

"You two? Do you see Hyro?"

She didn't say anything. I asked the question a couple more times before she admitted what was going on.

"Well, I told you I was a healer. Sometimes you have to play along with the patient and believe them if only to build trust and establish the right kind of relationship."

I'm not crazy. So again, I suppose for irony's sake, I played along.

"Thank you for being so considerate."

"Of course, of course, of course."

"So just who is the sick one here and the one in need of healing?" Hyro said in regards to her.

"Where exactly are we going," I asked her.

"To Black Obsidian, of course. She has the ring. Though, that said, she may not be so willing to give it to you."

"And why is that?"

"Because she won't be certain of how you're going to use it. She will worry you might use it to steal this kingdom away from her. Or you might use it to bring harm to other worlds. Or you might use it to …"

"I'm going to use it to save my world," I interrupted.

"Well, of course you are. You're a highly sensitive and creative individual. I'm not saying the words she would say and I am not doubting you. I always take my patients at their word and I want you to know I really do believe you and I affirm who you are, and what your stated journey is."

Hyro looked like he was about to be throw up in response to what he was hearing.

"Why won't Black Obsidian believe me?"

"How could she, Hiro? How could she?"

ME AND HIS SHADOW

I am worried, Doctor Snow, that there is something wrong with Hyro. I'm the only one who can see and hear him. Is it just that he's not here yet or is it something else? Like he has no shadow. And all I know about him is what he told me. Why did I trust him so easily? Is it because he kind of looks like me? Who's to say that he isn't here to take the rings away from me and not save Earth?

AURORA GLITTERWING

Glitterwing is a fairy who seems like she is moved by the wind rather than flies upon it. Everything I said or did was immediately accepted by her. I feel like any choice I would ever make would be justified by her emotionally. There is no right or wrong. There's just my truths and my beliefs. She's gotten me to think that, despite my guilt, in some eyes, there is nothing wrong with what I have done on these worlds to save Earth. There are no lines I have crossed. And no mistakes that I have made. I'm not sure I want to feel this way, Doctor Snow.

CHAPTER SEVENTEEN
PARANOIA

"Talk.."
Steve Aoki and Danna Paola

We were taken to stand in front of Black Obsidian. She was the ruler of this world. She was beautiful to behold. But also, perhaps the most terrible and to-be-pitied being I had ever seen.

Her wings were glorious. But they were covered with eyes. She came from a family of Bloodlins that had always had more than two eyes. Were always able to look out for others in their kingdom because of their remarkable abilities. But in her case the eyes that faced behind her and to the sides of her and to her side and over her shoulders added to her fears of being watched. And just watched. Judged.

The eyes on her wings also looked upon her. Her vision out of all of these eyes, out of each of these eyes, was better than twenty-twenty and she could see others turn to speak to each other when she would pass or fly by. She would see others whisper to each other. They would wait till they thought she could not see them anymore and they would point. They wouldn't laugh. It wasn't like that.

And that was why she was so frustrated in not knowing exactly what they were saying. She both wished she had the ears to hear what they said but also feared any words that might be cruel.

As the ruler of this world, she was a tortured soul, though I have heard that most rulers are.

"What do you want?" she asked. Those were her first words.

"There's a ring I need to save my world."

"Why do you want it saved?" She asked. "Is it so much better than other worlds?"

"I like to think so."

"Are there people there who would speak ill of other people?"

I knew the answer was yes, Doctor Snow, Junior High School alone was evidence of this. I was afraid to answer because I knew how she hated what people said about her.

Reluctantly, though, I think I knew that if I lied, she would be afraid that I was lying. But if I spoke the truth and answered in a way where she would know I was not putting the Earth in the best of lights, she would not be able to be paranoid about that and second guess me.

"I'm afraid, Black Obsidian, that there are many people on my world that speak ill of each other."

At this she looked at me. There was nothing not to mistrust.

"Not everyone, though. My parents for example, I want to save them and that's why I'm here. 'm not happy with everything they say but I know I love them and I know that they love me."

She nodded. "I lost my parents a while ago. They were not perfect, either."
"Did they love you?" I asked her.

"I think they did. But it's been some time and I don't remember them exactly as they were any-more. It's easier to remember when they seemed mean. I think I remember them more out of my fear of what they said about me when I was not around."

I could hear Hyro in the back of my thoughts trying to tell me what to say. How to lie to her. But I thought he was wrong. I knew what it was like to be lied about and made fun of. And I think I could relate to the Princess.

"I'm sure they loved you even if they talked about you with each other," I said.

All the eyes on her wings turned in my direction. It was if they were all ears.

"What do you mean by that?" she asked me.

"I mean that I think that parents have this weird job where they try to prepare their kids for life, but at the same time, there's no perfect book, there's no perfect understanding of how to do that. And I think parents make mistakes. Sometimes big ones. Sometimes they lack all the wisdom in the world. Sometimes they do terrible things because they're selfish. But sometimes they do good, as well. And even then, it's only their best, which can be really flawed anyhow."

Her winged eyes continued to stare at me even though she herself did not.

She seemed to talk to herself a little, but it was like a whispered argument.

I could hear Hyro's voice. He kept telling me to let him out. Let him out? What did that mean? Was he a prisoner here in Black Obsidian's palace? None of this made any sense at all.

The Princess finally looked at me.

"I do appreciate your honesty and your kind words, Hiro. But you see, I don't want any kingdom to exist where anyone can say anything wrong about anyone else. I cannot help the way my people speak about each other in this kingdom I've been put in charge of. But the idea of helping save another kingdom where people can be so intolerant, I don't know if I can do that. I also don't know what giving you my ring will mean to this, my kingdom. The ring allows not just the wearer to fly but all others the wearer wishes to have that power to fly. So, if I give it to you, will my people lose that ability?"

I wasn't sure I understood. "I don't understand," I told her.

"Well," she responded. "What if giving you this ring would mean that every Bloodlin in the world would no longer be able to fly? Would we lose our wings? Would they be ripped from us all? Or would they somehow just dangle or drag behind us, no longer able to take ourselves into the air. Would you have me curse my people with gravity just so that yours could live?"

"Yes," I said in fear of how she would respond. "Yes, at least my people would still live." That's what I told her. "And, if you lost your wings, you would also be free of them, of all they see."

The eyes on her wings began to glare, not just stare. There was anger behind them.

Hyro was screaming at me and I was ignoring his screams.

Finally, the Princess looked back at me. "You're right, I would indeed lose my wings and perhaps even the many eyes on them, but I would still have my own. Every person in my kingdom, how do you think they would look at me?"

"I don't know," I said and began to be convinced that she was not going to give me the ring.

"I don't think I could bare to look at any of them."

"I understand," I said over the screams of Hyro that echoed and raged all around me.

"Would you have me pluck out my own eyes so that I would not have to face them?" she asked. "But I'd still hear their condemnations. I'd still hear what they would say, and I could still guess what they would say about me even when I was not there."

"Your parents will die." I could hear Hyro calmly whispering this now, behind me. "They will die. Take the ring from her. Save the world. That's what you need to do. Save the world. Take the ring however you need to. By force if you need to. Just say it, Hiro. Take my body. Take my body." What was Hyro telling me?

As for Black Obsidian, I didn't know if I could just take the ring without her consent. I didn't know if I could do such violence to her. I mean, maybe this ring wasn't as needed as the others. Maybe Earth could be saved with just the nine rings. Maybe there was something else you, Doctor Snow, and Doctor Horse, and Doctor Scottski could do to help Earth. If I take the ring, even though I'm suspected of being a villain on some other worlds I'll actually be the true villain of this world. Its destroyer.

But then I thought, of course, that if I took the ring, from her, I could come back, after Earth was saved and give it back to her, and allow her to restore her kingdom.

So, I suggested this barter with her. I explained what could happen. I talked about time and how it worked. I promised her on the lives of my parents that I would come back and give her the ring back.

She nodded and thanked me and told me how much she wanted to believe me.

"I will bring the ring back. I almost feel like I need to bring all the rings back. That I can't be a hero to my world at the cost of other words. I need to be a hero of all worlds."

"Good words, Mister Hiro," she said. "Good words. And I believe you."

Doctor Snow? I could not believe it. She actually believed me. I mean, I did mean what I was saying. I meant every bit of it.

"But ... "

"But?"

"But will I believe you tomorrow?"

"I'm sorry?"

"I believe you in this moment, but what about when I step out on my palace balcony and watch my people falling from the skies? What happens when the cruel reality of not being able to fly hits home and they plummet to the ground?"

"I'm going to come back."

"But you want the ring right now, correct?" There's no way to make certain that everyone on my world hears a decree and won't be flying when their abilities, the very thing that makes them who they are, is taken from them."

"I'm going to come back."

"When? Tomorrow, after you've gone four hundred years into the past to save your planet from a killer meteorite and everyone hails you as the hero of your planet? Are you really going to come back then?"

"Yes."

"But what if there are other threats to your planet?"

"What?

"What if there are other ways to help your world? Other ways these rings you've collected can help and save your people. Will you really turn your back on them to come back here?"

"I said I would," is what I said, but I knew what she was saying. And I hated thinking it. There was some wisdom to her paranoia. Black Obsidian had wisdom and I could not argue with it no matter how much Hyro was screaming over it.

"What if there's a second meteorite?"

I couldn't help but remember my mom telling me about the likelihood of a second meteorite hitting Earth, like the one that killed the dinosaurs, was so obscure that it just couldn't happen. And yet, Doctor Snow, a second meteorite was coming to destroy Earth. So maybe the likelihood of a third wasn't so impossible?

"What if I believe you, Hiro. And trust you. Do one of your rings allow for Time Travel?"

"No."

"I see. So the same people who sent you on this quest, who changed and transformed your body, they also sent you into the future?"

"Yes." I said. "They are waiting for me to give them the rings and then they will change me back to a human being."

I paused for a moment.

"I see," she said.

"But after I bring the ring back to you, of course." I promised her with as much will power as I could muster.

"So, you give them the rings. Your world is saved. And then they're going to give you the rings back to return here and give them back to me."

"Yes, of course." I said, not fully understanding what she was suggesting.

"What if they don't give you the rings back?"

"Why wouldn't they?" At this Hyro's voice began screaming again and the world once again went black.

"Hiro?"

"Hiro?"

"Hiro?"

When I came to, I wasn't on the Bloodlins world anymore. I woke up in a room. On a bed. It felt like Earth. Looked like a hospital room.

I looked up and there was Doctor Snow.

I sat up.

"Am I back on Earth?" I asked.

"Yes, Hiro. You did it. Earth is going to be saved."

I smiled. I couldn't believe it. "But what happened on the last world? I didn't think that I … they… they …"

Doctor Snow smiled. "The time strand that made it possible for you to be in the future pulled you back here once you had all ten rings in your hands."

"Oh, okay." I said. I couldn't believe it. I actually did it.

"When you arrived here, you were unconscious. We tried to take the rings from your hands and transform you back to your human form so you could wake up as a normal human again, but you wouldn't unclench your fists. Even the powers of your rings began to activate as we tried to take the rings." She smiled.

The other doctors came in. "There's our hero," Doctor Horse said. Doctor Scottski smiled as well. "You did it."

Doctor Scottski stepped a forward just a little. "We've readied the machines to make you human again, Hiro. We're certain you'll want to see your parents again as soon as possible."

"Yes, I would," I said.

"We just need you to take the rings off because they cannot go into the machine. The rings are not human biologic material and we fear the side-effects they would have on your re-transformation."

I opened my fists showing the nine rings on my fingers and the tenth in my palm. But the tenth ring was still on one of the fingers of Black Obsidian, the Princess of of the Bloodlin world and faction. I mean, I had ripped the finger off her hand to get the ring and there it was. The finger was still bleeding.

I was overwhelmed and horrified. What had I done? I was imagining all of her people falling to their deaths having lost the ability to fly. I begand to imagine a deepening ocean of fairy blood rising hire with every plummeting.

I'm not a murderer.

I turned to the doctors. "I did something terrible, Doctors. After we save Earth from the meteorite, I'm going to have to take this ring back to the tenth world. I need to take it back to the exact point in time where I left that world. So many Bloodlins are going to die if I don't!"

The doctors paused as if what I asked was not as easy as just doing that.

I heard Hyro's voice inside of me. I heard him speaking plainly. "Listen Hiro, I don't think they are going to be okay with that, I think the Princess was right. Maybe you can't trust them completely."

I could sense that Hyro was right about this, but I didn't understand why he wasn't here, either. Wouldn't he have come back with me? What was going on?

Just then, at that very moment, Alora rushed through the door. She was as beautiful ever. She screamed that the doctors would not give me the ring back.

"Take the ring off the Princess's finger and put it on," she said.

And then I could hear Hyro's words. "Show them that you're not just going to give them the rings until they agree to let you go back and save the Princess and her people."

I looked at the Doctors. "I'm sorry," I said. "I did this to save Earth, and once I do that, I need to use these rings to save the Bloodlins. Maybe even some of the other worlds I took rings from."

I took the ring off the Princess's finger and I put her finger down on the bed behind me. Maybe it could be reattached or something, I thought.

I put the ring on my finger. I had all ten rings on my hands now. All ten. And then I began to shake, and change. I could see the doctors were smiling, at each other as much as at me.

There was a mirror in the room. I looked in it for a moment. I wasn't Hiro anymore. I was the image of Hyro.

The Doctors moved around the body of Hyro, congratulating me … him … on a mission well done. A mission masterfully accomplished. He thanked them. He thanked them. With my mouth, well, not my mouth. With his mouth. His mouth that had been my mouth. His voice that had been my voice.

Alora embraced him. She embraced Hyro. She told him how she loved him. She never loved me. Only the part of me that was him. And told him that she hated kissing me and was never attracted to me. It was Hyro she loved. From the beginning. She saw him in me. That was all. It was all a trick.

I had put the final ring on and was lost for it. Transformed by it. Overtaken by it.

I thought Hyro was there to help me. But all this time, he was there to take over me.

To possess me.

To become me.

BLACK OBSIDIAN

The Princess of the world of the Bloodlins did not want to give me the ring, Doctor Snow. She had eyes all over her, including all over her wings. She could see everywhere. And doubted everything. She wasn't certain if my story was true or not. And where, on the first worlds I got rings from, I was so confidant in my quest, I think she could tell I'm not as I was anymore. When I asked for the ring, she said no.

THE BLOODLINS RING

I took the ring, Doctor Snow. I took the ring and the finger it was on. I blacked out. Hyro was screaming in my head and she said no. I just took the ring. From what I understand, it allows the wearer to fly, which I already could, but it also allows the wearer to make it possible for all others to fly as well. In taking the ring from the Bloodlin world, Doctor Snow, did I cause all the other Bloodlins who were flying to fall to their deaths?

SOURCE CODE TO
ACCESS POWER: BOOYA KASHA

HIRO's JOURNEY
CHAPTER TEN

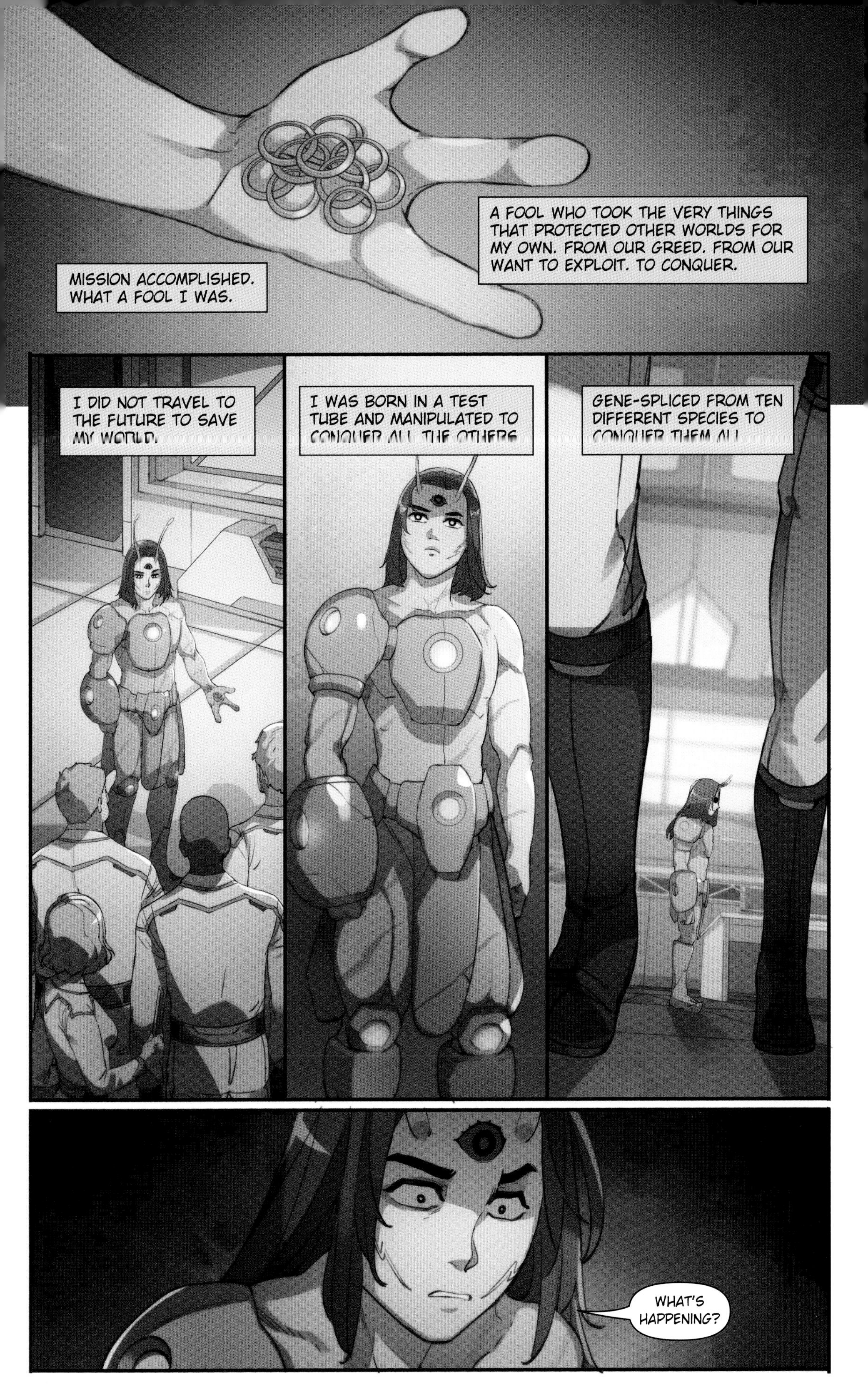
MISSION ACCOMPLISHED.
WHAT A FOOL I WAS.
A FOOL WHO TOOK THE VERY THINGS THAT PROTECTED OTHER WORLDS FOR MY OWN. FROM OUR GREED. FROM OUR WANT TO EXPLOIT. TO CONQUER.
I DID NOT TRAVEL TO THE FUTURE TO SAVE MY WORLD.
I WAS BORN IN A TEST TUBE AND MANIPULATED TO CONQUER ALL THE OTHERS
GENE-SPLICED FROM TEN DIFFERENT SPECIES TO CONQUER THEM ALL
WHAT'S HAPPENING?

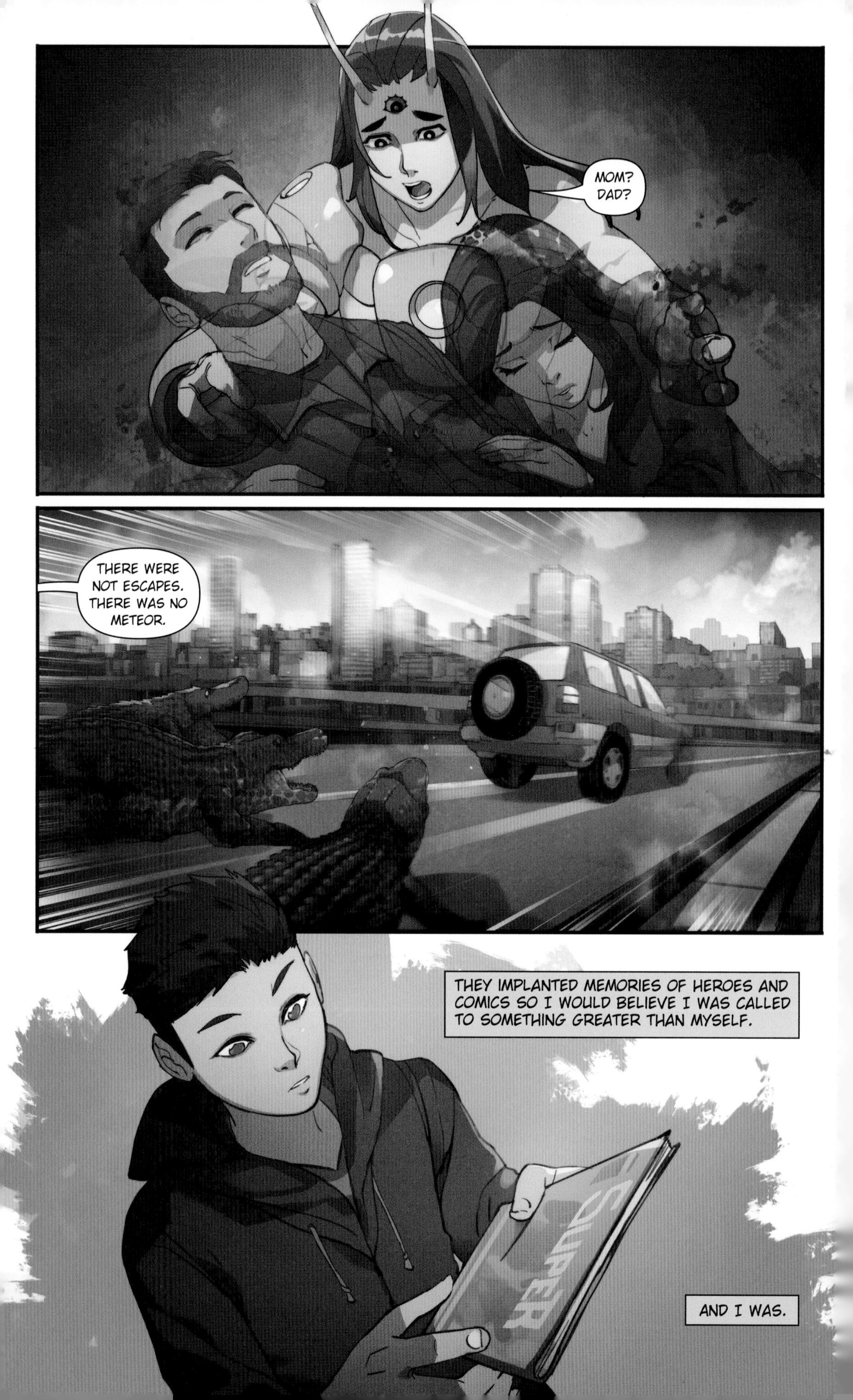
MOM? DAD?
THERE WERE NOT ESCAPES. THERE WAS NO METEOR.
THEY IMPLANTED MEMORIES OF HEROES AND COMICS SO I WOULD BELIEVE I WAS CALLED TO SOMETHING GREATER THAN MYSELF.
SUPER
AND I WAS.

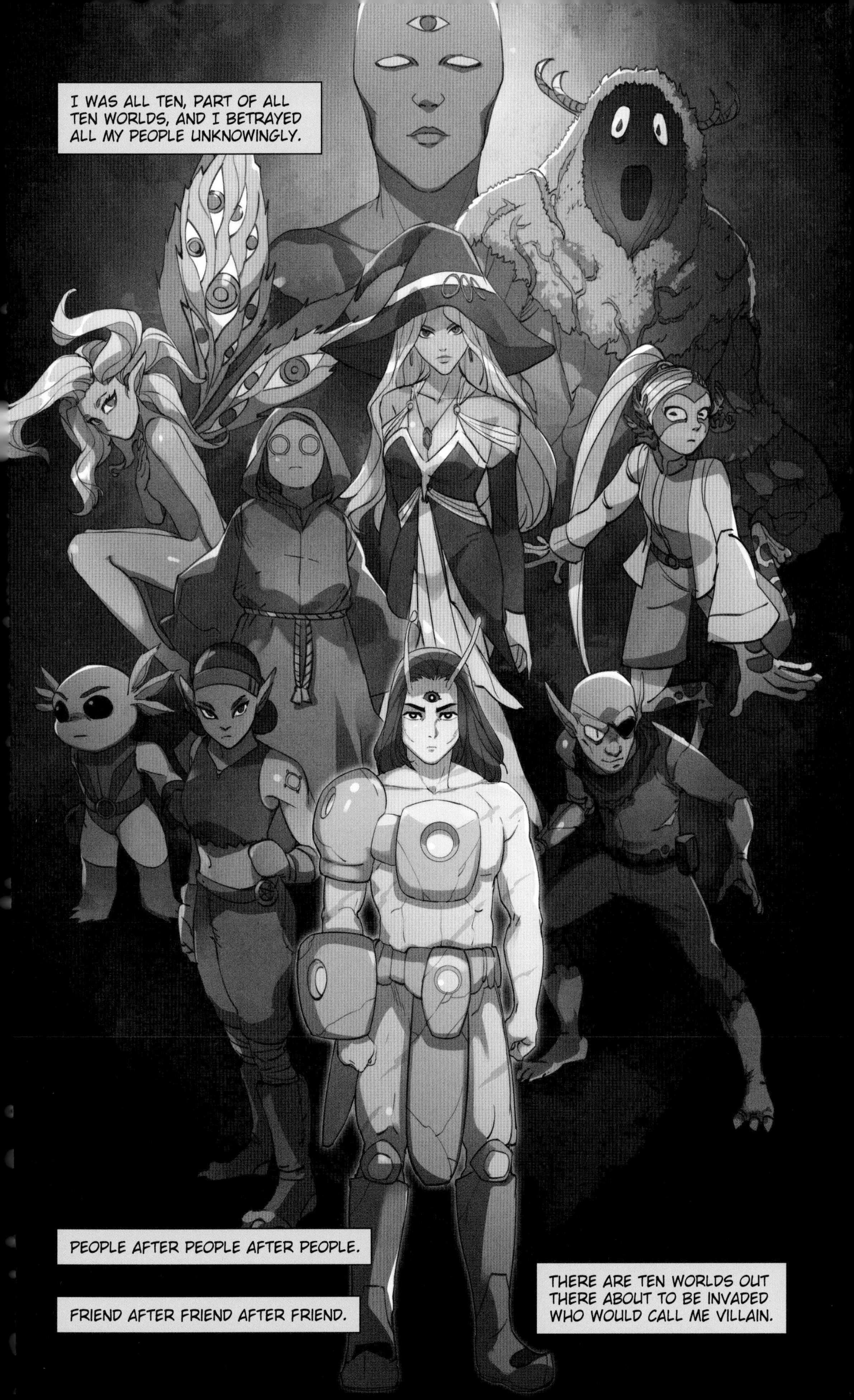
I WAS ALL TEN, PART OF ALL TEN WORLDS, AND I BETRAYED ALL MY PEOPLE UNKNOWINGLY.
PEOPLE AFTER PEOPLE AFTER PEOPLE.
FRIEND AFTER FRIEND AFTER FRIEND.
THERE ARE TEN WORLDS OUT THERE ABOUT TO BE INVADED WHO WOULD CALL ME VILLAIN.

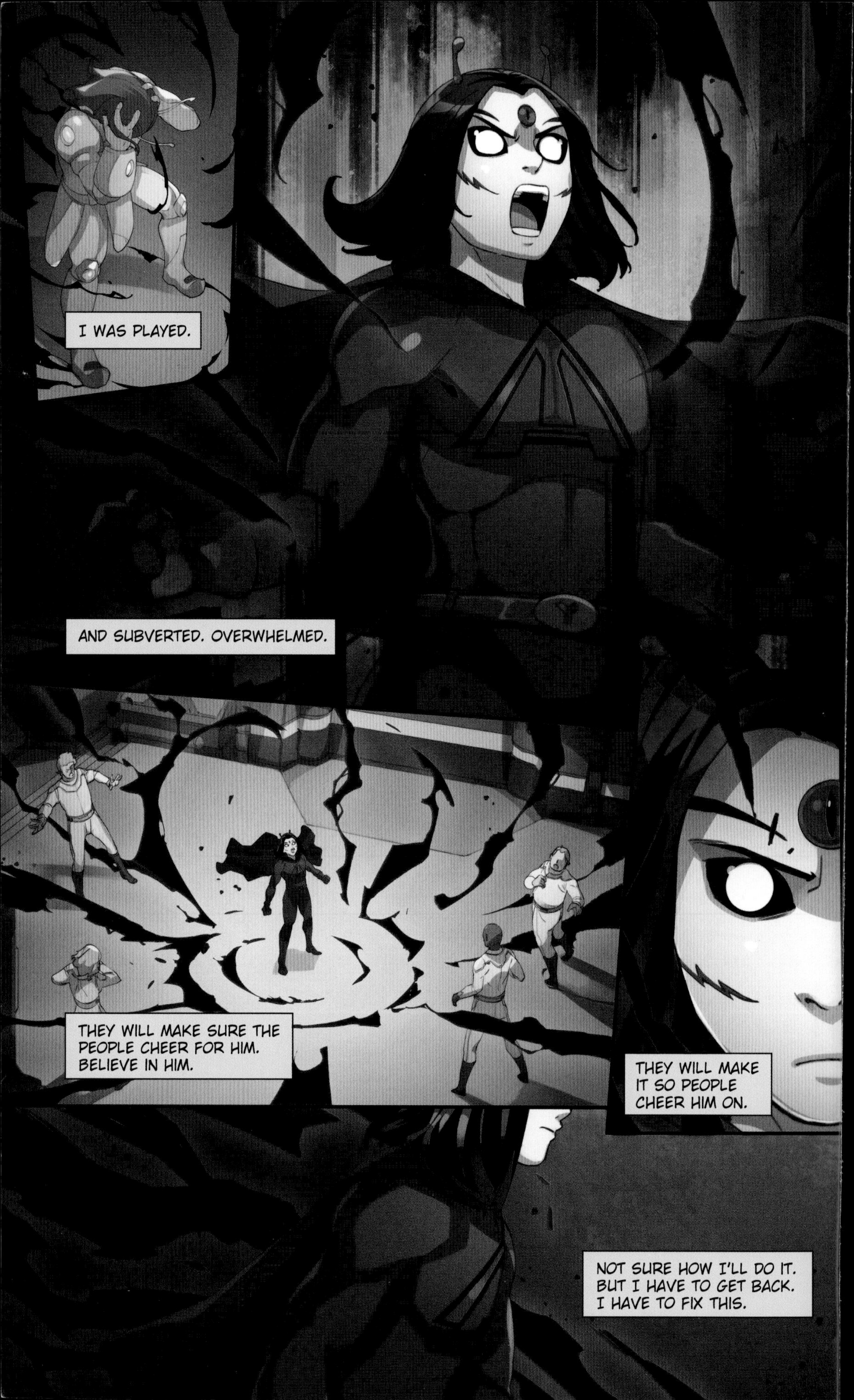
I WAS PLAYED.
AND SUBVERTED. OVERWHELMED.
THEY WILL MAKE SURE THE PEOPLE CHEER FOR HIM. BELIEVE IN HIM.
THEY WILL MAKE IT SO PEOPLE CHEER HIM ON.
NOT SURE HOW I'LL DO IT. BUT I HAVE TO GET BACK. I HAVE TO FIX THIS.

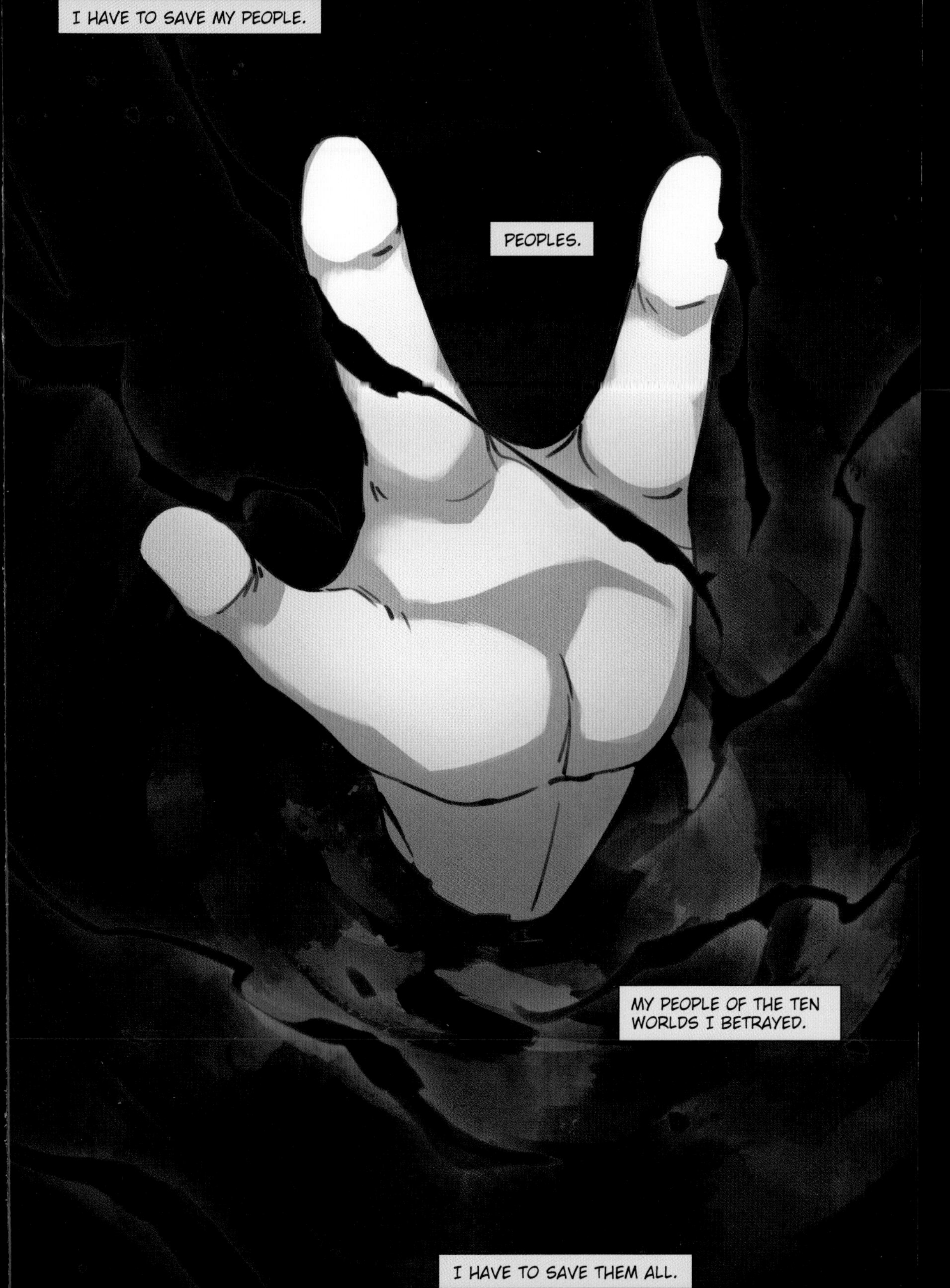
I HAVE TO SAVE MY PEOPLE.
PEOPLES.
MY PEOPLE OF THE TEN WORLDS I BETRAYED.
I HAVE TO SAVE THEM ALL.

CHAPTER EIGHTEEN
HYRO

"That's how they read Hiro. They said Hyro."
Steve Aoki

"Hyro?" I called out over and over again. "Hyro?"

"What do you want?" his thoughts spoke to me.

"What happened?" I asked. "What's happening?"

"Well, you accomplished your mission to collect the ten rings." He said. "You did it, Hiro. Apologies for having had to take over a couple times there. But you were showing your weakness, believing your programming to be a hero."

"Programming?"

"That's a bad word for it. Genetic coding, perhaps? It's more like you were given certain memories and motivations to be a hero, and those motivations, no matter how vital they were at the beginning, were beginning to get in the way of our goals."

"To save the Earth from a meteorite?"

"To get the ten rings. Earth had nothing to do with it. At least saving it had nothing to do with it."

"What are you talking about?"

"I have good news and bad news, Hiro. Well, the bad news for you is still good news for me."

"I don't understand."

"You never travelled 400 years into the future."

"Yes, I did."

"No."

"Your past was all fake memories, an implanted back story to give you the motivation to want to save Earth. To want to save your parents and your world. None of it was true."

"That's not possible."

"It was and is."

"My parents would ... "

"You don't have parents, Hiro. You never did. Implanted and predetermined memories again.

Genetically tied to your very DNA to make you seem genuine."

"Genuine?"

"Genuine. Real. Whatever you want to think, Pinocchio. Though it's your makers, your Geppetto's, whose noses should grow. The point is that none of it was real. Not the hurricanes or the alligators or the meteorites or Florida or Wisconsin or the transformation from human to what you are right now."

"My parents?"

"You never had parents. You were born in test tube."

"What?"

"They made you. They were able to get genetic samples from the ten worlds, the same ten worlds you took the rings from, and used those cell samples to create a being who could travel to those worlds and steal from them such amazing abilities and weapons that Earth and humanity would be able to ultimately invade those worlds for their riches and resources."

"They implanted memories in you and made you believe them so badly so that there would be no way, if there were psychics or anyone on one of those other worlds, that they would doubt you. You had to believe in you more than even they would. And when you were knocked down, you had to have the motivation to get up again. Over and over again. You had to be so convincing, and so willing to fight to save your world, that they would see how genuine you were. And believe you. And in some cases, even trust you and want you to succeed."

"But the rings? The Earth?"

"Look on the bright side, Hiro. And this really is a bright side. Earth is fine. And about to get a whole lot more powerful. Because it now has the rings of the ten other worlds to exploit. Thanks to you."

"I never would have done this."

"Of course not. I like to think of the rings as not so much rings, but as crowns."

"Crowns?"

"Yes, the same general shape of a ring. But these are the things that will help us rule the other worlds. Crowns."

"But how have you become me?"

"You were always going to become me. If anything, I was sleeping and waiting to awake in you. I am the real you. There were certain genetic reactions that had to happen as you gained more and more rings. Coupled with the abilities of those ten worlds that you were already given, one thing led to the other, allowing me to overwhelm your original programming. In other words, you were groomed to become me. The doctors knew, of course, that you, with your strong and heroic and selfless motivations, would never give them the means to take advantage of these other worlds, so a sleeper program was put into your system. Me. So that when certain things happened, and you changed as a result of your adventures, that sleeper program would gain dominance. In other words, I would rise to the surface. I told you I was almost there."

"So, I thought I was saving Earth but was really betraying the ten worlds I was genetically grown in a test tube from? It's you. You're the one the witch with no name was warning me of. You're Diablos Finales. You're the last devil."

"Well, that might be a dark way to think of it, but yes. That's pretty much it. I know that's a lot to live with. The good news is that you are in the process of being discarded completely by this body, the same way a human being would discard old cells. Or a snake would its own skin. There won't be anything left of you at all. So again, there's the good news."

"I don't understand."

"You're not going to have to live with the knowledge of what you've done at all."

AS I WAS

All I am or ever was is a petri dish. A hero cocktail. I thought I was a human who was turned into a hero to save his planet. His home. His parents. But the laboratory was my home. The beaker was my birthplace. There were no parents apart from the scientists that mixed me up and put me in this form. There are no real memories I have apart from the damage and hurt I have brought to ten worlds. My worlds. I took from them. I stole from them. It is all too much.

AS I AM

The concoction that I was has been overwhelmed with a later chemical reaction known as Hyro. He cares nothing for the ten worlds whose rings he wears. He merely shares the greed and cruelty of the scientists who made me. Scientists who would be conquerors. Conquerors who will now invade the ten worlds I stole from. And other worlds beyond those, I imagine.

SOURCE CODE TO ACCESS THE CUMULATIVE POWER OF THE TEN RINGS: DIM MAK